Los Morenos

Also by SHELLEY HALIMA

Azucar Moreno

Los Morenos

SHELLEY HALIMA

STREBOR BOOKS

NEW YORK LONDON TORONTO SYDNEY

Strebor Books
P.O. Box 6505
Largo, MD 20792
http://www.streborbooks.com

Cover design: www.mariondesigns.com

ISBN-13 978-1-59309-049-4
ISBN-10   1-59309-049-8
LCCN 2005920189

First Strebor Books trade paperback edition January 2006

10   9   8   7   6   5   4   3   2   1

Manufactured in the United States of America

For information regarding special discounts for bulk purchases,
please contact Simon & Schuster Special Sales at 1-800-456-6798
or business@simonandschuster.com

ACKNOWLEDGMENTS

It's that time. Time to thank all of those who gave me love, support, and guidance.
Mi familia:

My parents, Dwayne, Nesey, Chavis, Marius, Timeaco, Walt, Aunt Pat, Aunt Barbara, Aunt Shirley, Aunt Willie M., Uncle Aubrey, Uncle Joe, Edith, Erica, Eric, Steve, Stacey, Cathy, Mona, Marsha, Dionne, Uncle Woody, Jan, Lynn.

Mis amigos:

Tina Brooks McKinney, Harold L. Turley II, V. Anthony Rivers, Nane Quartay, David Bernard, Darrien Lee, Allison Hobbs, Debra Ingram, Deanna Thomas, Darren J., Enrique O., Sheri and Barb.

Mi Amor:

Brad, thanks for putting up with a neurotic writer. You've been such a blessing.

Mil gracias:

Zane, Strebor Books, Charmaine Parker, Chris Webber, Kima, Laisha Webber, Jawn Murray (a big hug), Marlena Martin, Nicole Boyd and the Page Turners (Detroit), Mizz Neisha and the Sistahs 'n Books, the employees at Ford, Linda Thomas, Cydney Rax and Book Remarks, Tee C. Royal and RAWSISTAZ, Angie Pickett-Henderson and Readincolor, Carla Dean & Jessica Tilles and Writersrx, LaShaunda Hoffman and Shades of Romance Magazine, Dawn Petty at Murphy Middle School, Ana Ulloa, Alisa Valdes-Rodriguez and the Sucias (Kim the Cuban Diva, Claudia, Desiree, Miriam, Renee, Valerie, Caro, Karen, Roberta, Mariposa,

Elsie, Cherise, Suezette, Jubie, Marissa, Gloria, Julie, Liz, Janis, Janette, Mariana, Joanne, etc.), Dr. William Roper (thanks so much for the info—you are wonderful), Linda Nieves-Powell of Latino Flavored Productions, Nick Alexander of Books & Poetry Café, Linda J., Nancy W., Ashirea B., Makisha G., Veronica A., D'Kaara, Dee Ceres, Christine S., Gaby, Exceptional, my peeps in the blog world, online at Supacindyonline, Latina, etc., Yolanda Johnson and Literary Wonders, Eileen Denz, the gang at Producto, Ri'Chari, Pamela Crockett. Anyone else I may have forgotten, please forgive me.

Funny How Time Flies

1

Nikki

Has it really been more than two years already? Earlier, I glanced at the calendar and saw that this week it will be two years and two and a half months since I left Detroit to come out here to L.A. to make my mark in acting. And making my mark has been a struggle, to say the least. I've lost track of how many parts I've gone after and didn't get. Until this past spring the most I had to show for my endless string of auditions was a couple of walk-ons and bit parts on soap operas and primetime shows. I'm very fortunate my agent Erica believes in my talent and is one of my strongest supporters. Early on, Erica and Mario formed a united front and wouldn't let me stay discouraged when I got rejected for part after part. There were a few times when I just wanted to give up, but those two weren't having it.

To say the competition out here is fierce is a horrible understatement. It's bad enough if you're Caucasian, but for a minority actor it's ten times worse. I have gone up against so many talented actors of color. You wouldn't know there were so many, though, by looking up on the big screen. Hollywood seems content with casting the same seven or eight minority actors in every picture. That's one barrier I've had to contend with.

The other barrier has been my looks. Being Black and Puerto Rican—a Blatina, if you will—I go up for parts calling for a Black female as well as parts looking for a Latina. This is where I catch hell. With few exceptions, casting agents are a clueless group of people whose ideas about casting for certain ethnic groups are based on ignorant perceptions. They don't seem to realize that Blacks and Latinas have a variety of shades and features. Yet I've still been turned down for Black roles because I was told that I look "too exotic." And I've been turned down for Latina roles because I'm brown-skinned. I had one asshole tell me that my coloring was "a little too dark for someone playing a Latina." Many people out here have it drilled in their heads that all Latinas look like either Jennifer Lopez or Salma Hayek. Never mind that in reality we range from milky white to coal black.

I've done some nonacting stuff, like a print ad for a hair relaxer. It was a bit of false advertising since I don't use any chemicals on my hair and the hairstylist simply blow-dried my curly hair straight. But hey, it paid some bills. And the voice lessons I took back in Detroit came in handy when I was chosen to do voice-overs for two commercials. One commercial is a national long-running one that I still get residuals from. I thought about going out for a couple of videos but I nixed that once I found out who the artists were. From looking at their previous videos I knew right off the bat they'd follow the tired format, which would more than likely involve me being scantily clad and propped on top of a car, money being thrown at the camera, a bunch of ass-shaking and showing off of rented jewelry. Thanks but no thanks. Besides, unless you're a known actress making a guest appearance or you're a popular and sought-after video vixen, they pay you about twenty dollars and a chicken snack.

My first speaking part was playing a waitress on *The Young and the Restless*. My complete lines were: "May I get you anything else, sir? Okay, I'll be right back with your check." Then, the following month, my next *big* role after the Jane Blow waitress was of a woman who witnesses the mob hit of an FBI informant and is later questioned by the police on the show *Wings of Justice*. That may not sound like much, but the night that show aired I was talking on both my cell and house phones, fielding calls from peeps back in Detroit and New York who were so excited for me. Even though Mami and Papi had always been opposed to my choosing acting as a career pursuit, they were very proud to see their little girl's face on television. They'd seen the commercials I did back in Detroit, but this was nationwide exposure. My screen time was only about two minutes but it was still a big deal.

My real break came about as a result of that role. Amber Woodson, one of the actresses from the popular African-American sitcom *Tapestry*, was guest-starring on the same episode of *Wings of Justice*. I ended up sitting next to her in the commissary and we struck up a conversation. I told her how much I enjoyed her show.

She gave me the heads-up on the impending exit of one of the actresses on *Tapestry* and let me know when the auditions would be held. I took my ass up in there and aced the audition and the rest is, as they say, history. Okay, so it wasn't quite that easy. Being a big fan of the show I wanted this part bad—and I mean bad. I was so nervous I screwed up my lines and then begged to do them over. After I got myself together and did it again, *then* I aced it. When I received the call from Erica that I got the part, I literally fell to my knees crying in a mixture of joy and relief.

My role is not directly *replacing* that of the previous actress, Kendall Randolph. She was fired before the season even ended because she was such a pain in the ass. Before landing her role on *Tapestry*, Kendall's biggest claim to fame was being one of the models that showed off prizes on a game show. She was up against established actresses who were also vying for the role. Instead of being grateful for landing such a prime part, I was told she walked onto the set in full-blown diva mode, treating cast and crew alike as if they were her minions. She managed to alienate everyone before the first show even hit the air. What precipitated her firing was, she went to England for a cameo in a movie. There was a delay in production and she decided to stay on the film set instead of returning to L.A. for the *Tapestry* taping. That was the final straw for the execs, who were fed up with getting a new demand from her every week and needed just one more reason to let her go. They didn't even try and make her honor her contract and finish the season. Her loss was definitely my gain.

Now here I am a co-star on *Tapestry*. Talk about feeling blessed! My first steady professional gig out here and on a major show no less. *Tapestry* follows the love trials and tribulations of a group of twenty- and thirty-somethings living in L.A. My character is witty and intelligent, which is great considering the large supply of demeaning roles for minorities. I'm very proud of my role and the show as a whole because there's nothing degrading about it. Audience reaction to my character has been very positive. I've gotten a lot of fan mail from guys who think I'm pretty hot. And since my racial heritage was written into the script, I've gotten great response from Blacks and Hispanics as well as those who are both who are pleased with how I'm representing. Of course everyone has detractors, and I saw a few on the message board of the show's website. They said they didn't like me and were going to start a campaign to get Kendall back. Oh well, you can't please everyone.

I've been on some sets and I've witnessed firsthand how many casts are not "just like a family" as they proclaim to be on *Entertainment Tonight*. One night I almost rolled on the floor laughing when I saw a certain bottle-blonde actress giving an interview and doing the "family" spiel. I was one of the extras on that particular set a few weeks prior and saw for myself: The cast was barely on speaking terms with one another! Also, the aforementioned actress held up production as she chilled in her dressing room, protesting that another actress on the show had more lines than her. Her agent had to be called to the set and coax her out by dangling the little carrot of possibly directing an episode.

Once the *Tapestry* crew saw I wasn't anything like my predecessor, just a down-to-earth homegirl from Detroit, they warmly welcomed me into their fold. I became fast friends with them—Amber, Paris, Leon, and Benjamin, as well as Joanne, who plays my mother. The girls and I try to have a sista night whenever possible. That's when we meet up at someone's house and just kick back and pig out, have some drinks and act silly.

Since the show is so popular I received instant recognition; I'm still adjusting going from being a relative unknown to getting recognized most of the time when I go out. I enjoy interacting with the fans, and for the most part they're very cool when they approach me. While some celebrities find it bothersome, I love signing autographs. There are times when it can be inconvenient, though. Like one night when Mario and I were out having a romantic dinner; we were holding hands across the table, looking into each other's eyes— lost in the moment. Then out of nowhere we heard, "Hey, don't you play Veronica on *Tapestry?* That's my favorite show! I watch it every Tuesday night! Can I get an autograph for me and my friend Pookie? She gonna trip!"

But I knew it was part of the package. To make it in this business there are going to be sacrifices. And inconvenience and loss of privacy are just two of them. It's a given. It trips me out when my fellow actors clamor for the major movie roles, awards, accolades, and magazine covers and then turn around and pull that Greta Garbo "I vant to be alone" bullshit. I'm not talking about putting up with the stalk-erazzi who take pictures through the slats of their window blinds and follow their kids to school, but dealing with the public who support your career. I've seen celebrities outright refuse to give autographs or even acknowledge their fans. They seem to forget it's the fans who helped them buy those fancy homes to show off on *MTV Cribs* and that fleet of cars they don't even drive. You don't get into this business and cry about the lack of privacy. If your privacy means that much to you then you get a job at Merrill Lynch or Kroger's and not in show business. If I'm out and about doing errands and not feeling particularly sociable, I'll hide behind some sunglasses. If I still end up being recognized then I suck it up and put on the sparkle.

Professionally I'm pleased with how things are progressing; things are great in the personal arena, too. Mario and I are very happy. Living together took a little getting used to, though. We both have habits and quirks that call for compromise. For instance, I hate going to sleep in absolute quiet. I have to have some music or the television playing in the background. But Mario likes it as quiet as a tomb. The way we work that out is I go to sleep with wireless headphones on, feeding my ears either Luther or Nick at Nite. We have our lovers' spats now and then but we follow the rule many old married couples have—we never go to bed angry.

You would think now that I'm on the show we can't spend as much time together but actually the opposite is true. Before, I was working for an answering service at night and going to auditions during the day and we only got to spend time with each other on the weekends. Now I go to work to run lines and rehearse Monday through Thursday and on Fridays we tape before an audience. I'm usually home a couple of hours before Mario. Plus, the show is on hiatus one week every month during the season.

Recently Mario began researching for a book on the beginnings of hip-hop to the state of it now, like the commercialism and how police agencies are using CoIntelPro-type tactics in targeting hip-hop artists. When he gets home he eventually ends up on his laptop working on it. He told me it wouldn't surprise him if it took him a year or more to complete because of all the research he's doing. I'm usually sitting across from him memorizing my lines or answering fan mail. Even though we're in our own zones it feels good to just be in the same space together.

⁂

I get a couple of steaks out of the fridge and marinate them for our dinner tonight, fix myself a small glass of gin and pineapple juice, and put on some Gato Barbieri. I then get out my script and begin to look over my lines. Right as I get started the phone rings. I'm so distracted by going over my dialogue that I reach for it without even looking at the caller ID—which is something I almost never do.

"Hello?"

"Hey, Miss Nikki!"

I toss my script to the side on the couch. "Odell! What's going on? I called you a couple of times but I guess The Diva was otherwise engaged."

"Engaged? Girl, you must be a damn psychic or somethin'! That's what I was callin' to tell you about!"

"Hey, cuz!"

"Rosie? Is that you?"

"Yeah, heiferlicious. Who you think it is? Odell and me got you on the three-way. Girl, we both got some news to tell you."

"Wait a minute now. Odell, you said something about me saying 'engaged.' Don't tell me you and Rosie are getting hitched," I tease.

"Please, chile. You know the only pussy I like has fo' legs and nine lives."

Rosie and I chortle.

"You tell Nik your news first, O."

"Okay. Girl, me and Aaron is gettin' married!"

"Ahh!" I exclaim. "Odell, I'm so thrilled for you!"

"I'm thrilled for me, too, chile!"

"You should see the ring this bitch got," says Rosie.

"That's great news. Rosie was telling me how good he is to you."

"Mm-hmm. After the three months of straight hell that little girl Jamal put me through, Odell was 'bout to give up on mens lemme tell you. And then 'fore that Robert was workin' my last nerve. I ain't even gon' mention the ones 'fore *him*. I feel like I deserve to have somebody like Aaron in my life."

"You sure do, honey. Be sure and let me know when the ceremony will take place. I want to make sure that I can make it back to Detroit for it."

"I sho will, girl. It's looking like it'll be next year sometime. Aaron wants to save up some more money for a house first. We both tired of renting." He sighs. "I already know my mama ain't comin'."

"Why?" I inquire.

"Now my mama has known that I was gay since I was playin' with blocks, and she always accepted me. She can handle me being in love with a man, but for some reason she just ain't comfortable wit' me makin' that commitment in a ceremony. But she glad I found somebody that makes me happy."

"And that's what matters," interjects Rosie.

"Really," I agree.

"Okay, yo' turn, Miss Rosie."

Rosie clears her throat. "I got a call from *Silk & Velvet* magazine and—drum roll, please!—they want me to head out to L.A. for some test shots with their photographer. I'll be out there in a couple of weeks!"

"Aw, heeelllll no!" I shout gleefully. "Are you serious?"

"Yeah, girl! I'm serious like a mutha."

"Congrats! That's a pretty classy magazine. They make the nudes look like works of art. Erica has been trying to get me to consider posing for them for some publicity but I couldn't work up the nerve. Plus, Mario would kill me. I can't believe my cousin will be in a national—wait, international magazine!"

"If the test shoot goes well, then hopefully they'll pick me. Besides, I enjoyed myself when I visited last year and I'm looking forward to coming back. I hope you don't mind if I stay with you and Mario for a few weeks."

"Heifer, remind me to slap you when you get off the plane. You know damn well I don't mind. I can't wait to see your knuckleheaded butt."

"I can't wait to see your nutty ass, either."

"How's Chico doing?"

"He's doing fine. His head is in the clouds over this pretty girl named Bisola he's been dating."

"Yeah, Mario told me Chico was getting serious about somebody. Where is she from again?"

"Nigeria. She's real sweet."

"That's good. I want him to find somebody cool to settle down with. What about my boy Alejandro? I haven't talked to him in a minute."

"He's all right. He's busy with the store."

"He's still finding the time to beat it up though, right?"

"Shoot, eat it up, too." She laughs.

"Rosie, you telling me about how y'all did it on the front porch over at his house that night got me tempted to take Mario outside."

"Mm-hmm," says Odell. "Rosie, you know I love to hear about y'all's little escapades. It puts all kinds of thoughts in my head. I was already crushin' on Alejandra. One time I fantasized I was cleanin' the house in nothin' but a thong and when I bent over to sweep up somethin' on the dustpan, he come up behind me—"

"Okay, buddy!" Rosie interrupts, giggling. "Stop right there. You lucky I love your ass or I'd be over there busting your head for telling me your fantasies about Alejandro."

"Chile, it's just a fantasy. My heart belongs to my boo. Oh! Speak of the devil, I see that's my baby Aaron callin' on the other line. I'll talk to you chickens later. Love y'all!"

"Love you, too," Rosie and I tell him.

"Hold on, Nik. Let me clear the line," she says. After a couple of clicks, she's back. "All right. So everything is going good for you?"

"Yeah. It's kind of crazy between rehearsals, taping, and doing appearances, but it's all good."

"That's great. I'm so proud of you, *mija.*"

"Thanks. That means a lot to me."

"In between all that you've got going on, do you think you can take a couple days and meet me in New York?"

"New York? Why do you want me to meet you there?"

Rosie clears her throat but doesn't say anything.

"Rosie?"

"Well, um. I need for us to hook up there next weekend. I'm going to see Lupe and I want you there with me."

"You're going to see your mother?!"

"No, I'm going to see Lupe. I talked to Raul the other night and he's flying out to New York next weekend, too. Lupe has breast cancer. She's, uh—she's scheduled to undergo a mastectomy."

"Oh no, Rosie! Raul told you the other night? Why didn't you tell me as soon as you found out about your mother?"

"'Cause I needed to think about this on my own for a bit. And Nik, quit calling her my mother—she's Raul's mother. Tía Sarah is the woman who pretty much raised me. Lupe stopped being my mother a long time ago. But now that this has happened I'm not going to completely turn my back on her. Even though that would be some karma for her ass. Anyway, I'm not staying long. I'll get there either

Friday night or Saturday morning and leave Sunday. I'll probably just fly back out to Cali with you. Raul is taking a leave of absence from the restaurant so he can look after her for a while. I really need my cousin there with me."

"Of course, girl. I'll go online and get a ticket tonight. And I'll call Mami and Papi to let them know we're coming. They must not know about your mo—I mean Lupe, 'cause I'm sure they would've called and told me."

"No, Raul said she hasn't told anyone else. He had to convince her to finally have the surgery. She wasn't even going to try to fight it. She was more concerned about having only one breast and he told her he would pay for her to have reconstructive surgery. He asked me if I would come and see her and I said yeah. I'm glad you're going to be there with me."

"Please, no matter what, you should know that I'd find a way to be there for you."

"Yeah, I know."

"Are you okay, Rosie?"

"Shit yeah. I'm cool. But I don't really wanna talk about it right now, okay, Nik?"

"Sure, I understand."

"Let me go and get ready. I have to put some final touches on my outfits as well as ones for two other girls for the show tonight. I got something else to tell you but I'll wait till we see each other in person."

"What does it have to do with?"

"Me. And that's all I'm telling your nosy ass."

I suck my teeth.

"Smack them lips all you want, I'm still not telling you till I see you, brat. Anyway, I'll holla at you."

"Just leave me hanging then. I love you."

"I love you, too, brat."

2

Rosie

I'm not looking forward to telling Nikki what's been happening on this end. She's going to give me straight hell when she finds out that I've broken up with Alejandro. I could just bitch up and tell her over the phone, but I'm going to do it in person. Hopefully she won't hear about it before we see each other. Odell is only going to be able to keep his big mouth shut for so long. I was crossing my fingers that he wouldn't slip and say something while we were on the phone. Nikki's already not going to be pleased when she finds out I haven't been honest with her. First of all, even though I may not tell Nik every single thing, I never lie to her, most of the time anyway. But I haven't been honest with her about two things. One being the status of my relationship with Alejandro and two, I lied to her about my true feelings for our old friend Crystal after the threesome between her, Alejandro, and me a couple of summers ago.

⁂

I've known Crystal since high school, but I didn't develop any feelings outside of friendship until a few years ago. I didn't let Crystal know how I felt because she was straight and I just knew I'd never get anywhere with her. Or so I thought. The night of our friend Rhonda's baby shower, me, Alejandro, and Crystal were chilling in the living room on the couch. Nikki was on the sofa opposite us plastered out of her mind. I had been drinking and smoking and was feeling horny as hell. There I was sitting between the two people in the world who each had a piece of my heart. Two people who also turned me on. I couldn't help but think how incredible it would be if I could get down with both of them. I semi-playfully mentioned that I was feeling freaky and asked if anybody would be down for a threesome and Alejandro said yes. That was no surprise. What man is going to turn down the chance of getting it on with two women—two fine women at that? But when Crystal said she was down, I almost fell off the couch.

Then I thought she was probably only going to do something with Alejandro and the most I'd get to do to her would be to sneak a touch here and there. Imagine my surprise when the supposedly Miss Strictly Dickly turned her attention to yours truly. I thought the trees I was smoking was causing erotic hallucinations. That would explain how Crystal kissed me, sucked my *tetas*, and then got busy on *mi chocha*. But it wasn't the trees, it was the real shit. It was when her and Alejandro started doing their thing to the exclusion of me that I was not a happy camper. Suddenly getting on with the two people that I cared about and was attracted to didn't seem like such a great idea. That shit looked a lot better on paper. I knew they would screw but actually seeing them fucking pushed all my jealousy buttons. After that I swore no more threesomes with people I have strong feelings for. It may sound crazy, but I think if you're going to participate in a ménage à trois then it's best to do it with people you're not attached to emotionally. When Alejandro left, Crystal and I went upstairs and had a party for two. The sex was out of this world. I didn't know if Crystal just had natural skills—like my first female lover said about me—but I had a strong feeling that this wasn't her first time taking a dip in the sapphic pool.

Early the following morning we got the horrible news of Rhonda's death. Some niggas retaliated against her boyfriend Dante for not repaying a gambling debt by shooting up him and Rhonda's house. We all piled in Crystal's SUV and headed to the hospital, where we found out baby Jada didn't make it, either. That was a hell of a blow for all of us. I still can't believe Rhonda is gone. She was my girl since grade school and I loved her like a sister.

Anyway, after the funeral I called Crystal to see how she was doing. She started talking about that night and how I got her drunk and high and I took advantage of her. Yeah, like I poured the liquor down her throat and blew the weed smoke into her lungs. She even had the nerve to say that she wanted to fuck Alejandro again, I guess to prove how much she loved dick. I told her some choice things about herself and then hung up in her face. I found out from Nikki that Crystal had been double-dipping and got busted in bed with some female by the chick's husband.

That girl hurt me and hurt me deep. So when my cousin expressed concern over me being in love with Crystal, I told her that she was mistaken; I had some feelings for Crystal but nah, I wasn't in love with her. What could I say? I was too embarrassed to admit how I really felt after Crystal out and out played me like she did. Nikki is the closest person to me, but I still couldn't find it in me to share that pain with her.

That's when I turned all my attention to Alejandro. At the time I was digging him a lot but holding him at arm's length, not only 'cause of my feelings for Crystal but also because I was cautious about getting into a relationship; I'd never been in a serious one before. I even stopped dating him for a minute because he was getting more caught up than I was ready for him to be. But after the fiasco with Crystal I said "fuck you" to caution and fell heartfirst into a relationship with Alejandro. I thought he'd be perfect to help me get over her. I know that sounds like I was using him and I was sort of, at first. But Alejandro was so sweet and kind—he was just what I needed in my life. It wasn't hard falling in love with him once I let my guard down. And damn, he is amazing in bed. What I told Nikki and Odell was no joke. We hit a few bumps in the road but overall we enjoyed a good relationship. I thought I would have to step out on him with a female every now and then but I didn't. My focus was completely on him. Even though I run into attractive men and women all the time, I had no trouble being faithful to him—until about a month ago. I called things off a few days ago by telling him I needed some space because the guilt was killing me. I couldn't take looking into his loving, trusting eyes knowing I'd started fucking around on him with someone else. The someone else being Crystal.

I ran into her last month. I was hanging out at T.G.I. Friday's with Odell's crazy ass. If there's one thing Odell loves to do more than live, breath, and suck dick, it's to talk about folks, especially lookswise.

"Miss Rosie, you always talk about how I don't know how to hold my tongue.

Lemme tell you, even I was amazed I didn't say exactly what was on my mind when that chile sat her three inches of hair ass in my chair wit' a picture of Ashanti talkin' 'bout 'I want my hair like this.'" He leaned over and let out a laugh. "I liked to fell out! How this crow wit' hair you can barely snap yo' fingas on gonna come up in my piece wantin' a hairstyle that goes past the shoulders? Bitch, please! I just went ahead and gave her a cute little 'do and sent her on her delusional way. Folks be killin' me thankin' they can make a king-sized comforter out of a handkerchief." He picked up his drink and took a sip.

I shook my head. "What are you going to get, O? I'm thinking about the buffalo wings."

"That's fine with me. You know I ain't choosy about what goes in my mouth. Say somethin' smart and I'll throw the resta my drank in yo' face."

A heavyset man and woman with two chubby kids walked past our table. I rolled my eyes up to the ceiling and waited for the commentary from Odell.

"Lawd, look at the Klumps," he whispered. "Girl, you betta hope they don't want no buffalo wings, too, else ain't gon' be none left for us. We betta hurry up and order just in case."

"Odell, be nice."

"They should go to one of them stomach bypass places like that big girl from Wilson Phillips went to. Shee-it, they asses probably can get a family discount."

"Odell…"

"Now you can see fo' yo'self they one mo' trip to Krispy Kreme's from being housebound."

I didn't want to smile at his stupid ass but I couldn't help it.

"Miss Rosie, did you hear about Sherry's little sister Tonya?"

"No. What about her?"

"She got arrested the other night. She was comin' back here from over in Canada."

"For real? What did she get arrested for?"

"Stupid heffa got caught tryin' to bring some dope over for her boyfriend. E'rybody know after 9/11 they don't play at that border and even if you an old lady coming back from playing bingo, they'll check you."

"*Ay, díos mío!* What the fuck was she thinking?"

"She wasn't and that's why her ass in the trouble she is. Lettin' that no-good boy get her in that mess. She wasn't caught with a joint or two either. She had a shitload of weed. These bitches gonna get enough tryin' to play that Ride or Die shit with these mens. That's why a lot of 'em *ride* in a police car to jail and gon' *die* of old age in prison."

"I know that's right. Oh yeah, what happened with Aaron's ex-girlfriend? Last you told me, she was begging Aaron to see her one last time."

"She gave him a guilt trip and he went on over there and tried to tell her for the fiftieth time that he done finally accepted the fact of who he is and he wit' me now. She still wants him to come back to her. It's been five months since he left her but she just won't let him go. I feel sorry for her but at the same time I'm trippin' 'cause she got a man in her face tellin' her he wants to be with another man and she still hangin' on. For what?! Chile, you know she even told him she was willin' to have anal sex."

My mouth dropped open. "Her man finally admitted to being gay and she thinks all she has to do is offer her ass and he'll stay with her?"

"Yes. Girlfriend ain't got a clue if she thankin' that's all it'll take. She could get one of them strap-ons you got and bend him over a chair and it wouldn't keep him." He glanced over at the bar. "Uh-oh. Check out this hot mess sittin' up at the bar. Why is she dressin' season retarded? It's chilly as I don't know what outside and she got on a damn halter top. Lawd Jesus. She need her ass beat."

The chick lifted her arm to signal a couple that came into the restaurant. When she did, she revealed an Afro puff growing out of her armpit.

"Ch-ch-ch-Chia!" Odell covered his mouth to suppress his laughter. "Girl, if I had a razor I don't know if I'd shave them pits or slit her throat fo' comin' out the house like that. That bitch all kind of wrong."

I put my head in my hand and lightly chuckled.

"Oh shit. Miss Rosie—look."

"I ain't looking at nothing, fool. Now you're gonna get enough of always talking about people," I chastised him.

"You ain't gonna believe who just walked up and through here."

The serious tone in his voice made me look to where he was staring and there she was. Crystal, with some dude, being led to a table. I guess I had made myself believe that I didn't care about her anymore for so long I was caught off guard when my heart jumped into my throat at the sight of her. She was even more beautiful than when I last saw her. The waiter seated them a few tables down from us. She had on a full-length leather coat and took it off to reveal a tight red sweater and blue jeans. The sweater had a V-neck and it gave me a peek at her silky dark brown skin. I couldn't help but remember how soft it felt. Crystal always had such style and she made that simple outfit seem like something off a runway. She put her coat across an empty chair and sat down with her back to me. The last time I saw her she had cut her hair short but it had grown and now just brushed the tops of her shoulders. I wondered who the hell the buster was she came in with.

"If it ain't Miss 'Liquor Made Me Lick Her,'" said Odell. "I ain't seen that trick since the funeral."

I called Crystal all kinds of bitches and *pendejas* but it irritated the hell out of me when I heard Odell call her a trick. I wasn't about to show it, though. I'd talked plenty of trash about her so how would I look if I said something to Odell on calling her out of her name? I didn't say anything. I just slipped on my cool face.

"That sho is a fine piece she got with her," said Odell. "I have to give it to her janky ass, she always did have good taste in mens. 'Member that male dancer Shawn who used to sling dick over at Henry's? Oh, you know 'cause he was dancing on one of yo' gigs when him and Crystal met. But this boy is even more cuter than him."

"Yeah, he's all right."

"All right? You need to schedule an appointment wit' yo' gynecologist, 'cause somethin' must be wrong with the tingle in yo' pussy if you can't see that that boy is fine."

"Whatever," I responded in my most nonchalant tone.

Odell and I got back to our conversation, though my mind was on the couple seated not too far from us. A little while later I noticed the dude with Crystal get up and go toward the restrooms.

"You know what, Odell? Since we're in the same space I'm going to go over there and just say hello."

Odell crimped his lips and tossed a suspicious glance my way.

"Mm-hmm. I had a feelin' you was itchin' to go over there. I say let sleepin' bitches lie, but you gon' do what you want." He waved his hand at me as if to shoo me off.

As soon as I stood my heart started beating crazy fast. I walked over to her table and tapped her on the shoulder. "Hey, stranger."

She turned around and looked up at me. Surprise and then a smile lit up her lovely face. "Rosie!" She stood up and gave me a quick but warm hug. "What are you doing here?"

"Same thing you and everyone else are doing here, putting food and drinks in my belly. I'm here with Odell." I pointed to where he was sitting. His eyes were trained dead on us of course. Crystal looked around, smiled, and waved at him. He put on what I knew was his best fake smile, waved back, and mouthed, "Hey, girl." As soon as Crystal turned back around the smile dropped from his face and he rolled his eyes.

"Rosie, I've—. Here, have a seat. I've wanted to call you, I really have. I heard through the grapevine and on the news about the situation with the club closing. That was crazy."

"No, that was some straight-up bullshit."

"Was it really like they were trying to make it out to be?"

"They exaggerated some stuff. I'm not saying Vito, the guy who I was running the club with, was a choirboy or that his hands were totally clean. But a lot of that shit the feds just piled on him to get his assets. They're just as crooked as some of the people they go after. I know they would've loved to pin some stuff on me but they just questioned me. I'm hoping they don't call me to testify when the racketeering trial finally starts because I don't know anything that could help them despite them trying to bully something out of me. I didn't have anything to do with money or receipts. I ran every aspect of the place except the cheddar part. I hired the girls, choreographed dance numbers, came up with the décor for the club, and made sure the customers were happy and shit like that. The whole thing has been a nightmare." I paused for a moment. "You just asked me what time it was and I'm telling you how the watch was made. I didn't mean to pour all that out."

"Girl, don't worry about that, I understand. I hope everything turns out okay. What are you doing now?"

"I'm back to dancing at my old club for now. I'm working on some other things, though."

"That's good." She looked down at the table for a minute before looking back up. "Rosie, this estrangement has been driving me crazy. I miss Chico and Nikki. I'm so happy that Nikki is doing well. I watch that show she's on whenever I can. She's really doing her thing." She paused and looked earnestly into my eyes and said in a softer tone, "Most of all, I miss you, honey."

Right then I knew I was in trouble. "Why didn't you pick up the phone or come through, then?"

"Same reason you didn't I guess—pride."

"No. I didn't call because you tried to make it seem like I took advantage of you that night."

"I'm sorry, Rosie. I was so confused about everything." She looked over my shoulder. "Lamont is on his way back. We need to talk. I still have the same number. Call me tonight, okay?"

"Yeah, sure."

"Hey, sweetie," she said to Lamont. "This is my old friend Rosie. Rosie, this is Lamont."

I stood up and shook his hand. I had to admit that Odell was right; this Lamont was a looker. He wasn't very tall, only an inch more than me—around 5'8"—and had a Tyson Beckford look to him. Not quite that fine but close.

"It's nice to meet you, Rosie. It looks like we're both running into old friends, Crystal. I just ran into a guy I used to work with." He turned back to me. "Would you like to join us?"

"Oh, no thanks. I'm here with a friend. Thank you for asking, though. Crystal, I'll talk to you later."

"Okay."

"Nice meeting you, Lamont."

"Same here."

I walked back to my table and answered all of Odell's nosy questions. He put in his two cents and said that I shouldn't call 'cause Crystal was trouble and I would screw up my relationship with Alejandro. But I knew I would. For the rest of the time we were there my mind was in another world. I wondered what Crystal and I would say to each other when I called her later and what would be the outcome of the conversation.

When I phoned her that night we both danced around the core issue for a while and caught up on old news. After a bit of that I was ready to get everything out in the open. I asked her was what was going on with her and why did she act like she did following our night together. She was silent for a minute, then she just spilled it and let me in on things she'd never shared before. I've known her for more than ten years and I was taken aback by what she told me. I thought her foray into lesbianism was something that happened a little before our night together. She shocked the hell out of me by telling me that her first girl-on-girl experience was back in high school.

∼✦∼

Every summer just before school began, Crystal's mother would take her on weekend trips to New York to get a few choice designer outfits. On one particular trip, they stayed at the home of one of her mother's old friends, Wanda, who had recently relocated to the area. The woman had a daughter named Lydia who was around 20 years old. Crystal and Lydia hit it off right away. They sat on the living room floor and began gabbing away while their mothers were in the kitchen talking. At one point in their conversation, Lydia told Crystal that she was very pretty and should consider modeling. Crystal was already flattered that the older girl didn't brush her off as some kid, and the fact that Lydia considered her pretty made her feel even more flattered. Crystal told her she doubted that would be possible unless she experienced a growth spurt in the next couple of years.

Later that day they went into Lydia's room to listen to her stereo until dinner was ready. When they entered the room, Crystal noticed Lydia lock the door. Lydia walked over to the stereo and turned the radio on and then plopped on the bed. Crystal sat opposite her and they began chatting again. Crystal made a joke about Lydia and in retaliation Lydia moved across the bed and put her in a playful chokehold. Soon they were in a wrestling match. At some point Lydia had Crystal facedown on the bed in a bear hold. Crystal felt that warm pressure in her crotch as she became excited from their physical contact. She then felt Lydia softly moving her groin against Crystal's backside. She put her mouth to Crystal's ear, and the feel of her warm breath excited Crystal even more. Then Lydia began to softly nibble on her earlobe and dart her tongue in and out of her ear. Just as Crystal was about to turn over so they could be face-to-face, Wanda knocked on the door and told them dinner was ready.

When they retired to Lydia's room for the night, Crystal lay in bed and eagerly waited for Lydia to make a move, but she didn't. Crystal didn't have the nerve to so she fell asleep, disappointed. She was awakened later that night. There was movement beside her; she saw Lydia, completely naked and masturbating. When Lydia saw Crystal was awake and watching her, she asked if she wanted to join her. Crystal didn't say anything; she just slipped her hand inside her panties and started doing it as well. Lydia leaned over and pulled Crystal's T-shirt up, exposed her tits, and started licking her nipples. Crystal said for a brief second she felt guilty and wanted to stop her but she enjoyed the feeling too much. Lydia then slid Crystal's panties down and off. She got on top of Crystal and in between her legs. They ground against each other till they both came.

Crystal said that she'd already begun to have a curiosity about other girls and this incident just stoked it. She and Lydia had sex again the next night before Crystal and her mother left. I asked her why she acted like she had such a hard time understanding when I first came out—talking all that "what can another woman do for you that a man can't?" bullshit. She didn't let on when she was having sex with guys so she wasn't going to say anything about dalliances with women.

This was the part where she gave me some insight on why she was like that. I knew Mrs. Johnson was on the staid side, but Crystal said it went way beyond that. She said her mother never missed the opportunity to tell her that sex was something despicable that only men wanted and women merely put up with. She told Crystal any woman who wanted, much less enjoyed, sex was no better than a prostitute. Crystal went real deep into how she was affected by her mother's mentality about sex. By the time she was through I understood a lot more about her than I ever did. She didn't even feel comfortable enough to express her sexuality toward men much less her growing attraction to women. That explained why she would lie to me, Rhonda, and Nikki about sexual encounters she'd had with guys. She'd play all innocent and shit, but yet we'd hear about her getting down with this dude or another.

It's like Nikki said on numerous occasions, Crystal illustrates how you can know someone all their life and not know them at all. I can spot family a mile away—yet here was someone that I'd known for years, and until the night of the ménage à trois, I had no clue Crystal swung both ways. Girlfriend was deep undercover.

We ended up talking for about three hours on the phone. Then she asked me if I wanted to come out to her place and finish the conversation. I knew what she really meant. I knew what was going to happen if I went out there; I'd end up cheating on

Alejandro. I loved him but I still had this love for Crystal, too. I loved her first and for the longest. I tried to ignore the guilt gnawing at me when I got in my car and drove out to Crystal's place. I just told myself that whatever happened would be a one-time deal.

We finished the rest of the conversation all right. In about ten minutes. After that it was on. She walked over to the chair I was sitting in and with a little smile on her face she dropped her robe and exposed her beautiful naked body. We ended up going at it right there on the living room floor. Eventually we made our way to the bedroom. The sex was even better than when we were together before. Any thought that I had in my head that it would be a one-time deal was shot to hell. Especially when Crystal let me know that morning she wanted to continue seeing me.

❧

During the last few weeks all my feelings for Crystal have come bubbling back up to the surface. Now here I am, in love with two people at the same time. Alejandro. It's fucking killing me to hurt him. He has no idea what's going on. All he knows is one day we were talking about moving in together and the next he's hearing a speech about me needing some space. Odell told me, "You need to get yo' lips offa Crystal's clit and back on Alejandra's dick. That bitch don't know what plate she wanna eat offa. I'm tellin' you, she gonna put you through mo' changes than Mary J. Blige's hair. I thought we both said that we was through with these DL bitches anyway. Crystal ain't nothin' but the female version of that Thomas that I used to kick it wit'."

I know what Odell is saying but it's not that simple. I can't help how I feel. And yeah, Crystal wants to kick it with me but she doesn't want anyone to know about it, so we're not exactly holding hands in public. I'm not feeling that at all. I know it's a big step for her to even admit that she likes women, but she only does to the women she's messing with. I don't live my life looking over my shoulder for approving nods and I don't waste time worrying about what peeps are thinking about me. I wish she could find it in herself to live the same way.

It's because of this whole situation that I was so happy to hear from *Silk & Velvet*. I need the opportunity to get away for a while. Maybe being in California for a bit will clear my head and by the time I come back I'll know who I'll be with—Crystal or Alejandro. Nikki is going to fucking flip when I tell her all this. I already know she's going to be against me fucking around with Crystal again. And she's really going to trip when she finds out I've lied all this time about my true feelings for Crystal.

3

Rosie

One good thing about all this drama in my love life is it's taken some of my focus off of Lupe. That woman had Raul beg for me to come see her. She's lucky that I agreed to it. After what she did to me, I'd be justified if the only time I saw her was to spit on her grave. I spoke to her for few a minutes after Nikki first left for California. I only did that after somebody in the family gave her the number to the house and she kept calling me. I finally answered the phone and told her to quit trying to contact me because I wanted nothing to do with her. She had the nerve to ask me why wouldn't I at least talk to her. I said, "Oh, I don't know, maybe it's because after it came out Tony was molesting me, not only did you go along with your husband Renaldo in denying that it happened, but packed up my shit quick to send me to live with Nikki and her parents—shipping me off like an unwanted puppy." She started sputtering about how sorry she was. That's when I hung up the damn phone. I wasn't trying to hear none of that. I picked the phone back up and put in the blocking code and her phone number. I should've done that in the first place.

Her trying to apologize at this point is out and out laughable. No matter how much she says she's sorry, it doesn't mean a thing to me. She betrayed me in such a way I'll never forgive her. Raul and I were already still reeling from the sudden death of Papi, when Lupe turned around and within months was dating Renaldo. Then a short time later she married him.

It was so fucked up to not even have time to come to grips with our father being gone before seeing another man in our house taking his place. Seeing him in the bed where our father had just been not long before. This *cabron* even had the nerve to parade around in some of our father's clothes. And to top it off he forced my brother and me to call him Papi. Wasn't that some shit? Then he had a nickname for me— Mamita Rosita, even though Rosie is short for Rosaura. I could not stand hearing him call me that because the only time he did so was when he was about to punish me for something. The sick asshole turned a name that could be an endearment into my call for punishment.

Of all the men to rush into marriage with Lupe picked this fucker. Every day he would have a list of duties for Lupe and me to do and had a time set for when he wanted the tasks completed. From time to time he even had one of his loser friends spy on us when we went to the grocery store and had them report back how long it took us to finish. If we ran over the allotted time our punishment were some smacks across the face and getting called every name in the book. He would even sneak off from work to come home and check on Lupe. He also isolated us from our family— Nikki was no longer allowed to sleep over—but his family had unlimited access to our home. How I hated that family. They were a bunch of loudmouth pieces of trash.

Raul was the son Renaldo never had so he was spared all of this. Renaldo was the king of the house and he anointed Raul the prince. At the time, Raul took full advantage of his favored status. Somehow, though he managed to overcome being raised all those years by Renaldo and has turned out to be a fantastic guy.

I'll never forget the night Raul had an asthma attack and Renaldo and Lupe rushed him to the hospital. As soon as Renaldo picked up the phone to call his brother Tony to have him come over to stay with me while they were gone, the feeling of dread came over me. I used to like Tony. I thought he was funny and much nicer than his brother. But he was just as much of a lowlife as his brother—he just hid it behind a nice-guy façade. He had begun molesting me a short time before that night. He convinced me that if I said anything everybody would think that I was bad and not love me anymore.

The night Raul got sick, Tony tried to take his molestation of me to another disgusting level. I can still remember the pain of him attempting to enter me. I lied and said I had to use the bathroom. When he let me up, instead of going to the bathroom I made a dash for the door. In the cold of that winter night, and in only my nightgown and slippers, I ran over to Nikki's. That's when I finally told Nikki and Tía Sarah what had been going on. I was already ashamed to relay everything to them but I was even more so to say it in front of Tío Miguel, so I asked if he could leave the room.

Tía Sarah told him later and the next morning they went to my house to talk with Lupe. While Nikki and I were waiting for them to get back, I envisioned what I hoped would happen: that Lupe would come and hold me and tell me that she still loved me despite what Tony did to me. She would finally see how evil Renaldo and his brother were. She would divorce Renaldo and kick him out of our home and everything would be all right again.

That's not what ended up happening, though. Between Nikki and me eavesdropping on conversations, we found out how it all went down. Renaldo said I was lying and Lupe agreed with him. Tío Miguel and Tía Sarah stood up for me, though, and said I was telling the truth. Tío Miguel wanted to press charges against Tony. Renaldo told Lupe if she went along with that he would divorce her immediately. Tío Miguel said if Lupe wasn't going to report Tony that he sure as hell wasn't going to let me come back to stay in that house. Right then and there Lupe made her choice on what was more important; staying married to an abusive asshole whose brother was molesting her child meant more to her than her daughter, who never needed her mother as much as she did then.

I can't even describe how hurt I felt when I saw Tía Sarah and Tío Miguel coming through that door with my clothes, toys, and other belongings. My so-called mother betrayed me to the utmost. My hurt quickly turned to anger. It may sound crazy but I believe my anger has been my saving grace. If I'd let myself give in to all that pain and wallow in it, I don't know how I would've made it. As mad as I was, I still tried to call home and talk to Lupe and Raul. Lupe told me that I wasn't to call there because Renaldo had forbade it and I would just make things bad on her. At the risk of emotionally getting kicked in the teeth again I still called here and there, but I finally gave up.

This is why I found it highly ironic that Lupe couldn't understand why I won't take her phone calls now. What the fuck could she have to say to me after all this time? A few years ago Renaldo left her for some twenty-two-year-old. It was after that that she began calling me with a vengeance.

I did feel I received a certain amount of justice as far as Tony is concerned. There ain't no such thing as shit staying behind closed doors, especially not in the old neighborhood, and the reason why I was living with Nikki and her folks got around. Tony's fiancée heard about what he did to me and dumped him, which was a good thing considering she had a young daughter from a previous relationship. It's nice to know to some mothers, their child's well-being and welfare take priority. When other people found out about it they treated him like a pariah. A few years ago he ended up going to jail for a credit card scheme, and word from the street got behind bars that Tony liked to mess with little girls. You know how it goes down when that happens. My cousin Enrique said his boy who was doing time in the same joint told him some guys ripped Tony a new asshole—or at least greatly improved on the size of his old one. He's spent the last few years on and off drugs. I wish I could say there was a part of me that felt bad for how his life turned out, but I can't. I think he got exactly what he deserved.

≈❀❁❀≈

Now I've got to prepare myself to go see Lupe. As much anger and resentment I feel toward her, I don't want her to die. If I hadn't found out she has cancer and might not make it, I could've gone the rest of my life not seeing her. Maybe I'll ask her why she couldn't be there for me and how could she just abandon me the way she did, Not that I care at this point. Still, there's no harm in asking, right?

Some people who know what happened have speculated that it's shaped the woman I am today. It's gotten back to me that some family members think because I was molested it skewed my sexuality and made me bi. Bullshit. I know other dancers who are bi and were molested, and close-minded peeps can put us all in a neat little clichéd package, but I remember having the same feelings for girls as well as boys since I was in kindergarten; before any molestation took place. I scribbled anonymous love notes of red hearts in crayon to both sexes in first grade. I even got the mighty sting of three rulers taped together when Sister Mary Alice intercepted a little scribbling I made for a little girl named Janice. It was only years later that I understood why she punished far more for that note than the one she caught me writing to a boy.

No, Tony molesting me didn't turn me into a bisexual. I could've easily been turned off sex altogether, but that didn't happen to me. There are still certain touches or words that trigger old memories, but I shake it off. I have to. I'm determined not to let what happened to me have that kind of power over my life. I was victimized but I'm no damn victim.

Now as for my being an exotic dancer, Alejandro once asked if that was one way of making up for the attention I didn't get from Lupe. I'd never even thought about it before but as soon as he said it, something in me clicked. I love the attention men and women lavish on me when I'm up on that stage. I mean, I love it like a crack-head loves the pipe. A lot of chicks have to get high to go on stage, but with me, when I'm onstage—that's when I get high. And when I really thought about it, there have been times when I'm performing I feel like I'm giving a big "how you like me now?" and "fuck you" to the woman formerly called my mother. So yeah, Lupe plays a part in that. But I also love the power I feel when I mesmerize the audience. I can make the stingiest, quarter-squeezing muthafucka come out his pocket for me. I make them all—even if it's just for the time I'm swinging on that pole—fall in love with me. They adore my sweet Puerto Rican ass. They haven't made a drug yet to equal that feeling.

4

Nikki

I get up and go to the kitchen and pour another glass of Seagram's and juice, then sit back on the couch. Damn, Tía Lupe has cancer. Despite their relationship—or a lack thereof—I know this still has to come as a blow to Rosie. Hell, I'm stunned. Even though they haven't seen each other in about twenty-one years, she has to be hurting 'cause that's still her mother. After we moved to Detroit, we went back to New York a few times to visit relatives and go to the Puerto Rican Day parade. However, each time we went we managed to never run into Tía Lupe. Rosie didn't want to see her and I felt like I would be betraying Rosie in some way if I went by. Until Tía Lupe married that prick Renaldo, I only have pleasant memories of her. I remember she was very affectionate; always giving Rosie, Raul, and me plenty of hugs and kisses. She would let Rosie and me help out in the kitchen and wouldn't get mad if we messed up a dish or spilled something. The woman I remember was loving and protective of her children. That woman was in complete contrast to the one who sent her child away.

I pick up the phone to dial my parents. After two rings Mami picks up.

"Hello?"

"Hey, Mami."

"Hey, honey. How's it going?"

"Good, I'm about to go over my script some more but I wanted to call you first."

"Nikki, you had me laughing like crazy the last time I saw the show. That was too funny when the lady who plays your mother came in and caught you and that boy messing around and you two fell all over each other trying to put your clothes back on. I almost peed on myself."

Normally I'd be eating a big ole chunk of Wisconsin cheese right now hearing Mami talk like this. But it's hard to feel happy when I have to tell her the news about Tía Lupe.

"You didn't hurt yourself, did you? It looked like it hurt falling down behind that couch."

"No, Mami. They have padding to break your fall; you just can't see it."

"Oh, that's good. I saw Miss Hernandez the other day at the bodega and she said to tell you how proud she is of you. She remembers you putting together little shows with the neighborhood kids. She said she could see you had a talent even then at that young age. And I do recall her bugging me and your father that we should try and get you in commercials."

"Wow, I had forgotten all about those little plays I used to put together. I thought my acting bug got started after we moved to Detroit and I was in my first school play."

"It was when you got up on that little stage and heard the applause that you began wanting to be an actress when you grew up. You always were a little ham," says Mami proudly.

"Who are you telling? Next time you see Miss Hernandez tell her I said thank you. But I might run into her next weekend. Me and Rosie are heading out there for a couple of days."

"You are? That's wonderful! I can't wait to see my two babies. What brings you both out this way?"

"To see Tía Lupe. Mami, I don't know how to tell you this so I'll just spit it. Tía Lupe has breast cancer and she's going to have a mastectomy."

"What?! How do you know this?!"

"She told Raul out about it a few days ago and he told Rosie. He's on his way to New York, too."

"How can this be? I just talked to Lupe the week before last and she didn't mention anything about this or being sick. She looked a bit frail, but she's been looking that way for years. Your father and I always get on her about not taking care of herself. I can't believe this! I just can't believe it!"

"Calm down, Mami. I know you're upset but don't get all worked up. You have to watch your blood pressure."

"Fuck my blood pressure!"

I'm a bit shocked by her language as I always am those rare times Mami spews an obscenity. Rosie and I can cuss like sailors at times, but it's not something we picked up from Mami. She only cusses when she's really upset about something.

"Lord, have mercy. I know Lupe has made some huge mistakes, but your father and I have still tried to reach out to her 'cause with Renaldo annulling their marriage, Rosie not talking to her, and Raul living out in Miami, she doesn't have anybody here to look after her. I just can't believe she didn't tell us about this. I'm a half hour away from her but you find out about it way out in California before I do. Wait, so Rosie is going to see Lupe?"

"Yes, Mami. That's why we're coming there, remember?" I say, exasperated.

"I'm sorry. You caught me off guard about Lupe. This is terrible. Maybe some good can come out of this, though. Maybe Rosie and her mother can reach some kind of resolution. They've missed out on so much time together."

"I know. I hope they can, Mami. Even with Rosie going there to see her, I'm not sure if we can hope for that kind of miracle after all these years. Rosie has so much resentment toward Lupe—she doesn't even refer to her as her mother."

"I haven't been to Mass in a few weeks but it looks like I need to go and do a lot of praying."

I jump on the opportunity to change this very depressing subject. "You know, I'm surprised you're still hanging in the Catholic faith. I didn't expect your conversion to last all these years."

"I still go to the A.M.E. church down the street once in a while. I miss the gospel choir. The one thing I don't miss is spending hours on end there. At least with Mass you're in and out in about an hour or so. I love the Lord and praise him every day and I don't think I have to prove that by sitting in church all day. If Momma were alive she'd probably hit me for saying that. Oh, she had a fit when she found out I was converting. She didn't speak to your father for months because she felt it was his fault."

"Where is Papi, by the way?"

"Him? Oh, he's gone to play pool with his friend Tomas."

I'm real good at catching tones in people's voices. They can say something that seems perfectly innocent and I'll hear hidden meaning in the sound of their voice, no matter how subtle. Even though all she said was Papi had gone to play pool, I definitely hear something in Mami's voice.

"What's wrong, Mami?"

"What makes you think something is wrong?" she says evasively.

"Because I can hear it and because you just answered a question with a question."

"You always were a bit too perceptive for your own good."

"Please, Mami. What's going on?"

"This isn't something that I should be getting into with you, Nikki, especially over the phone."

"Mami, if you don't tell me, my imagination will go into overtime and I'll be thinking all kinds of things. Now what is it?"

After a few moments she says, "Nikki, I love your father. We've been together for almost thirty years now. But the fact of the matter is…"

"Is what?"

"No one ever said marriage was easy. You go through the highs and lows. Right now we're going through a low period, and I've had this feeling like I just want to pack it up even if it's just to make him wake up."

I just sit there holding the phone, too stunned to speak.

"I'm sorry, sweetie. I guess this conversation has brought us both things we didn't want to hear. Nikki, perhaps I shouldn't tell you this—and trust me, if you didn't bring it up I had no intention of doing so. There are issues in our marriage. We have our good days, but then there are times like now that I want to go it alone for a while."

Go it alone? I can't believe what the hell I'm hearing. What the fuck?! My parents' marriage is my role model. Having grown up in a sea of kids from divorced homes, my parents, along with Mario's, are who I looked to as proof that Mario and I could make it for the long haul.

"I'm not ready to be put out to pasture yet, Nikki. I still have some years in me and I don't want to spend the rest of them not being as happy as I could be. I'm trying to hang in there, baby, because I love your father very much. It's just hard sometimes."

"Mami, that's in all relationships. You have good days and bad ones, it doesn't mean you should give up on it. Why haven't you said anything to me before now?"

"This is something I'm trying to work out with your father. Like I told you, I had no intention of bringing it up, but I'm glad it was because I need someone to talk to."

"I'm thinking everything's just nigga-dory on the home front. Then out of the damn blue I find out that I could call home and possibly find you two are no longer together 'cause you've decided to 'go it alone' somewhere seeking your fulfillment. Thanks for the heads-up, Mami."

"Nikki, first of all, I'm not one of your friends so don't take that sassy tone with me. And secondly, don't use that n-word around me. I don't know where you and Rosie get using that word. You certainly didn't learn it in our house."

"We grew up in New York and Detroit, Mami."

"There are plenty of people in New York and Detroit who don't use that word."

"Really? They're certainly outnumbered by the ones who do. Anyway, I just found out that Rosie's mother could be dying and that my parents' marriage is in trouble, so excuse me if I'm not trying to get into a PC debate over the use of the n-word."

After a few moments of silence, she continues. "I wish you could understand. There have been so many nights that I've cried myself to sleep over this. A part of me feels like I've missed out on things. You know your father is the only man I've ever dated and well, you know, been with."

"Are you telling me the reason things are strained in your marriage is because you've got the itch to be with other men?" I ask incredulously. "What, are you going through a midlife crisis?"

"Nikki, if you don't watch how you're talking to me, we can end this conversation right now," she says firmly.

"All right. I'm sorry. You've got to understand how I feel hearing this. You still love Papi, don't you?"

"Didn't I just say I did? And my comment about having only been with your father doesn't mean I'm going to go out and mess around—especially in this day and age. I do have curiosity, though, but that's it. I think my curiosity has been piqued because up until recently your father and I have had a very active and satisfying sex life."

"Aw jeez, Mami. I totally don't want to hear about that."

"Sex isn't just for the under-thirty crowd, Nikki."

"I know that but I don't wanna hear about my parents knocking boots," I whine.

"Well, there hasn't been much boot knocking lately. I think your father needs some Viagra or something. I want to suggest it to him in a way that doesn't offend that Latin machismo of his. It seems like my sex drive has gotten stronger and his has tapered off."

I squirm uncomfortably on the couch. I'm so ready to wrap up this portion of the conversation.

"That's not the only problem. The main thing is I just wish I'd done more and been to more places before I got married. And your father's a stay-at-home type and doesn't really want to do anything other than play pool a couple of nights a week. I've saved and made some good investments from the money I got making outfits and doing alterations at home. This would be the perfect time for us to travel but he doesn't want to. His excuse now is it's too dangerous to fly. I had to practically drag him on the plane when we visited you.

"At least I'm hanging in there, Nikki. Not only because I love your father, but also because I'm afraid of what might happen if I were to leave. I don't know how he would handle it. You know what he did that time…I'm sorry, baby," she says softly. "I'm so sorry. I didn't mean to dredge that up. Just understand that I'm in the prime of my life and I should be out there living and doing things I didn't do when I was younger. I feel so…so stuck! If I can't get your father to go along with me, what's going to be the price?"

"Mami, can't you go and travel on your own? It doesn't mean you have to leave your marriage just because Papi's not willing to go along with you. Maybe after he sees the fun you're having he'll want to start coming along."

"You're right. It's funny, but I didn't think of that. We've always done things together so I guess my mind-set has been all or nothing. What if I start doing that and we end up living separate lives? I don't know. I have a lot of thinking to do." She pauses for a moment. "I've got to go, baby. I don't mean to drop this on you and leave. But I need to get out of here—the walls are closing in on me. I'm going to go for a walk and clear my head."

"You and Papi can make it, right?"

"That's all I want. I'm going to stop by church and light a candle for Lupe. And say a prayer for your father and me. And pray that you will understand what I'm going through. I miss my little girl so much. I don't care how old you are—you'll always be my little hardheaded girl. I wish you were here right now. I could use some of your strength. I never told you this but I admire the chutzpah that you and Rosie have. I may not agree with all the choices you two make at times, especially that exotic dancing Rosie does, but you both have a clear vision of what you want to do—and hell or high water, you do it. If you had listened to your father and me you wouldn't be out there in Hollywood and on television. I'm sorry we gave you such a hard time about acting. We shouldn't have tried to get you to give up something you love so much. As parents, you want your child to have as stable a future as possible, so it's kind of hard to be supportive when they choose to do something where the chances of succeeding aren't in their favor. I'm so pleased you've found a way to beat the odds and you're—what is it you kids say now? Oh, you're doing the damn thing."

"Thank you, Mami." I want to say more than just "thank you." I want to tell her how much what she just said means to me. That it's something I've waited years to hear. That I haven't always been as strong as she thinks, because if Mario hadn't come to Detroit and given me the push I needed, I'd probably still be there doing plays and commercials, dreaming of Hollywood. And how I was then is the same as she is now—stuck inside a comfort zone, wanting more but settling for less. But the words in my head don't connect with my vocal cords. My mind has drifted to a long-ago incident.

"Mami loves you. I'll talk to you later. Tell Mario I said hi. I can't wait to see you and Rosie. Bye-bye." She hangs up.

I continue holding the phone and listen as the silence turns to a dial tone and then the recording comes on— "If you'd like to make a call, please hang up and try your call again. If you need help…" I finally hit the off button on the phone and put it on the coffee table. I look at it like it's a backstabbing friend. The bad news I've gotten through it about Tía Lupe and the situation with Mami and Papi has overshadowed the good news about Odell's engagement and Rosie's trip out here for the photo shoot.

Here I am a grown woman but I might as well be a kid again, faced with the possibility my parents might separate. Even though I couldn't find the words to tell her, I do sympathize with what she's going through. I don't want her to be miserable. Her mentioning how Papi reacted to her attempt at leaving him once has dug up a long-buried memory. There are certain painful things from our childhood that to this day Rosie and I don't talk about—and what precipitated our move to Detroit is one of them.

5

Nikki

Rosie and I were playing out in front of our apartment. It was the first day of the season that we could go without our jackets. We were in the midst of a heated competition of ball and paddle when Mami threw off our concentration by calling us from our second-floor window.

"Nikki and Rosie! Get in here and get washed up so you can eat dinner!"

I whipped around and looked up at her and smacked my lips. "Dang, Mami! You made me mess up!"

"Girl, you smack them lips and talk to me like that again and that paddle is going to be hitting a lot more than a little red ball! Now y'all gather up them toys and get up here."

"Make me sick," I muttered under my breath as I started gathering the toys.

"What did you say?" Mami asked.

"Nothing."

"That's what I thought. And Rosie, you can get your hand off that little hip and uncurl your mouth. It'll be enough heat left on that paddle to put some fire on your behind, too, missy."

As I picked up my Etch A Sketch, I noticed Marcela Jimenez sashaying across the street toward us. Every neighborhood has a resident hoochie and Marcela was the chick who held the title in ours. She and her four kids lived in the apartment across from us. She had three boys and one girl named Yesenia who Rosie and I played with. We never held Marcela's reputation against Yesenia. She couldn't help it if her mama was a ho. Other kids weren't so understanding, though, and Rosie and me had to stop them from picking on Yesenia. They used to surround her and sing horrible little ditties like "Yo' mama is a slut! Who takes it up the butt! She can't stop, from selling her cock, up and down the block!"

At that age all adults seemed like giants but not Marcela. She wasn't much taller than Rosie and I were at the time. I guess God decided that since He shortchanged her in the height department He would compensate for it by giving her an extra helping of boobs and ass. And she made sure to wear outfits that emphasized her attributes. The only time you didn't see her in something that showed off her top and bottom assets was when winter forced her to wear a coat. She was light-skinned with long hair dyed a hideous brassy blonde color. Still, she was very pretty despite getting a little too happy with the eyeliner and lipstick and having hair that was the envy of the two-dollar hookers in Times Square.

Marcela had on a skintight black Lycra minidress with a blue and black bolero jacket, and pink house slippers. She looked like she was a change of shoes away from going to party. She didn't acknowledge Rosie or me. She looked up to the window where Mami was still standing.

"Yo, Sarah! Can you buzz me up? I need to talk to you a sec."

"About?"

A wicked smile crossed Marcela's overly made-up face. "About Miguel, honey."

I looked at Mami and saw the strangest expression on her face. Marcela didn't wait for an answer from Mami; she just walked up the steps and opened the first set of doors leading to the vestibule. Moments later we could hear the buzzer and she entered through the second set of doors.

"Nikki, what do you think that hoochie-coochie wants to talk to Tía Sarah about?"

"I don't know. Let's hurry up and go see."

Just then Mami came back to the window. "Nikki. You and Rosie stay down there till I tell you, okay?" She disappeared from the window again.

Rosie and I sat down on the steps holding our toys. Suddenly, we heard shouting from our apartment through the open window. Rosie and I stood up and looked toward it.

"Get the hell out of my apartment, you lying tramp!" Mami shouted.

"I'm not lying, bitch! When your husband gets home you talk to him and find out who's the liar! Have him tell you whose apartment he's really been at when he comes across the street to supposedly play cards at Woody's!"

"Bitch, you got two motherfucking seconds to get out before I put my foot so far up your ass I can't pull it out!"

"You mean to tell me you'd beat up on a pregnant woman?"

"Get out!"

"Fine, I'll leave! But just in case he doesn't tell the truth, find out how I know about the clover-shaped birthmark inside his thigh and how his dick curves to the right!"

We heard the door slam. Soon Marcela came stomping out of the building. When she got to the street, she turned toward our apartment window even though Mami wasn't standing there.

"You let your husband know that he ain't just gonna hit it, then quit it! Shit ain't over till *I* say it is!" She walked quickly back across the street; her massive behind was rolling, trying to keep up.

Rosie and I sat back down on the steps waiting for the signal from Mami that we could come up. After a few minutes I grew anxious and impatient.

"Come on, Rosie. Let's go."

We rushed up the steps and into the building. We had to hit the button a couple of times before Mami finally buzzed us in. When we opened the door to the apartment we looked around the living room and dining room and didn't see Mami. We dumped our toys on the couch and Rosie went to look in the kitchen. She came back out and shook her head. We both went to my parents' bedroom.

Mami was sitting on the edge of the bed with her hands in her lap. She was looking down at the floor. Rosie and I went over to her; I sat on one side; Rosie, the other. Mami's jet-black hair, which was cut into an asymmetrical bob, was hanging in her face. I leaned forward and swept her hair back.

She lifted her head and looked at me. Tears were streaming down her beautiful dark bronze face. Mami put her arms around me and Rosie and we hugged her tightly. I laid my head on her chest and listened to her fast-beating heart; silently wishing it to return to its normal pace. I could smell her signature scent—Chanel No. 5. She wore that perfume almost daily. It didn't matter if she was going to the grocery store or to church. It was one of the few luxuries she allowed herself.

"Look," Mami said softly. "I need for you two to be my big girls tonight, okay? I want you to wash up and fix your own plates and take them to your room to eat. Unless you have to use the bathroom, I want you to stay there until I say so. Mike and I need to talk in private when he gets home. Now you two go on." She kissed us both on our foreheads. Rosie and I got up and hugged and kissed her. As we were leaving the bedroom, I turned and looked at Mami. She gave me a half-smile that didn't even halfway comfort me.

Rosie and I finished eating our meal rather quickly. You would think that we wouldn't have had much of an appetite, but we ate like it was going to be our last meal. As if we were giving ourselves some sustenance to carry us through the storm that was brewing.

We were lying across the bed watching television when we heard Papi come in. Rosie and I both sat up. I went over and turned the volume down and sat back on the bed. I heard Papi in the kitchen. He always stopped there first to see what was for dinner. Soon there was a tap on our bedroom door, then it swung open.

"Hey you two. Why so quiet in here? Are you feeling all right?"

"Yes," I answered as I shot him an evil look.

Papi's eyebrows knitted together and he gave me a quizzical look. "What's wrong with you, Zuzu? Why are you looking at me like that?"

"Why don't you go ask Mami?" I grabbed the bedspread and bunched a fistful in my hands. I was so angry with him for doing bad things with that nasty Marcela and making Mami cry I could've just run up to him and kicked him till his legs bled. I glanced over at Rosie and she looked like she wanted to do the same. Papi looked back and forth at us again before closing the door.

"Sarah! What's wrong with the girls?" I heard him ask.

Then, for what seemed like hours, we sat frozen on the bed and listened to my parents alternate between shouting and crying. Papi kept saying things like, "It didn't mean anything," and "It'll never happen again." Somewhere in all of this was the sound of glass shattering—Mami had thrown something at Papi. A short time later our bedroom door flew open, causing both Rosie and me to jump. It was Mami. Her eyes were red and swollen but no longer wet with tears. Instead, they were full of fire, like she wanted to do a lot more to Papi than kick him in the legs.

"Put together some clothes—we're leaving."

Papi appeared behind her. "No! Don't pack anything! No one is going anywhere! Sarah, come on, let's talk about this. Please!"

Mami turned around to Papi. "There is nothing more to talk about! You son-of-a-bitch! What else is there to say, huh? You want to talk about how you slept with that filthy whore and about how she might be carrying your child? Huh, Mike? Is that what you want to talk about?"

"Please, Sarah. She's lying. If she is, you know, pregnant, it's not mine because it only happened once and I used something." Papi looked over at Rosie and me. "Let's not say any more in front of the girls. They shouldn't be hearing this."

"Ha! Why should we hide this from them? They're going to hear all of this anyway! You know your nasty little whore hangs out her panties for the whole neighborhood to see! I'm sure everyone in Spanish Harlem knows about this. You motherfucker! You've humiliated the kids and me! We'll be the joke of the neighborhood!" She turned back to us. "Do as I say and put some clothes in a bag." She pushed past Papi and stomped toward their bedroom.

Rosie and I started gathering some clothes in our Barbie overnight bags. I just stuffed a few random things in there; I didn't take the time to see if anything matched or not. I put on my shoes and sat back on the bed; waited for Mami. Rosie followed suit. Mami came back to the door with her purse slung over her shoulder and carrying a suitcase.

"Let's go."

We picked up our bags and Mami held out her hand to wave us ahead of her. Just when we got to the front door I heard Papi say from behind us, "I'll kill myself if you leave me, Sarah!"

"Oh my God, Mike!" Mami screamed.

I turned around and saw Papi standing where the living room and dining room joined, holding a handgun to his head. I dropped the overnight bag. Mami dropped her purse and suitcase too. She walked slowly toward Papi. It didn't even seem like I was a part of what was happening. I felt myself disconnecting from what was going on—like I was just watching it all on television.

"Mike, please put the gun down."

"I can't live with-without y-you, Sarah," he sobbed. "I have n-nothing to live for if you and the girls l-leave."

"Mike, don't do this, think of the kids." She held out her hand. "Give me the gun, babe. Please. I promise we won't go, okay? Just give me the gun."

"You promise me!" Papi screamed; his body was shaking. "Promise me, Sarah! Promise me! Promise me!"

"I promise Mike! I promise!"

Papi slowly took the gun from his head and gave it to Mami. She took it and gingerly placed it on a nearby table. Papi grabbed her and fell into her arms, crying. He then slid down to his knees, hugging Mami around the waist. He said how sorry he was over and over.

I had felt numb to all that was going on and then the reality of everything came crashing down on me. I began screaming at the top of my lungs and the held-in tears unleashed down my face. I felt Rosie grab and hold me; I could hear Mami and Papi saying it was going to be all right, everything was going to be okay. All three of them encircled me, in a ring of solace. Still, it took a minute for my screams to die down and even longer for my tears to stop. Papi picked me up and held me. Everything went blank after that. I don't know if I fainted or what. Next thing I knew I woke up later that night and I was in my parents' bed. Rosie was there, too, and we were in between my parents. I fell back into a deep slumber.

⋘⊚⋙

I've said it before and it bears repeating: Parents always think they can hide the things they do and say from kids, but that's almost never the case. Even though my parents told Rosie and me that we were moving because Papi got a new job, I knew from catching pieces of conversations that Mami told Papi the only way they could try and save their marriage was to move back to her home state so they could start over. Her father had pulled some strings to get Papi a job at the company he retired from. As Mami had predicted, the affair between Marcela and Papi became neighborhood knowledge. A few kids tried to give Rosie and me grief about it. Unfortunately for a couple of them, their own fathers had had dalliances with Marcela. Don't think for a minute it didn't get thrown right back into their faces. And it turned out Marcela was not pregnant like she claimed.

Within a matter of weeks we'd packed up and settled in our new house in Detroit.

It was a while before things got back to normal in our home. My parents were normally very huggy-kissy with each other but I never saw my parents exchange any form of affection again until after we'd been living in Detroit for a few months. I saw Papi making affectionate advances but Mami rebuffed them. I'll never forget the day when I came in the house to get my gloves and they were in the dining room kissing. I was so happy to see the first real sign that things were back on track that I interrupted their kiss by squealing in delight and running up to them and throwing my arms around them.

Now that I'm looking back at what happened through the glasses of retrospect, I'm not sure if Papi would have pulled the trigger. I know he was truly distraught over us leaving, but I don't know if the gun was just a last-minute ploy to get us to stay. If it was a ploy, it was one that worked. But I wonder if it ever crossed Papi's mind what the image of seeing him with that gun to his head did to me. How it made me feel so helpless and scared. And I'm sure Mami and Rosie felt the same way. It's strange how it was never talked about. I can see Mami still remembers. How could she forget? The question is, what if it *wasn't* a ploy? What if Papi really *can't* live without Mami?

Even though that incident was never talked about, it's always been with me. In fact, I use it in my acting; if I need to show anguish, I go back to what I felt on that long-ago evening. It may seem like I'm pimping a painful memory but that's what actors do. To bring out an emotion, we draw from a memory that mirrors it.

Seven is supposed to be a lucky number but it was during our seventh year on earth that Rosie and me went through some real shit. Rosie went through traumatic events at home and then she and I came close to seeing my parents break up and witnessed Papi with a gun to his head, threatening to blow his brains out right in front of us. Following close behind that, we had to adjust to living in a brand-new city, going to a brand-new school, and making brand-new friends. I'm surprised we made it out of grade school without being institutionalized. My parents sent Rosie to counseling to help deal with what she'd gone through with her mother, stepfather, and Tony, but they should've popped for a couple of sessions for me.

I'd give anything if my parents can get through this. I want both my parents to be thrilled—and damn it if it makes me a selfish bitch—I want them happy *together.*

6

Nikki

J ust as I start setting the table I hear Mario's key in the door. I walk around the corner to greet him. He looks dead tired, poor thing. After all these years of knowing him, it still bowls me over how gorgeous he is and how attracted I am to him. I've lost count of how many times I've run my fingers through his short, curly, black hair. Or how many times I've gotten lost in his beautiful green eyes—mesmerized by the golden flecks dancing within them. Mmm, don't get me started on those sexy, slightly full lips. I can't imagine even after forty years that I'd tire of kissing them. I think the reason I haven't grown tired of his masculine beauty is that his spirit and intellect are even more beautiful. A man with a keen mind and a generous heart is automatically appealing and will do nothing but boost what he's got going on outside.

And if I may walk down Crass Street for a minute, him having a nice thick nine-incher that he knows how to work sho don't hurt any, okay? Also, I love the casual and cool way he dresses—none of that bling mess. He has on beige Dockers, white shirt rolled up at the sleeves, and black loafers. His brown suede messenger bag with his laptop in it is slung over his shoulder.

"Hey you," I say.

He just turns the corners of his mouth down in a playful pout and opens his arms. I go to him and wrap my arms around him and feel his envelop me.

"What a day," he sighs.

"A rough one, huh?"

"Yeah, baby. I'm glad to be home."

I give him a peck on the lips. "Put down your bag, kick off your shoes, and come eat some dinner and tell me all about it."

"Sounds good to me. I can taste on your lips that you've started on the after-dinner drink early."

"Ah, no lectures."

"It wasn't a lecture, just an observation. What are we having?"

"Porterhouse steaks, stuffed potatoes, salad, and rolls."

"Mm-hmm. That sounds good 'cause I'm starving."

He washes his hands at the kitchen sink while I put the food on the table. We both sit down to eat. Mario says a quick blessing and proceeds to rip into his plate. I consider myself a thoroughly modern woman who will have my own career and not depend on a man for my livelihood. And I'm a woman who will only walk beside my man, not one single step behind him. I have views that would make Glorias Steinem and Allred proud. But at the risk of putting my feminist card in jeopardy, I love taking care of my man and one of the ways I do that is by making him a delicious meal. It's reciprocal so it's all good. He pampers me, too. Breakfast is the meal that's his forte; let me tell you, his scrambled eggs put mine to shame.

"So babe, tell me about what's going on at work," I say.

"You know how we've got a new owner, right?"

"Yeah."

"At first we were all just happy to keep our jobs. But now it's been a battle with this dude to not turn the magazine into some big gossip and bling-bling rag. One of the reasons that I was happy to get a job at *Urban Report* is because of the quality of the articles, you know? They covered things that affect our communities, like government policies and police brutality. It had entertainment articles but that was just a small part of what the magazine was about. Lloyd is trying to flip it and make it all about who's fucking who in show business and doing photo layouts of some celebrity's mansion. He's steering away from what this magazine is all about. I'm not saying there shouldn't be a gossip column or interviews with singers, athletes, and actors. We can have that, too. But our people need information that's going to empower; especially the information that doesn't get coverage on the evening news."

"I hear you, baby. When I read the latest issue this morning, I noticed it had a lot more lightweight type of articles. And they pushed your article on how people have been hurt by the Patriot Act way in the back of the damn magazine. I had to go through thirty stories about rappers and big-name jewelers and stuff like that to get to yours. I had to look on the cover a couple of times to make sure I was reading the right magazine."

"That's what I'm talking about. That infuriates the fuck outta me. Running a big-ass story about where to buy diamonds instead of how we got peeps dying in Africa so that we can floss ice. Now I know why Lloyd turned down my article on Sierra Leone. Before Diane retired, she would've had us writing about how stupid that kind of shit is, not glorifying it. I'm not feeling working at *Urban Report* at all right now. The stuff we were writing about before were things to educate and try and guide our people away from this nonsense of chasing trinkets and baubles, to show that our focus should be on purchasing things like stock and land—something we can leave to our kids. What the fuck are we gonna leave to the next generation—rusted rims and diamond necklaces?"

I nod, smiling in agreement and admiration at the passion Mario has.

"What?" he asks. Then he grins back at me. "Am I going off on one of my tangents again?"

"Yes, but I love it. Your tangent is more than justified. I wholeheartedly agree."

"See, that's what I'm saying." He makes the eye-to-eye gesture between us. "We right there. There might be some hope, though. I heard from a couple of people who field e-mails from our readers that many are complaining already about the content of the last issue and it just hit the stands. We're having a meeting next Tuesday; some of the other writers and I are going to try again to talk some sense into Lloyd and use those e-mails to back us up. If that doesn't work and things keep going like they are, I'll start putting out my feelers for a new job. Once I'm sure where I stand on my j-o-b, we can start looking for a house. I know that we could get one now 'cause you got a steady gig, but I want to be able to contribute, too. We've outgrown this apartment and we need more space."

"Speaking of space, we're going to have someone taking up some for a few weeks."

"Who?"

"Rosie. *Silk & Velvet* wants her to come out here for some test shots. I'm excited for her."

"Hmm."

"'Hmm'? What does that mean?"

"Nik, you know I love Rosie like a sister, but I don't understand why she wants to be in one of those magazines. I know *Silk & Velvet is* one of the more upscale skin mags, but it's still exploitive to women as far as I'm concerned."

"It's what Rosie wants and I support her."

"Don't *you* think those magazines are exploitive to women?"

"I told you that my agent wanted me to pose for that very magazine."

"I like and respect Erica a lot, but I completely disagreed with her suggesting that. Thank God you didn't do it."

"Only because I couldn't work up the nerve and I knew you would've tripped."

"You know it. I bet you wouldn't like it if I posed for *Playgirl.*"

"Look, I'm not saying that I one hundred percent approve of posing for those magazines, but I'm not about to sit up in judgment of my cousin. Whatever makes her happy makes me happy."

"So even if she's exploiting her body, you're happy?"

The temperature of my blood has risen by a good ten degrees. He's starting to piss me off and dropping a notch or two off my buzz to boot.

"Don't look at me like that, Nik. I'm just asking a question. I know that Rosie went through a lot as a kid and you're protective of her—"

"Anyway," I say, cutting him off. "I'm going to New York on Saturday."

"To visit your parents?"

"That, too. But mainly it's to meet Rosie there. Her mother has cancer and she's going to see her finally. She wants me there with her. We should be back Sunday afternoon or early evening. She said she'll probably just come on out here with me."

"That's too bad about her mother."

"Yes, it is."

"I hope she makes it through."

"Me, too."

We finish the rest of the meal in silence. Even if he hadn't ticked me off, I wouldn't really want to talk about what's going on with my parents. Not right now anyway. I just want to do anything I can to not think about that. I get up and start clearing the dishes. As I'm rinsing off a plate before putting it in the dishwasher, Mario comes up behind, turns off the water, and takes the plate from my hand, placing it in the sink. He puts his hands on my hips and turns me around to face him.

"Look at me, baby."

I lift my head and look at him.

"I didn't mean anything by what I said. I love Rosie and I'm not trying to put her down. I just think she's capable of doing more than showing off her body. I know she's back to dancing, but before the feds went after that guy Vito and shut down all of his clubs, Rosie was almost single-handedly running the one in Michigan, right?"

"Yes, she was." I reach over and dry my hands on a towel.

"That shows that she has a good business mind. She told me once that she had the place packed damn near every night. She respects what you say. You should use your influence to guide her in a more productive direction. It was lucky for her that all the FBI did was question her and let her go. They could've tried to pin on her some of what they got Vito and some of his other partners on. It's not just you that goes for the okey-doke as far as Rosie is concerned, either. Tell me if I'm wrong, but it seemed like your folks gave you more grief about acting than they did her about dancing. While they were busy nagging you, they just ignored what Rosie was doing. Right?"

I don't say anything. What can I say? Mario is right.

"I've known the both of you since we were all kids. Your father was always the main one getting on you two for coming in late or getting into fights and whatever, but from what I could see you got punished more when it was just you doing something. I know for a fact that even though you were the quieter one and you followed Rosie into devilment, you pulled Rosie into a lot of stunts, too. And I think you did that 'cause you knew that if you got caught, the punishment wouldn't be as bad if she was involved. Tell me I'm wrong." He tilts his head, grinning at me.

"Whatever."

"Don't try to hold back that smile."

I finally give in to the smile tickling my lips. "Shut up. I hate how well you know me."

"I understand the fact you all were accommodating of Rosie because of her mother not being around. But that doesn't mean you have to co-sign on everything she does."

"You're forgetting how upset Papi was when he found out she was bisexual. Mami dealt with it okay, but Papi didn't take it too well. He wanted me to move back home from the apartment Rosie and I were sharing."

"True. But that lasted a hot minute. After that he just turned a blind eye to it and tried to pretend that her bisexuality didn't exist," he points out.

"My family is pretty good at turning a blind eye to things we find uncomfortable. I think it's a genetic trait. I hear what you're saying. But I'm still going to support her if she does get chosen for this magazine. I refuse to put her down for it. It's not like someone is making her do this, she's doing it on her own."

"Is a hooker any less of a hooker if she doesn't have a pimp?"

"Hey, I know you're not calling my cousin—"

"No, I'm not calling her a hooker. I would never do that. I'm just saying there's not much difference between exploiting yourself and someone making you exploit yourself. Okay, I'll keep my comments to myself as far as her posing nude and stuff. By the way, despite how I may sound, you know that I'm not trying to put her down, right? I'm only looking out."

"Yeah, I know. You made a good point."

"So, you're not mad at me, are you?"

"No, idiot."

"Good, 'cause I really need some tonight."

I giggle and punch him lightly in the stomach. "You're so nasty."

As he leans in to kiss me, he whispers, "You know you like it."

"I never said I didn't. Just making an observation."

Mario pushes me backward against the counter. He puts his hands on my ass and pulls me closer to him, pressing his lips against mine—drawing me into a deep kiss. I slide an arm around his shoulder and the other around his waist. We take turns tracing each other's lips with our tongues and exploring the other's mouth. He presses his hips against mine. I rise up on my toes a little so that his growing erection is rubbing against my mound. We move against each other, kissing and filling the other's mouths with moans. Mario moves his mouth down to my chin and then my neck—running his tongue up and down it. He unbuttons my blouse, takes it off, and drops to the floor. He then gently bites my nipples through my bra. The sensation is both great and teasing: It feels good but it's making me crazy 'cause I desperately want to feel his mouth directly on me. After a couple of minutes of him doing that, I can't take it any longer and I remove my bra myself.

Mario grins. "I knew I was driving you crazy."

He bends his head to my breast and it's almost an orgasmic relief to feel the warmth and wetness of his mouth. He twirls his tongue in firm circles around my engorged nipple, sending vibrations throughout my body and causing a soft groan to escape from my lips. He turns his attention to my other breast—planting kisses all over it before putting his mouth on my nipple. He lightly runs his teeth over it, making me involuntarily jerk with delight. He moves his mouth back up my neck to my ear. He kisses it, moving his tongue in and out in short and quick strokes. I reach down between us and stroke his rigid dick through his pants. He takes off his shirt while I unbuckle and unzip his pants. I push them down till they fall to his ankles. Then I slide his boxers down past his hips, exposing his hardness. I lean over towards the sink, turn on the faucet, and dampen my hands. I rub my hands together to warm them and take him into my hands. I move my hands up and down his dick, twirling my hands in an opposite direction, in a motion like I'm twisting a lemon— applying more pressure around the head. Mario leans his head back, his eyes tightly shut and his mouth open. The look of pleasure is caressing his face. After a few more strokes, he puts his hands on mine to stop my movements.

"Whoa, baby," he whispers.

He holds me for a minute as he calms down and then kisses me again, lightly sucking my bottom lip. He unbuttons my jeans, unzips them, and pulls them off, along with my thong. He kicks off his pants and boxers and gets down on his knees in front of me and begins kissing my belly as he strokes my thighs. He moves his mouth and kisses my pubic area, which is free of hair thanks to my first Brazilian wax. He takes his hands and spreads my lips, exposing my passion-soaked clit. He tongues it, alternating between circular and up-and-down motions. I tightly grip the edge of the sink as he begins to gently suck my clit. I take one of my hands and put it to the back of his head—pushing it deeper to me. He switches from sucking my clit back to attacking it with his tongue.

"Oh shit, baby! Don't stop! Keep your tongue right—right in that spot!"

A few minutes later I'm in the epicenter of a fiery orgasm. I loudly moan through gritted teeth and grip Mario's hair, bucking against his face. My orgasm is short but electrifying and my knees feel like they're going to buckle. Mario kisses my thighs and moves his way up my body till we're face-to-face.

"What did I tell you about holding back, Nik? You know you wanted to scream."

"I know, baby." My breathing is still erratic. "I can't help but think about the neighbors sometimes, though."

"I told you to forget about the neighbors. Who cares if they hear? Hell, they don't care about making noise when they're doing their thing. Don't think about that. It's just you and me making love. Just us." He kisses my neck. "I want to hear you, baby. Don't hold back. Please."

Mario turns me around and bends me over. I feel his hardness enter me, sliding in the wetness from my orgasm. He grabs my hips and begins pumping inside me in long, slow strokes. I move my hips in a soft circular motion and soon his movements and mine join together in sexually heated synchronicity. He quickens and deepens his strokes— pumping me harder. I cry out from the pleasure of it. I speed up the circular motion of my hips to keep in time with his movements. Somewhere outside my own cries of pleasure, I hear Mario's. I then feel the sweet sting of him slapping and rubbing my ass a few times. The momentary pain is an exquisite complement to the pleasure. Mario slips out of me, turns me around to face him. He takes one of my legs and lifts it to his waist. With his other hand he grabs my hair, wrapping it around his hand. He knows that when we're getting a bit wild I like for him to pull my hair—kind of rough but not to where it hurts.

He pulls my head back slightly and I look up at him. His eyes are open and directly on me. The passion raging in them mesmerizes me. Even though our lovemaking is feeling good as hell, I know that I'm not going to come again right now. So I just concentrate on Mario. With one hand I trace my nails across his nipples. His eyes narrow and he bites his bottom lip. I lean toward his neck and firmly run my tongue up and down the side of it. Mario makes a sound close to a whimper. I move back and grip the counter again. I thrust my hips toward him, moving in deep, concentrated circles. He can't maintain his eye contact any longer. His eyes shut tightly and he bites his bottom lip again. The pumping of his hips increases. He then pulls me to him and moans loudly as he orgasms. He slumps against me, trying to catch his breath. "Damn, baby," he says, his breathing ragged. "Damn."

I close my eyes and hold on to him, running a hand through his hair, which is damp from perspiration. I focus all the energy that I can on him and this moment. I needed to lose myself in this. Not allowing any painful memories or anything else intrude on it.

I'm in a
New York
state of
mind

7

Rosie

"Rosie, honey!" Tía Sarah shouts through the bedroom door. "Raul just called, he said he'll be here in a few minutes!"

I snap closed my phone.

"Ok, Tía Sarah. Thanks!"

I shouldn't even have called Crystal. I just got off the plane last night and already this morning she's got Lamont over to her place. I know I ain't got no claim on her, but shit—I can't help but feel jealous. I called her for a little bit of comfort because when Nikki gets here, me, her and Raul are going over to Lupe's. I should've called Odell or Chico instead. But no—I had to call her ass and hear that fucker answer the phone. Just then my phone rings. It's Crystal's home number. I pop open my phone.

"*Que carajo quieres?!*" I snap.

"What did you say? It doesn't sound like it was something nice," Crystal says.

"What do you want?"

"Didn't you just call here?"

"Yes, Crystal, I did."

"Why did you hang up?"

"I heard that you had company and I didn't want to interrupt."

"Rosie, we're just about to have some breakfast, baby," she says in a hushed tone.

"Why are you whispering?"

"I'm not."

"Whatever. Look, I've got to go. My brother will be here any minute."

"Okay. Give me a call later. I'll be here."

"In bed fucking, no doubt."

"Rosie, don't be like that. Are you still going straight out to California when you leave there?"

"Yeah, I told you that before I left."

"When are you coming back? Huh? Hold on, Rosie."

I hear her talking to Lamont in the background. "Yeah, just get a bottle of orange juice and a carton of eggs. No, that's it, thanks. Hurry back, sweetie." I can't help but cringe.

"Okay, Rosie. I'm back. Now when are you coming home?"

"I told you when I left that I'd be gone for a few weeks. I'm sure you won't be wanting for company in the meantime."

"Why am I getting this jealousy trip from you? What do you expect for me to do? Am I supposed to be alone?"

"You can't stand a few weeks by yourself? I told you I need this time to figure what I should do."

"See, that's what I'm talking about. You act like I'm supposed to sit here by myself while I wait to find out whether you can be cool with the way things are."

"And how's that, Crystal? Explain that again for me."

"With us still being friends, only friends who…you know…enjoy great sex together," she finally gets out.

"And that's it? Friends with benefits?"

"You make it sound so meaningless when you say it like that."

"Crystal, I want more than for us to go shopping, do each other's hair, and fuck. I'm in love with you. Do you not understand that? I ain't trying to be your best friend and fuck buddy. Why can't you give us a try? I mean a real try. Let's see how we would be in a relationship together."

"Whoa. I'm not into that, Rosie. I think I told you that. I can finally admit to you that I enjoy having sex with women, but I can't see myself in *that* kind of relationship—not the kind that I've been in and will continue to be in with men. I thought I made myself clear."

Talk about déjà vu. This is almost verbatim what Odell told me that bastard Thomas told him when Odell wanted a relationship.

"Obviously not clear enough." A tear rolls down my cheek. "In other words you'll give me your pussy but not your heart, right? Is that what you're saying? Answer me," I say through gritted teeth.

"Rosie, I hope that you don't think that I've led you on. I know I wasn't clear with you before. But the last few weeks that we've been back in contact, I thought that I let you know how much I enjoy being with you and making love with you. And I do, baby. You and I have great chemistry in bed, plus we're great friends out of bed. Why can't that be enough?"

"It just isn't. You know what? You remind me of a lot of men who tell a woman one thing, then act totally opposite to what they say. You know exactly how I feel about you and you use that shit to your advantage."

"And just how the hell do I do that?"

"For instance, when you say shit like 'making love,' it makes me think things have moved to another level. And when we're together alone you treat me like you're feeling me in the same way I'm feeling you—the way you caress me, look into my eyes, and hold me. And what did you tell me when I left?"

"What do you mean? I said a lot of things."

"Don't play with me. When we were in bed after just fucking, making love, or whatever you want to call it, you whispered in my ear that you loved me. Do you know how happy that made me? Then a few hours later you're spending time with somebody else."

"Rosie, I do love you. You're one of my best friends."

"Oh, okay." I take the phone away from my ear and take a deep breath. A lightning bolt full of clarity has just hit me in the ass. I put the phone back to my ear. "I shouldn't have ever called you when I saw you in the restaurant. I shouldn't have even acknowledged your damn presence. After we talked that night I thought you had changed, Crystal, I really did. I thought that since you were able to at least cop to the fact that you're bisexual—"

"Wait a minute! I never copped to a damn thing! Just because I mess around with women, it does not mean that I'm bisexual!"

I shake my head and laugh softly. "You're still as confused as ever. Think about what you just said. Let it marinate in your brain for a second and see if it makes sense. I thought since you weren't trying to blame sex with me on alcohol or dope, you acknowledged it. My bad. I can't believe that I broke up with Alejandro for *this*.

I guess I got what I deserved, huh? I was happy, Crystal. I really was and in a matter of weeks of letting you back into my life you've turned it upside-down."

"You couldn't have been all that happy with Alejandro if you dumped him at the first whiff of my pussy," she hisses. "And another thing. You have a lot of nerve calling me confused when on one hand you say how s-o-o very happy you were with Alejandro, and then you break it off with him to chase after me. Telling me how much you love me and that you want a relationship with *me*. Now how confused is that? Hmm?"

"You know what, Crystal? *Vete alcarajo!* It's called being in love with two people at the same time. That shit happens. I don't need your head trips. I'm done. I want to thank you for one thing, though."

"And that is?"

"Thanks for making me see once and for all that no matter how beautiful you are on the outside, on the inside, in your heart—a *chupacabra!* You best believe I won't be letting your ass back into my heart, my bed, or my life! Have a nice one trick. Oh, and of course you know to delete my number, right?" I slam my phone shut.

I'm so goddamned stupid! Why didn't I listen to Odell? Fuck! I should've just left her ass alone. I could still be with Alejandro. I toss my phone on the bed and put my head in my hands. I messed up big-time. I left a perfectly good relationship. And for what? To roll in the hay and feast on the little crumbs Crystal threw my way. What was I thinking? I called Crystal for some comfort before leaving and instead she adds even more bullshit on my head.

I hear from the commotion outside my door that Raul is here. I already wasn't looking forward to seeing Lupe and now I gotta go over there with my mind even more screwed up from Crystal's bitch ass. I can't wait for this to be over and done with. Damn.

8

Nikki

I settle into the cab that I had to hustle my ass for. I don't know why I didn't arrange for a car to pick me up. LGA is a mother to navigate, and I thought LAX was bad. When we finally get away from the airport I roll down the window a bit as I reacquaint myself with not only the sights and sounds of New York, but also the smells—good and bad. I think this city was custom-made to awaken and assault the senses. This is the first time I've been here since Rosie and I came for our cousin Eva's *quinceanera* and to see the PR parade about three and a half years ago. To say this trip is going to be interesting is like saying it gets a little nippy during Alaskan winters. I'm looking forward to seeing my parents, but I'm apprehensive about what's going on with their marriage. I haven't talked to Mami since I called to tell her about Tía Lupe and she in turn dropped her little bomb on me. She's called me twice from her cell but I didn't answer the phone. Avoidance. I think that's the word. Hell, I knew I'd have to deal with it when I got here.

I wonder how my cousin is doing. She got in on the red-eye a few hours ago and is over at my parents' house. We're going to see Tía Lupe later on today. Rosie must be a nervous wreck 'cause I know my stomach feels tight with tension. I need something to help me relax. I take off my sunglasses and put them in my purse. I reach in and get out a little sample bottle of Grey Goose. It's one of the few types of liquor I can take straight. I drink it and then find a piece of gum to pop in my mouth. I settle in my seat some more and feel the liquid course a warm trail through my body. A part of me wants to be here to see my parents and other family members. I can't wait to see Raul after all these years. But it's the shit going down with Mami and of course Lupe that has me itching to hightail it back to L.A. Back to work and back to my baby.

☙❧

"Miss! Miss, we're here!"

I snap awake. Dang, I guess I fell asleep. Between the drinks in the plane and here in the cab, New York noise or not, I dropped off. I look at the fare box and give the cabbie the cost plus tip. I get my overnight bag out of the trunk and walk up the steps of my parents' brownstone and ring the bell. I can't help but smile as I stand here and smell the aroma of food and hear the music of the man I grew up listening to—Willie Colón. I recognize the tune playing is "Calle Luna Calle Sol." Even though this isn't the same place we lived when I was a child, I still feel like I'm home. Soon I hear the sound of footsteps. The door opens and Papi greets me.

"Zuzu!" Papi looks like he could just burst from joy. The last time he saw me in the flesh was last year when he and Mami came out to L.A. for the Christmas holidays.

"Papi!" I playfully mock him. I fall into his arms and he gives me a big hug, lifting me off the ground. He puts me down and goes back and forth kissing both of my cheeks. I see he's got a little more girth to his belly and more gray hairs around his temples. Other than that he still looks like my papi and the Puerto Rican twin of Cuban trumpeter Arturo Sandoval.

"You look tired. Here, give me your bag."

"I got it, Papi. It's not heavy at all."

"Give it."

I hand over my bag and we walk down the foyer toward the living room.

"Your mother is cooking up some lunch. Your cousins are in the living room. Raul is giving me grief about my music. He only likes that rap stuff. Not all youngsters are like you and can appreciate the *salsa vieja* by Johnny Pacheco, Ray Barreto and others."

"Hey, I used to hate that music as a kid. I didn't start appreciating it until a few years ago."

When we get to the living room, I peek around the corner and wave.

"Trouble comes to Harlem," Rosie says. She gets up from the couch and gives me a long hug.

"How are you doing, cuz?"

"Better now that you're here. Nikki, here's someone you haven't seen in a minute. Hey, get over here, *manito.*"

Raul is standing over by the stereo. He puts down some CDs he was looking through. Oh *coño!* This is why people need to know who their relatives are. If I were single and saw this man out somewhere, it wouldn't take two seconds for me to jump up and holler at him. He's just under 6' with a medium build. His complexion is somewhere between my golden-brown tone and Rosie's olive one. His eyes are a golden shade that kind of reminds me of a lion's. He doesn't really look like Rosie, but he does look almost exactly like the pictures I've seen of their father Guillermo. His long, dark hair is pulled back into a ponytail. The smile he's flashing begs that he be placed in toothpaste commercials. Rosie told me that he was juggling a few females down in Miami and I can see why. He gives me a warm hug.

"It's good to see you again. It's been too long."

"Same here. You've grown into a handsome young man. Ain't he handsome, Rosie?" I look around at her.

"Yeah, your *primo* is quite handsome." We smile at each other. I knew she would catch my drift.

"People don't believe me when I tell them I'm related to a famous actress."

"I'm not exactly famous yet. But I'm working on it."

"Nikki, honey!" Mami says as she comes into the living room.

For a woman who recently turned fifty-four, Mami doesn't look a day over thirty-five. Her pretty, dark bronze face is smooth and practically wrinkle-free. God really blessed her with great metabolism, because even though she can sometimes give Papi a run for his money at the dinner table, she still has the same trim figure. She started dyeing her hair black in her thirties, when gray hairs started coming through. But now it's dyed a flattering dark auburn color. She has it in cute twisties. I walk over to her and we hug, rocking from side to side.

"I'm so glad you're here, baby."

"Me, too, Mami."

She pushes me to arm's length and looks me up and down. "I see you need some eyedrops. Your eyes are red. And you've lost weight."

"My eyes—you know how dry the air is on the plane. My weight—only ten pounds. It's the whole TV-adds-ten-pounds thing. I lost that much to make up the difference."

"Looks like you've lost more than ten pounds to me."

"Mami," I groan.

"Yeah, you have lost some bricks from your brick house, girlfriend," says Rosie.

"Thanks a lot, Rosie," I say, looking over my shoulder at her. "I already hear enough from Mario complaining about that."

"That's okay. I've got something in the kitchen to remedy that," Mamie reassures me. "Of course there's only so much I can do in two days. Hollywood is not going to turn my child into one of those stick figures I'm always seeing in the magazines. Not if I have anything to say about it. Come on, everyone, and let's eat."

"Zuzu, give me your purse and I'll take it along with the bag into the bedroom."

"Thanks, Papi."

⚜

I'm eating like the last time I ate was a week ago. I didn't realize how hungry I was. Mami made fried chicken, black beans and rice, corn, homemade biscuits, and iced tea. Once I slow my roll after getting full, I covertly glance around the table. Rosie and Raul are eating but their minds seem to be elsewhere. No doubt they're thinking about our visit to Lupe later. Mami and Papi are laughing and talking like nothing is wrong. I don't notice any tension whatsoever. I guess they're having one of their good days. Mami even feeds Papi some corn from her plate. They look like a typical happily married couple, pleased and content now, but tomorrow it'll probably be a different story. I mean, Mami was just on the phone griping about the state of their marriage.

"Zuzu, how's Mario doing?" Papi asks, interrupting my thoughts.

"He's great. He's still working on that book I told you about."

"Good, good. Are you two any closer to walking down the aisle and making me and your mother *abuelos?*"

I roll my eyes and throw up my hands. "I knew that was coming. You and Mami did good this time. You waited a whole twenty minutes before you started in on me. What are you grinning about, Rosie?"

"Hey, better you than me."

"By the way," Mami says, "what about you and Alejandro? When are you two getting hitched?"

I stick my tongue out at Rosie. "Nah, eat cheese with that."

"Well?" Mami and Papi ask Rosie in unison.

Rosie looks like she wants to make a quick getaway. "We'll just have to wait and see. Get back on Nikki; she's closer to hearing the sound of wedding bells than I am." She laughs nervously.

My parents turn back to me and ask, "Well?"

Rosie, Raul, and I can't help but laugh.

"When Mario and I make that decision we'll let you know, okay?"

"No, that's not good enough, Zuzu. If you love each other enough to live together—"

A phone rings. Raul pulls his cell off his belt. He excuses himself and takes the call in the hallway.

"Saved by the ring," I say.

"For now, anyway," Mami says with a wink. "Here, Anna. Have some more to eat." She passes me the chicken.

"Why you call me Anna?"

"Anna Rexic," she says with a devilish grin. Rosie and Papi start laughing.

"Mami, that's cold! How you gonna cap on me like that?"

She gets up and comes over to me, bends down and hugs me from behind. "I love you, honey. You know I'm only teasing you. You haven't gotten that skinny—yet." She picks up a drumstick and puts it to my mouth. I smile, cut my eyes at her, and take a bite of the chicken.

Raul comes back into the room and sits down. He reaches and takes Rosie's hand in his. "Rosie, that was my old friend Jarell on the phone. He's gonna drop us off at Mom's, remember? He said something's come up and he's got to come by here earlier to pick us up. He'll be here in a few minutes. Is that all right?"

"Yeah, whatever. That's even better. We can get this over with sooner." She gets up from the table and starts out of the dining room.

"Rosie? Are you okay, sweetheart?"

She turns around and gives Mami a little smile. "Yes, I'm just fine, Tía Sarah." She leaves the room. We all look after her, knowing otherwise.

9

Rosie

We all thank Jarell for the ride and get out of the car. Raul tries to give Jarell some money, but he refuses it. Nikki takes my hand and I look at her. She gives me a reassuring smile. We walk up the steps to the flat and Raul unlocks the door. He turns around to me, takes my head in both his hands, and kisses me on the cheek.

"It'll be all right, *mija*. Me and Nikki are right here, okay?"

I nod. I feel an incredible love for them both. It's times like this that set apart who's really down for you and the fake-ass bitches like Crystal. We proceed to the apartment where Lupe is waiting. As soon as we step in we see her. She's sitting in a huge chair with her feet up on an ottoman. The woman I see is nothing like the one I recollect. Her features had faded from my memory years ago. But when I was last here in New York, I was flipping through one of my cousins' photo album and came across her picture that was taken shortly after she married my father. The woman in that picture was robust with smooth fair skin, flowing dark hair, and sparkling eyes. This woman—oh my God. If I had to pick Lupe off the street I would've passed her by. She looks small and frail. Her skin that used to be like porcelain has a jaundiced appearance, and her formerly dark hair is almost completely gray. She looks a good ten years older than her age of fifty-one.

Lupe is looking right into my eyes. Her hand lifts up and she turns off the television with the remote—not for a second breaking her gaze. Her eyes fill with tears and she silently mouths, "My Rosaura." The last damn thing I ever wanted to do was shed a single tear. Yet, that's what my eyes are threatening to do. I try to stave them off with all the will I can conjure. Nikki lightly shakes the hand that I'm holding. That's when I realize that I'm squeezing her for dear life. I loosen my grip. Lupe reaches her thin arms out to me. For some reason it never occurred to me that there'd be any physical contact. I don't know why, it just didn't.

"It's okay, Rosie," Nikki whispers.

My feet finally decide to move and I go over to Lupe and sit on the edge of her chair, facing her. She reaches out and strokes my hair, tears streaming down her prematurely aged face.

"My beautiful baby," she coos softly. "So beautiful. I'm so happy to see you. My sweet Rosaura, thank you for coming. Thank you."

She wipes away the tears I so stubbornly tried to hold in but are now rolling down my face. I rest my head on her shoulder and begin to cry like a baby. She gently rocks me and tells me that it's going to be okay and how much she loves me. She says all the things that I wanted her to say after that horrible night all those years ago. A short time later we are both spent. I leave her embrace to sit on the sofa near her and motion for Raul and Nikki to come sit next to me. Nikki looks like she's been crying as much as I have. Before sitting down, she hugs Lupe.

Lupe beams at her. "You both have grown into such beautiful young women. You could be on the covers of those beauty magazines."

"Thank you," Nikki replies.

"Why did you give me away?" I ask suddenly, cutting to the chase. I'm pissed off at myself for weakening like I did. I didn't plan on crying and I sure didn't plan on crying on her shoulder like that. It's too late for that shit. Twenty-one years too late. But what's done is done. I just want an answer to my question.

Lupe closes her eyes for a moment and bites her bottom lip. "I was weak."

I shrug. "Tell me something I don't know. I want to know specifically why you did what you did. This is not the time to be vague."

She leans back into the chair and looks down at her hands. "Please let me tell you some history first. I met you and Raul's father when I was seventeen after my father moved his business to San Juan. Guillermo, he was the love of my life. Sometimes it hurts to look at Raul because he is the mirror image of him. Guillermo and Miguel were two of the most popular boys in the neighborhood. All the girls loved them and all the boys wanted to be them. I had such a crush on Guillermo. I admired him from a distance because I was much too shy to even speak to him. He used to come into the *taberna* and I'd sneak peeks at him from the kitchen. Then one day I literally ran into him when he was entering and I was leaving to go home because I wasn't feeling well. I bumped right into him. I apologized and he said, 'That's okay, Lupe.' I was stunned. I asked him how did he know my name and he said because he'd asked someone who I was." She puts her bony hand over her mouth and suppresses a girlish giggle.

"Even though I was sick as a dog, I felt like I was floating on a cloud to hear him say that he asked someone about *me*. Anyway, to make a long story short, we started dating. People who'd never seemed to notice me before were paying attention to me now that I was on Guillermo's arm. It was so strange to have the girls be jealous of me because I was his girl. I felt a change within me as well. People said I suddenly had a glow about me. It was because Guillermo told me all the things that were the complete opposite of what my father always told me.

"For as long as I can remember my father told me that I was ugly, stupid, and didn't have a talent in this world. He told me I should pray that a man would take pity on me and have me as his wife because I wasn't capable of taking care of myself. But Guillermo was different. He told me that I was beautiful and smart. He said I was the only girl that he could talk about politics with—we could talk for hours about Pedro Albizu Campos and Juan Marí Bras. Even if we didn't agree on certain points, your father respected my opinion. He gave me the self-esteem I never had before. Next to the births of you and Raul, my wedding day was the happiest of my life.

"I married a man who was the exact opposite of my father, which of course was a joy. It was a few years of trying before we were finally blessed with you, Rosaura, and then later with Raul. Your father doted on you both. We were such a happy family. When my Guillermo died, I wanted to be with him. I would've joined him, too, if it weren't for my children. After he was gone I was so lost. My father called and told me to come back to Puerto Rico with the two of you. He said I was incapable of taking care of a cat, much less two children. I believed him because I'd never really worked. I didn't think that I could get a decent job with only having cooked at my father's place from time to time."

"People make decent livings working as cooks," I interrupt her. "You could have easily gotten a job in a restaurant. Look at Raul. He started off as a cook and now he's part-owner of a restaurant."

She looks proudly over at Raul, then turns back to me. "Rosaura, I didn't believe that I could at the time. You have to understand that all the self-confidence that your father gave me died with him. After that I was right back where I began. I didn't want to go back home but I didn't believe I could take care of you two on my own. So when—" She pauses for a moment. "So when Renaldo came to me and told me he had been in love with me for a long time and offered to marry to me, I accepted. He had a good job and I thought he'd be a decent husband and stepfather."

"Come on," I scoff. "Even as kids me and Nikki knew he was an asshole. What the hell made you think he'd be a decent anything?"

"He was there. He offered what I thought at the time would be some stability and a roof over our heads. Your father only had a small insurance policy and after funeral expenses and flying his body back to San Juan, there wasn't much left. The money was dwindling and I needed to keep a roof over your heads."

"I'm not buying that," I spit bitterly. "We have a lot of family here. Tío Miguel and Tía Sarah would have looked after us. Stop acting like you were all alone in this world with no one but that bastard to help us. It's been nice hearing about how you met Papi and everything, but I want to know why you let Renaldo treat me and you like he did and why you sent me packing."

She looks down again and wrings her hands. "Just as Guillermo was nothing like my father, Renaldo was everything like him. The only difference was where my father only hurt me with words, Renaldo took it a step further."

I let out an exasperated breath. All I'm getting are excuses and woe-is-me bullshit instead of answers.

"Please bear with me, Rosaura. Renaldo said that he'd been in love with me for years, but he was no more in love with me than I was with him. He saw me for the weak person I was. Someone he could easily take advantage of and control and—"

I hit the coffee table with my fist, making her jump. "Enough, Lupe! I'm tired of hearing about how weak and defenseless you were! I want to know why, when you were confronted with the fact that Tony was molesting me, you did not believe it! Why?!"

"It's not that I didn't believe it as much as I didn't want to believe it!" She begins to cry. "I didn't want to believe that someone could hurt my baby like that."

"When it came down to having Tony reported to the police or for me to go live with Nikki, why did you pack up my shit? That's what I want to know! Why did you choose to have me leave? Why did you abandon me, Mami?" Shit, did I just call her Mami?

"I knew that you'd be better off living with Nikki's parents. You know how Renaldo was. He favored Raul, so he was safe. But you, he always found fault with everything you did. It was much better for you to be away from here."

"Was it also much better for you to not even accept my calls? Was it much better for you to cut off my contact with you and my brother?" I look at Raul. "Me and my brother missed out on so much together. Until he got in touch with me we were virtual strangers." I turn back to Lupe. "I'll tell you what would have been much better. If you had not been such a damn mouse and grew a backbone and put the welfare of your kids ahead of your fear of being by yourself! I tried to deny that I even wanted to know why you handled things the way you did, but I was lying to myself. I wanted to know. I thought that I'd walk up in here and get some great revelation from you. Instead all I get is a bunch of wack-ass excuses."

Lupe looks at Raul pleadingly. "Raul, you remember how Renaldo used to take it out on me when he knew Rosaura had called, don't you? I'd hear it for days on end." Raul doesn't say anything; he just stares at the facing wall. "I did sneak and call you whenever I could. As a matter of fact, he beat on me even more after you left, Rosaura. He was always so angry at how people were treating Tony after they heard about your claims of him touching you. And then—"

"Wait one goddamned minute!" I leap up from the couch. "What the hell do you mean by my *claims* of him touching me?!"

"Rosie, calm down," says Nikki.

"Hell no! I'm not calming down! I think Lupe needs to be schooled on a few things. It sounds like she's trying to blame me for having the fucking nerve to want to have a relationship with my own mother and brother! Like I'm supposed to feel sorry for her because she chose to stay with a man who used her as a human punching bag. And to top it off she has the audacity to talk about my *claims* of Tony messing with me! Look, *Mother.*" I put my hand on the edge of her chair and bend down to her till we're face-to-face. "You wanna talk about claims? I got some claims for you. Tony would make me touch his nasty dick." Lupe winces at my words. "He would make me jack him off. Then he tried to force me to use my mouth on it."

69

"Rosie…"

"Shut up, Nikki!" I say without moving my eyes from Lupe's face. "And the night I ran out of the apartment, he was trying to take my virginity. Now how's that for a claim, Lupe? I was a child! A fucking child! As my mother, it was your job to look out for my best interest no matter what. Instead you chose to stay with a man who verbally and physically abused you and me. At least most women who stay with men like that do it because for some damn reason they love them. But by your own admission you didn't even love Renaldo. And this is the shit that kills me: If he hadn't left you for some barely-out-of-her-teens chick, you'd still be with him, wouldn't you?" Lupe starts sobbing even more. "You would. And I wouldn't be standing here right now because he wouldn't want me here. Because you were sick, I finally decided to come see you. I hate to admit this, but there was a little part of me that hoped we could somehow squash a lot of the stuff from the past and forge some kind of relationship. But I get the feeling that if Renaldo were to come knocking on that door right now, you'd take him back and kick me to the curb again."

"No, Rosaura! I wouldn't do that!"

I look past the tears of denial in her eyes and can't find it in me to believe her. I kiss her on her forehead and whisper, "Good-bye, Lupe." I start for the door.

"No, Rosaura! Please don't leave! Please!"

I turn back to her. "I don't pray very much, but I'll pray that you have a full recovery. I'll do that every day. I'll make sure Raul keeps me updated on your progress. But you've caused too much pain in my life and I can't risk you bringing some more. I just can't." With that, I walk out the door and out of the building and keep stepping till I can no longer hear her calling my name and begging for me to come back.

"Rosie!"

I turn around and see Nikki and Raul running toward me. When they get to me, Raul grabs me and holds me. "I'm so sorry, 'mana." Nikki is standing behind me, stroking my hair.

"I'm sorry, too. I can't risk being hurt by her anymore. I was really hoping there'd be better reasons for her…"

"I've asked her so many times about the past and she always said it hurt too much to talk about it. I was feeling like you; I thought she had this earthshaking reason and that there were things we didn't know about," he says.

"I need to get back so I can lie down. I got a mutha of a headache. Nik and me will walk up to the Ave and get a cab. You go back to Lupe, okay?"

"All right. I'll call you later to see how you're doing."

"Hit me up on my cell. Everybody wants me and Nik to show up at Enrique's for a family get-together later on. Swing by if you're up to it."

"I'll do that." He kisses Nikki and me on our cheeks and walks back to the flat.

"Rosie, I apologize for interrupting you when you were telling Tía Lupe what happened to you. It was hard for me to hear about it again," says Nikki.

"Please, girl. It's cool. I didn't mean to snap at you, I was just caught up. Do me a favor, though."

"Sure, what is it?"

"I don't want to bring up what happened in there ever again. When we get back to the house, please let your parents know that I don't want to talk about it. You can fill them in, but I don't want to talk about it."

"No problem."

I put my arm through hers and we start walking. Walking away from all the pitiful excuses that make for a disappointing ending to a twenty-one-year-old story—away from my mother.

10

Nikki

I walk out of the bedroom and find Papi at the dining room table reading the paper. "Morning, Papi." I kiss him on the forehead.

"*Buenos dias.* Your cousin still sleeping?"

"She was finally stirring when I left the room."

"You two got in late. Some things never change." He shakes his head. "How was the get-together?"

"It was fun, of course. You know how we do it."

"How you do what? Party?"

I chuckle. "Yeah, Papi. Party. What is Mami cooking? It smells great."

"Your mother can't take credit for that. Raul came over and he's whipping up a meal for us."

"Uh-oh. Let me go check it out."

I walk to the kitchen. Raul is at the stove. "You are making me hungry, bro," I say.

"I hope so. I wanted to show off some of my skills to my sister and cousin before they leave."

"I ain't mad at ya." I put a hand on his shoulder and peek over to see what he's making.

"I thought I'd cook up a variety of stuff. These are some of our most popular brunch dishes at the restaurant. I'm making *tortilla de patata Catalina, torrejas, huevoltillo de chorizo, and jamon Serrano.*"

"You go, boy! How much longer? I'm starving."

"It should be done in about ten more minutes. Tía Sarah went out to get some juice. Where's Rosie?"

"I think she's about to get up. I'll go in there in a minute to make sure."

"How's she doing?"

"As well as can be expected, I guess. Last night she did what she usually does to escape—she partied even harder than usual."

"I hope she'll be okay. I love my mother, but I'm very disappointed with her answers yesterday. I can only imagine how Rosie must feel."

"Can I ask you a question?"

"Sure."

"How did you manage to grow up into such a great guy? I mean, with Renaldo's influence and all. It's not like Tía Lupe had the nerve to step up and do anything to stop it."

"Once I got a little older, I really started to hate how he was treating my mother. When you grow up in that atmosphere, you see the game and learn how to play. So I would try and use his favoritism toward me as a way to shield Mom from as much as I could. It didn't always work but I tried. I began to despise Renaldo. But I knew that house would be hell if he turned against me." He finishes piling the food onto the platters. "I left home as soon as I turned eighteen. I felt real guilty about leaving Mom behind. I tried with all my heart to get her to move to Miami with me. She wouldn't do it, Nikki. Even after I got established and everything, she still wouldn't leave. I know we don't really understand it, but I think her father messed up her head so much she felt she didn't deserve to live better. Perhaps my father was a temporary reprieve, but Renaldo gave her what she'd been used to most of her life. All I know is I was as happy as you know what when she called and told me Renaldo had left her.

"To finally answer your question—I wasn't influenced by Renaldo because I tried too hard not to be. He stood for everything I despised when it came to being a man."

"I'm back!" Mami says as she enters the kitchen. She comes and looks at what Raul has cooked. "Boy, are you trying to run me out of my own kitchen?" She pinches his cheek.

"No way. After that dinner you made me the other night, I could learn some things from you." Raul turns to me. "Hey, you better go get Rosie. Everything is about ready."

"Okay."

I walk into the bedroom. Rosie's bed is empty. Just then she comes out the bathroom.

"Morning, knucklehead," I say.

"Morning yourself. Hey, did you bring some shampoo? I don't feel like going through all these bags looking for mine."

"Yep." I turn to get it out of my bag. I scrunch up my face and look over my shoulder at her. "Dang, hurry up and close that bathroom door. Girl, it smells like something crawled up in your ass and died."

"I should've known better than to drink dark liquor. It always messes with my stomach. And I was slinging back dark rum and black vodka like an idiot."

"You need some aspirin or anything?" I hand her the shampoo and conditioner.

"I already took some that was in the bathroom cabinet."

"Raul has just finished brunch so come on. You can take your shower when you finish eating."

"Uh-uh. I'm taking it now. I feel too yucky. Tell Raul to keep it warm for me."

"We'll just wait for you. Hurry up," I say as I leave the room. I turn back around to her. "You okay?"

She looks at me, her eyes smeared from eyeliner and mascara. "I always am, Nikki."

I close the door.

⚜

"Papi, I need to talk to you." I take the remote control and click off the television.

"Hey! What are you doing? I can talk with you with the game on."

"No, you can't. Now listen up, this is important."

He looks a bit exasperated.

"I haven't told Mami yet, but as soon as I get back home, I'm making arrangements for you two to go on vacation in Greece."

"Greece? Zuzu, are you crazy? Why would I want to go to Greece?"

"Because Mami wants to. She's always wanted to travel there and you're going with her."

"No, I'm not." He shakes his head stubbornly.

"Yes, you are," I insist. "If you value your marriage, you'll go."

"What do you mean, if I value my marriage?"

"*Mira,* you need to get up off your behind and focus on your marriage. Mami is ready to travel and you're going with her. Now, you can sit it out if you want. But don't be surprised if you look up and Mami's living a life totally separate from you. I know you can see that Mami's not happy spending her days begging for you to unglue yourself from the couch. I'm not saying that you have to travel every single place, but you're going to at least make an effort. I'm going to help Mami in every way I can 'cause I can't stand to see her unhappy—and you shouldn't want to see her unhappy, either."

"I don't! You know I've always done what I could to see she's content, Zuzu."

"Then why are you being so stubborn about living with her?"

"What are you talking about—living with her. I do live with her. You're not making any sense."

"No, Papi. I don't mean *live* with her as in under the same roof. I mean live as in experience all the things you didn't before you settled down and got married. Live, damn it."

"Watch your mouth, Zuzu." He strokes his mustache with his forefinger, which is what he always does when he's giving something a lot of thought. "I take it your mother has voiced her unhappiness to you."

"Yes."

"It must be really bad if she's taking it to you. I'll think about it."

"While you're thinking about it, think about how it would be if Mami starts doing her thing without you and she meets a man who shares her interests. In the meantime you're here watching television or playing pool with Tomas."

I can tell by the look on Papi's face that I struck a nerve. Good. I didn't want to put that in his head but he obviously needs some extra incentive.

"How long is this vacation going to be?"

"I don't know, maybe a week or two."

He sighs.

"I know you're not looking forward to this, but I really think that once you get in the mix of it you'll enjoy yourself," I say.

"When I retired early, I was anxious to relax for once, not run around the world. I don't want to risk losing your mother, though. I love her too much. I don't know what I'd do without her."

"Then do this, Papi, please," I say, almost begging.

He puts an arm around me. "Honey, you look like you're about to cry. It'll be all right. Your mother and I will be fine. I'll go to Greece, okay?"

"I want you both to be okay. I love you, Papi."

He pats my shoulder. "Uh, well, you know I feel the same. Me, too."

I can't help but smile. Papi can be affectionate and loving in many ways, just not when it comes to saying "I love you." I don't know; it's as if he has a block. For instance, he can tell me that he loves Mami, yet can barely say those three words directly to her. Oh well, that's just his way. We all know he loves us.

"I'd better gather my things. We have to leave for the airport in a bit."

"You sure you can't stay another day? This visit was far too short."

"I wish I could, but I have to run lines tomorrow." I get up from the couch. Papi grabs my hand.

"I'm not going to lose her, Zuzu. If keeping her means I have to follow her around the world, so be it."

I give him a smile and squeeze his hand. Knowing how much he needs Mami is both touching and frightening. As much as I've loved coming here and seeing my parents, I'm just ready to get my stuff and Rosie and head back to Cali.

Goin' Back to Cali

11

Nikki

I look at Rosie in disbelief. I'm dumbfounded by what she's just told me. "So let me get this right. You broke up with Alejandro, a man you're in love with and who loves you, to run up after *Crystal? Crystal*, of all people? This is a really early or really late April Fools' joke, right?"

"Nikki, please. You can't make me feel any more fucked up than I already do. I know I made a mistake."

"A *huge* mistake. What the hell were you thinking?"

"What did I tell you? I already feel bad enough as it is."

"I'm sorry but you should feel bad. And don't roll your eyes at me, either. If you're expecting a pat on the back from me, forget it."

"I ain't expecting shit from you. I didn't even want to tell you. I knew Odell wouldn't be able to keep quiet much longer."

"Oh, so Odell knew? What does he have to say about this?"

"Same thing as you."

"Did you honestly think Crystal was going to act right?"

"I thought…Hell, I don't even know what I thought anymore. All I know is I wish to God I'd never hooked back up with the trick."

"Just a few weeks ago you were telling me you and Alejandro were discussing you moving in with him."

"I know," she says sadly. "I don't want to talk about this anymore."

"Of course not. Keep it in. You got that honest, because for the most part all our family has done is keep shit in. So why wouldn't you? 'Rosie, do you need to talk about your mother?' 'No, I don't want to talk about that.' 'Rosie, do you want to talk about why you walked away from a perfectly functional relationship to run after a crazy one?' 'No, I don't want to talk about that.' It goes on and on. It's our fucking legacy. Just keep shit in and don't deal with it until it's almost too late."

She looks at me like I've lost it. "What the fuck are you going on about? What's wrong with you?"

"I don't want to talk about it," I answer sarcastically. "I just don't understand why you wouldn't tell me what's up. You made me think all this time that you weren't in love with Crystal. I thought we told each other everything. Why wouldn't you tell me about your true feelings for her?"

"Because the bitch played me, all right! There I was in love with her and after we got together she acted as if I took advantage of her. I was embarrassed. Even in front of my cousin who I just about tell everything to. I'm sorry I didn't tell you."

"So what's your next step?"

"What do you mean?"

"Duh. I mean are you going to try to reconcile with Alejandro? Or are you still pining for Crystal?"

"Please! I ain't thinking about that ho. I'm truly done with her this time. I want to call Alejandro and make things right, I'm just scared to. Plus, I feel so guilty for hurting him."

"Were you feeling guilty for hurting him when you had your head between Crystal's legs?" As soon as the words leave my mouth I wish I could take them back, especially when I see the pained look on Rosie's face. "I'm sorry, Rosie. I shouldn't have said that."

"Damn straight you shouldn't have said it. I don't care if you get mad, I don't want to talk about this anymore. I'm beating myself up bad enough without you adding punches."

"I'm sorry for being so harsh. I know what you've been through and I want you to be with someone who is going to love you like you should be loved. And treat you like you should be treated. I've always wanted that. So hearing you tell me about what you did, it pisses me off that you would walk away from what was best for you. You know I love you and just want what's good for you. Admit it, if I were in your shoes, you'd be blunt as hell and upset with me, too. Right?"

"Yeah, you're right."

"I don't mean to lecture you, Rosie, but you can't keep doing this."

"Keep doing what?"

"When Crystal flaked on you, you turned to Alejandro. Now her ass is tripping as usual and you want to turn back to him. Now, do you really love Alejandro or are you only using him to get over Crystal—yet again?"

"Yes, I do love Alejandro. The thing you don't get is I was in love with him *and* Crystal. If you had unresolved feelings for Jaime and they were just as strong as your feelings for Mario, you could've ended up in the same predicament so don't fucking judge me. I had the misfortune of being in love with two people. And I finally found out that one of them wasn't worthy of me loving them. All I want to do is make up for what I did to Alejandro."

Just then the phone rings. I reach over for it and see on the caller ID that it's Amber's cell.

"What's up, girl?"

"I'm downstairs. Get your butt in gear, lady."

"All right, we'll be down in a minute. 'Bye."

I click off the phone and turn to Rosie. "That was Amber. She's waiting downstairs. You're still coming over to hang with us?"

"Naw. You go."

"Come on, Rosie. You shouldn't sit around here moping."

"I know. I just don't feel like going out tonight. You go and have fun—have enough for me, too."

"Are you sure?"

"Yes, now go. She's waiting for you."

I gather up the coupons I'd been cutting before Rosie came in with her news and put them along with the scissors on my nightstand.

"Nikki, why are still clipping coupons?" She grins at me. "I could see you doing that back in Detroit. You're a television star now, you don't need to penny-pinch."

"I don't care if I get million-dollar bank, I'm still going to cut corners where I can. And shoot, do you know how expensive it is out here?"

"All right, Miss Penny Saver."

"Speaking of finances, Mami wants to get with you on asset allocations. You know how she is about investing. So be sure to give her a call or e-mail her."

"Tía Sarah should've been on Wall Street instead of making dresses and doing alterations. She's a freaking whiz at stocks and stuff. It makes my head hurt just thinking about it."

"I know. It's because of her that she and Papi can afford that brownstone. Anyway, I feel funny going over to Amber's having a good time when you're here feeling down."

"Don't. I'm cool. I need a little downtime by myself to sort things out. So go." She gets up off the bed and shoos me out the door.

"As long as you're sure you really love and want to be with him this time, go ahead and call him, Rosie."

"It's not that easy. He doesn't know all that's been going on, but I do. Maybe I don't deserve him."

"Yes, you do. Push aside all your fears and go after your heart's desire. When you get him back, love him with all your being. Embrace with him your soul." I flutter my eyelashes for dramatic effect.

"Reading them damn romance novels again, huh?" She smirks.

"*Mira*, I was playing around but at the same time I'm serious, too. Like I said, as long as you know for sure he's who you want."

"I do. Now get. Have a good time."

"Tell Mario to call Amber's if he needs to get in touch with me. My cell phone is dead and it's charging."

"You can use mine."

"No, that's okay. Call him, Rosie."

She kisses me on the cheek and pushes me out the door.

When I get downstairs to the parking lot, Amber's black Eclipse is waiting by the door. When she sees me she starts honking the horn.

"You're not in the country, girl," I say as I get in.

"Honey, I'll always be in the country in my heart."

"Are Paris and Joanne at the house?"

"Uh-huh."

After a couple of minutes of silence, I ask, "What's the matter? You seem distracted."

"Girl, my sister Renie is back on that shit again."

"Oh no, Amber! She was doing so well."

"I know. I called over to her place and her boyfriend answered the phone sounding all funny. I asked what was wrong and he said she came home high the day before, they got into an argument over it, and she stormed out. He ain't seen her since. I actually felt bad for him. I never approved of their relationship because they met at one of them meetings. All I was thinking was he'd slip up and drag her down with him. But now I'm worried that *she's* gonna get *him* back on the pipe. Anyhow, something told me to look around my place 'cause she came over a few days ago. Sure enough, some pieces were missing out of my jewelry box. I really didn't care about any of it except the tennis bracelet. I can't believe she took it. She knows my baby gave me that. I still ain't told him, but I'm going to have to tell him soon because I gotta put in an insurance claim. Shoot, that bracelet is expensive as heck. Her ass gonna be smoking for a while on that alone."

"I'm so sorry to hear that." I gently pat her leg.

"Nikki, I'd just started to trust her being in my house unsupervised. 'Cause you know before I'd practically go into the bathroom with her. All I can do is pray for her. I tore my hair out about it the first couple of rounds she was strung out. I got my own life. I ain't got time to be sitting up somewhere biting my nails worrying about her. I can't do it. It took too much out of me before. That's why I called up all you broads and said come on over. I need something to take my mind off that mess. Plus, Benji is in New York filming that guest spot on *Law & Order*. Wait a minute. My mind is so gone I forgot to ask—where is your cousin? I thought she was coming over."

"She's got the blues over her ex."

"She really should have come over there. Ain't no use in sitting home crying about it."

"That's what I tried to tell her."

We merge onto I-5 and I take this as my cue to shut up. Amber is from a small city in Tennessee and even though she's been out here for ten years, she's still not used to the traffic on L.A. freeways. So whenever she gets on one, she has to totally focus on driving. She reaches over and turns the radio down even lower. Amber is a sweetheart. She's about 5'7" with a voluptuous figure. Her not being a size two hasn't stopped her from getting as much fan mail from men as Paris and me. Sometimes more. She has a beautiful, blemish-free complexion the color of honey. She wears her reddish-brown, medium-length hair natural. Today she has it in a soft 'fro with a scarf wrapped around her head like a headband. She's got big, beautiful expressive eyes. Amber has one of those contagious smiles that even if you're PMSing, pissed at your man, and having a bad hair day, you can't help but smile when you see hers.

Amber has been living with our co-star Benjamin for the past year. That man adores her. He's not the best-looking guy in the world—his personality is what gives him his appeal. Still, he has a strong female following. And though his agent tried to get him to play the unattached bachelor offscreen, Benjamin was never down with that and has made his love for Amber known.

"So, what do you think we should order to eat?" she asks as we exit the freeway.

"I wouldn't mind some Chinese. I'm in the mood for some General Tso's chicken."

"Oh, girl. That sounds good. The place not far from me has pretty good food."

"Hey, what happened with Paris and her husband, well, ex-husband Bernard? Did they come to terms in the settlement?"

"That buster wouldn't settle for anything less than the half he was supposed to get."

"See, I don't think it's fair when women run after money they didn't earn and I *especially* hate it when men do it. He hasn't worked in years; on his own he ain't got a pot to piss in or a window to throw it out of. Too bad they didn't have a prenup. But I'm sure drawing up papers wasn't on her mind when she married him, considering she said they were both frying up chicken and making waffles at Roscoe's at the time."

"Mm-hmm, I know she didn't. Hell girl, he walked off with half. *Half.*" She honks the horn at the car ahead of her. "Light ain't gon' get no greener. Paris said she got some juice to tell us."

"Any idea what it is?"

"Nope. She said she also needs some advice from us."

"Hmm. Sounds interesting."

"By the way, I know I'm usually the designated driver but tonight I need a couple of drinks. So I'm going to be sending your behind home in a cab."

"That's cool."

Soon we pull into the driveway of her 1930s Spanish villa-style home. I see Paris' and Joanne's cars parked on one side of the driveway. Amber parks in the garage and we enter the house from there.

I love the way Amber has her home decorated—a mixture of ultra-modern and Afrocentric. She uses a lot of bold colors that catch the eye but don't overwhelm it. Once we get to the living room, we find that Paris and Joanne have gotten a head start on the drinks. They're sitting on the plush burgundy couch sipping on what look to be daiquiris. Joanne Clarkson claims to be in her mid-forties, but we suspect that since she wasn't ten years old when she did some of those Blaxploitation movies in the '70s, she's a bit older than that. She still looks great, though. She's attractive, about 5'6" with a medium brown complexion, about one hundred-forty pounds and short dark hair.

Paris Deveareax—whose real name is Shanita Jones—is the same height as me, 5'9". She has a light complexion, dark blue eyes that are real and not contacts, and a long, thin frame. Her shoulder-length hair is dyed dark blond, which complements her complexion very well. I don't know why she slaved in restaurants before getting her break in acting because she could've easily been on a runway.

"All right now!" Joanne says in a voice whose huskiness comes courtesy of a two-pack-a-day habit. "It's about time y'all got here. Amber you better get your ass on that phone and get some food up in here." She looks at me. "Do you know this chile ain't got nothing in her refrigerator but baking soda and two dried-up kiwis? If me and Paris didn't bring the liquor, we'd be sipping on California tap."

"Don't even try it, Jo. I told you Benji had some tequila and beer in there. Listen, Nikki and me decided on Chinese. Is that cool with you?"

"Hell no! I ain't trying to eat no stir-fried cat!"

"Jo!" Amber laughs. "Now you know that's not right. Don't say racist stuff like that."

"Racist my ass. If it makes you feel any better, I don't trust them Jamaicans to whip up something, either. You got to be careful with them there foreigners. You never know what kind of weird food shit they be bringing over here trying to cook up for us. Order me some pizza. There's an Italian pizzeria close by."

Amber puts her hand on her hip. "Oh, so you trust the Italians? They're foreigners, too."

Joanne pauses to think for a second. "Aw, shut the hell up and order my damn pizza."

Amber, Paris, and I laugh. I go sit on the couch next to Paris.

"I'll go with you two," says Paris. "I'll have some Moo Goo Gai Pan."

"Okay, Jo," says Amber. "I'll order us Chinese and get you a pizza. What all do you want on it?"

"Just extra cheese and pepperoni."

Amber goes into the kitchen to find the restaurant listing and to order the food. I pour myself a glass of Corona.

12

Mmm. It feels so good soaking in this tub. I'm mainly a shower person but when I slip into a warm bath, I have to wonder why I haven't converted to them full-time. I'm still a little pissed at my cousin for coming down on me, even if she was right. I don't need any reminders of how I fucked up. That's why I haven't called Odell. Oh brother, I can just hear his "I told you so" mess already.

I'm not usually scared of anything. I got a bigger sac than a lot of men I know. The only two things I've ever been afraid of is falling in love and messing up if I did let myself fall in love. I think I've managed to kill two birds with one stone on that. What if I have a bit of Lupe in me after all? Maybe there's a part of me that feels I don't deserve the best. That would be a better explanation of what I did rather than just being stupid. More fucked up, but better. No, I'm not claiming that. I made a terrible mistake and I know I've learned from it. If I were to get another chance with Alejandro, it would be no more screw-ups. But if I don't, I'll know not to mess up like this again with someone else in the future.

I miss my sweetheart Alejandro. No matter what I was doing with Crystal, I still miss him. I loved putting my head in his lap and having him stroke my hair. I'd fall asleep just from him doing that. It got to where whenever I was having trouble going to sleep he'd start stroking my hair until I dropped off. He's the only person who ever served me breakfast in bed. Well, other than when Nikki did it when I was sick or something. Alejandro and I had developed a deep bond and the thing is, I know in my heart he wouldn't have done to me what I did to him. I can't say that about a lot of men but I can say it about him.

This may not seem like much but he was also the best kisser I ever had. I've had the worst luck with kissers for some reason. This one guy, I swear, he almost asphyxiated me with his tongue. It filled up my whole mouth and somehow made its way down my throat. Yuk. Then there was this chick that damn near sucked my tongue out my mouth. I was scared to let her get anywhere near my clit. Crystal was all right, but her technique could've used some work. In everything else, she knew exactly what to do. It's like that, though. I've been with people who couldn't kiss but were good sexually. You would think if they couldn't handle the basics they wouldn't be able to throw down elsewhere. Kissing is truly a lost art. Seems like everyone's so focused on the pussy or the dick they don't realize the eroticism of a good kiss. Yet, Alejandro could make me tingle at the mere thought of his kiss. Aw shit. Now I'm sounding like one of them romance novels. There have been times when we didn't even fuck, just would lie in bed running our hands over each other's bodies and kissing till our jaws were tired. Don't get me wrong; I enjoyed his lovemaking—shit, don't get me started on that!

That man had amazing control. He could hold off his orgasm for the longest till I came. And if for some reason I couldn't cum from the dick, he took care of me with his mouth or fingers. He was in no way a selfish lover and never went to sleep until his baby was satisfied. One dude I kicked it with tried that 'I got mine so I'm about to fall asleep' shit with me. I told him he wasn't going to cop one motherfucking Z until he got me off. That bastard had a lot of nerve especially considering how much he was begging for this *punani* to begin with.

I want nothing more than for Alejandro to be here now telling me he loves me and wants to be with me. I miss not only his love but his touch as well. Being in this tub gives me a flashback of one of the times we took a bath together. He was sitting behind me—stroking me. Mmm, that was the bomb. I close my eyes and relive that scene. I pretend my hands are his. That he's caressing my face and his hand is traveling down my neck and to my breasts. Lightly touching my nipples, circling his finger around them, causing them to become more erect. His fingers then softly pinch them, twirling them between his thumbs and forefingers. *Mm, yes baby—don't stop. Pinch it a little harder. Yes, like that. I want you so bad, baby.* He leaves one hand on a breast and with his other hand he caresses my belly, then the insides of my thighs. *You know how sensitive they are. Okay, my pussy is ready for you now. Yeah, flick your finger on my clit. Ssssssss—good, so good.* That warm, sweet feeling is traveling through my body…

Hold up a minute. I need a little something extra. Fuck, I forgot to bring my little friend. I know Nik has one, but—unlike hairspray or shoes—that's not something you borrow. I guess I'll have to continuing using my finger—or maybe not. I hop out of the tub and quickly semi-dry off. I open my toiletry bag on the sink and get out my battery-operated toothbrush and turn it on. I never noticed how loud it is. Good thing Mario's not home yet.

I put down the toilet lid and sit. I open my legs wide, part my lips with my left hand and apply the back of the vibrating toothbrush head against my hot little button. Now we're talking. After a few moments the moans I'd been containing begin to tumble from my mouth. I apply more pressure with firm, even circles. My hips begin gyrating and pumping. Shit is feeling good. I take the toothbrush off my clit and turn off the brush. I want to savor this feeling for a minute before I come. After a minute I return the brush to my spot and again enjoy the vibrations, reigniting that fire. I picture myself and Alejandro fucking in our favorite doggy-style position: me on my knees near the edge of the bed and him standing up. We're going at it crazy. He's grabbing my hips and pounding my pussy, hitting my G-spot. *Fuck me, baby. Fuck me harder.* I feel his balls slapping against me. I want to stave off my orgasm again but I don't move the toothbrush away in time. A red-hot orgasm rips through my body. I let out a scream and say Alejandro's name over and over.

It takes me a minute to regain my composure. That was amazing. Who would've thought I'd get off on a toothbrush? That was the first time I ever did that. I found out about it from this girl I used to know. I was curious about it but never got around to testing it for myself since I've always had a little friend on standby. Learn something new every day. Whew! I hope the tenants don't complain about all my moaning and carrying on. Oh well, if they do. I'm just glad I have an extra toothbrush with me.

13

Nikki

"There's one thing I hate about these girl-night things," Joanne says after pouring us all a glass of Hpnotiq.

"What's that?" asks Paris.

"Four bitches sitting around listening to soul music, drinking and acting the fool. Reminds me of *Waiting to Exhale*. I hate being reminded of that movie."

None of us say anything. We just give each other furtive glances. We already know the reason why. We've heard her gripe plenty of times about how she had her heart set on the role of Bernadine and it killed her seeing it go to Angela Bassett. And how insulted she was when they offered her instead the role of Whitney Houston's mother, which she turned down. Joanne is a terrific actress but for some reason she can't see that she was a bit, um, mature for the role of Bernadine.

"Paris, didn't you say you had some news for us?" Amber asks. I can tell she wants to steer the conversation away from Joanne's whinefest over her long-lost role.

Paris sips from her drink. She looks up at us over her glass. "You all know how I went to read for that new Devin Jenkins movie?"

"Yeah," we all respond.

"Although I didn't get the part, I did get to read with Jabari Thompson—"

"Ow!" hoots Joanne. "That young boy is gorgeous!"

"Really!" says Amber. She fans herself. "Fine piece of dark chocolate."

"Anyway," continues Paris. "Since the reading, we've, uh—kept in touch." She smiles coyly.

Amber stands up and points at Paris. "You're sleeping with him!" she exclaims.

Paris winks at her. We all hoot and holler.

"Why, you little slut you." Joanne laughs. "Do you know how many women would kill to be in your spot?"

"Yeah, her G-spot," says Amber. We all roar.

"Mario would kill me if he heard this," I say. "But Jabari has put some dampness in my panties. Oh, I thought I'd come just from watching in him in that love scene in *Catching Dreams*."

"Yes! That was the bomb," says Amber. "Paris, you lucky bitch."

"Is that Negro as good in bed as he looks like he is?" asks Joanne.

"He is by far the most sensual man I've been with. You all know my marriage to Bernard was over long before it was over and even when it was going good, I can't say I've ever enjoyed sex until now. The closest I've ever been to almost having an orgasm has been with Jabari."

"Wait a minute." Amber holds up her hand. "Almost? You haven't come yet?"

Paris shakes her head. "The only orgasms I've ever had have been from myself. But understand this, I actually enjoy sex with him. I feel things I've never felt before. This is where I need your help."

"Sure," says Joanne. "I'll fuck him. Bet he can make me come."

She and Amber give each other the high-five.

"No!" Paris laughs. "That's not what I meant."

"You know how Jo is," Amber says. "You walked right into that one."

"What I meant was, I need any advice you can give me in opening up sexually. I can tell from the sex talk we've had before that you guys are comfortable with your sexuality. That's how I want to be. I know if I can totally relax and open my mind, I could orgasm with him. How do I do that?"

Amber and I look at each other and shrug our shoulders.

"What's making you not relax?" asks Joanne.

"I'm always wondering what he's thinking. If he'll think bad about me if I do certain things. Like, he's excellent at oral sex—"

"You mean to tell us you haven't had an orgasm from oral sex?" asks Amber. "Even though he's good at it? Girl!"

"I know, I know. Not only that, but there are things I know he likes and I can't bring myself to do."

"Such as?" I ask.

"When he's going down on me I want to return the favor, but I just can't do it."

"What?!" exclaims Joanne. "Honey, you better wrap them lips around that dick and commence to sucking, especially if he down there French-kissing your kitty. Reciprocate, bitch, reciprocate! What's wrong with you?"

Amber and I laugh. Paris covers her face and falls back on the couch cushions.

"Seriously, though," says Amber. "What do you think the hang-up is? Were your parents Quakers or something?"

"No, silly. They were pretty open-minded. I tell you what it was—my no-good ex, Bernard. That man messed me up. At the time I married him, I was born-again; yeah, I know I've backslid. Anyway, we didn't have sex until our wedding night."

"Were you a virgin?" I ask.

"No, I was celibate. But I had only been with two other men a few times and that wasn't exactly mind-blowing. Sex with Bernard wasn't any better, but I still wanted to please him. I'll never forget this; this was the beginning of the end. He had asked me to go down on him and I was hesitant because I'd never done that. One day I decided I would finally do it. When I visited my parents' house I went into their closet where I knew they kept their stash of porno magazines and sex manuals. I looked at the pictures and read up on giving head till I was confident enough to do it. I even practiced on a banana."

I slide off the couch laughing. "A banana?"

"Oh hush, Nikki." Paris giggles. "So, I surprised Bernard a few nights later. He was going crazy, y'all. I had his ass wiggling. I knew I was working it. I even let him come in my mouth—I didn't swallow, I ran into the bathroom and spit it out. I came out of the bathroom thinking he's about to give me my props and instead he was sitting there looking at me with absolute disgust. I thought he was mad because I ran to spit that jism out. He asked me why I had lied to him. Now I'm totally confused, right? I asked him what he was talking about. He said, 'Why did you lie to me about never having done that before? How many other dudes you sucked off?'"

"That's fucked up!" says Amber.

"Tell me about it. I was almost in tears. I swore to him on my parents' lives that he was the first man I did that to. He said he didn't believe me because I did it too well. He started calling me all kinds of freaks and saying ain't no telling what else I'd done with other men. If I wasn't so stupid and naïve, I would've dumped his ass right then and there. But no, my dumb ass stayed married to him. By the time we were in our second year of marriage, I was so repressed sexually it wasn't funny. What tripped me out was he would get on me for just practically lying there. Yet, I was scared if I moved my hips too much or too fast he'd call me a whore.

"In my head, I know he had the hang-ups and I shouldn't let it affect me, but I can't help it. I've loosened up to the point where I can enjoy sex with Jabari, but not all the way like I should. And"—she looks at Joanne—"I do want to wrap my lips around that dick and commence to sucking, I just can't do it without all that old shit popping in my head."

"It's true what they say," Amber says. "The biggest part of sex is mental. I don't know what to tell you, Paris. You just have to free your mind and your wet ass will follow."

"You're so crazy." Paris laughs.

"For real, girl, when you're getting busy, completely focus on you and Jabari. Don't think about your screwed-up-in-the-head ex-husband and his issues."

"And they were his issues," I interject. "Some men are just like that—they can't handle a woman who can express her sexuality. Oh, a lot of them talk that shit about how they want a freak in the bedroom—but when they get one, their fragile little male egos can't handle it."

"Preach on it!" says Joanne, holding up her drink.

"That's right," agrees Amber. "I can't stand insecure men like that."

"My ex-boyfriend Jaime back in Detroit was that way to a certain extent. I didn't do half the shit with him that I've done with Mario because I didn't feel comfortable enough to. I dated Mario first and Jaime would sometimes ask if something I'd do to him I'd done to Mario. He was insecure about Mario because he knew Mario had been my only serious boyfriend before him. To spare his feelings, a couple of times I lied to him. I should've been like, 'Motherfucker, don't worry about if I did this to Mario or anybody else. Just lie back, curl your toes, and shut the fuck up! Your ass is getting the benefits now, that's all you need to be concerned with.'"

Amber, Joanne and Paris all break into laughter.

"You can tell Nikki is lit!" Amber laughs. "She gets all rowdy."

"I'm serious, y'all. I can't focus on what I'm doing or feeling if I'm all worried about my man thinking something bad about me. I don't need that head shit. I'm glad Mario isn't like that. I can be my old freaky self. I'll just be happy when we move into a house so I don't have to worry about the neighbors hearing us. That's my only hang-up."

"We were meant to enjoy sex—it ain't just for having babies," says Joanne. "We were given clits for a reason. Ain't no other physical purpose for a clitoris but for pleasure. I finally had a realization a little over a decade ago. I used to have hang-ups, too. Do y'all know I used to pretend that I didn't even want sex? I'd let the man beg for it and act like I was only doing it as a favor to him. I wouldn't let 'em know I was enjoying it. Plenty of times I wanted to scream my dang head off and wouldn't because I didn't think that was 'proper' or 'ladylike.'" She takes a swig from her drink. "And I ain't even proper or ladylike. Then I went to one of them weeklong female sex seminars down in Carlsbad that I let one of my white friends talk me into. Let me tell y'all—it changed my life. It didn't happen overnight but I eventually let go of all that crazy stuff and I'm feeling more sexual now than when I was in my twenties. Maybe you should go to one of them seminars, Paris. I heard they still have them."

"I'm willing to go. Shoot, I need the help. Give me the information when you get a chance. It's not only with Jabari but whomever I marry next time. I want it to be totally different sexually than in my last marriage."

"Joanne, do you plan on getting married again?" asks Amber.

"Hell no! All I need is a lover and companion, not a husband. I've been down that road three times and that's enough! All I want is what I got now—somebody to come touch it up every couple of weeks. Let me know I'm alive, then they can take their ass home."

Amber, Paris, and I guffaw.

"That's another thing I learned," continues Joanne. "Marriage ain't for everybody. You young women gotta stop thinking you have to be married. Paris, the ink is barely dry on your divorce papers and here you are with your mind on your next. If you feel you ready to get married again and most importantly *want* to get married, then fine. Just don't let your friends, family, or society make you feel you gotta do it. The only reason I ever married was because I thought I should be." She reaches for the bottle of Hpnotiq. "All right, I'm jumping down from my soapbox. No more speeches tonight."

"You made a good point," Paris responds.

"Yeah," says Amber. "I think every single one of us have felt that pressure to walk down the aisle."

"The last time I was in New York my parents were bugging Rosie and me about that shit. We'll get married when we get married. Oh, before I forget. Y'all know who taught me how to suck dick?" I say.

"Who?" they ask in unison.

"We're up here talking about marriage and she got her mind stuck on dick sucking," Paris says to Amber.

"Janet Jacme—the porn star. She is a good teacher."

"For real?" asks Amber.

"My cousin gave me some tips, but I really learned something when I was watching one of Janet's tapes. That girl sucks a mean dick, let me tell you. She's so into it. And that's what men like. They don't want somebody who's gonna play around with it, acting all scared of it. They want you to suck it like the rent is due!"

"Nikki, you are crazy!" says Amber.

"Wait a minute," says Paris. "What's her name again?"

"Janet Jacme," I laugh. "Write that down. And don't forget about Heather Hunter. That woman is fierce! I may sound like a lesbo for saying this but Heather is one sexy-ass woman. Rosie wants to meet her so bad. She said all she wants is one night with her and she can die happy."

Amber chimes in, "She's got it going on. Benji and me watched a few of her movies together. She is gorgeous. Let me stop because I sound a little lezzie, too. Okay, let's do a check of the sista night agenda. We've eaten and drunk till we have double vision. Nikki has had enough to have triple vision. And we've talked about sex. So what are we leaving out?"

"Gossip!" shouts Joanne.

"Oh! I have something!" says Paris excitedly. "I saw Lena Dobson heading for Stage 4—you know she's dating the director of *Lost Lives*. Anyhow, that girl has messed up her face! I couldn't believe it when I saw her. I can see you having a little something-something done to enhance your looks but that girl has lost her mind with that plastic surgery. Next time ya'll see her, you'll barely recognize her."

"What has she had done?" asks Amber.

"She's got her lips plumped up with that silicone crap. Her nose is messed up— nothing but a thin bone with two holes in it—and I swear her eyebrows were damned near on her hairline. She looks like she's always surprised."

"She didn't need to do any of that. She was very pretty," I assert.

"I know. That's why I was so shocked when I saw her."

"I'll admit that I've had a little nip and tuck," says Joanne. "I had a browlift, and a good one at that. Some of these browlifts have people looking like they just walked in on a surprise party. Plus, I brought the kids back home up north and got 'em perky again, but I knew when to stop. I run into folks I've known for years and I barely recognize them 'cause they done rearranged their faces so."

Joanne must be as wasted as I am if she's talking about having had plastic surgery. I know she has a vanity streak a mile long and wouldn't admit to that during sober conversation. Damn, this Hpnotiq ain't no joke. I think I'll make an Incredible Hulk. I reach for the Hennessy and pour some into my Hpnotiq.

"You all know in the regular world it's hard not to feel pressured to look a certain way," says Amber. "But here in La-La Land the pressure is ten times as hard. Even the beautiful feel inadequate. When I first came out here I had a roommate named Chidori. She was Asian and simply stunning. That girl could walk into a room without a stitch of makeup wearing a potato sack and still turn heads. One morning we were getting ready for work and I noticed her putting little pieces of clear tape on her eyelids—"

"What for?" I ask.

"I'm about to tell you, you little lush. This child knows she's high," Amber says to the others, laughing. "Anyway, I asked Chidori why she did that and she said to give herself a crease in the eye."

"Are you serious?" asks Paris.

"Yes. She was obsessed with having this crease, too. It was sad because instead of seeing how stunning she was, she was focused on wanting to have a darn crease and more round American-type eyes. Do you know that girl worked three jobs to scrape up enough paper to have eyelid surgery? She was so happy when she got it done, even though I didn't really notice a difference and doubt if anybody else did, either. It gave her added confidence, though—for a minute. Then she started saving up to get her boobs enlarged. See? Never satisfied. I'm very fortunate my parents instilled in me that I was beautiful inside and out. That's why I don't care how many closed-door meetings the new head has about me losing weight—screw him!"

"Go on now!" shouts Joanne.

"I'll go! Don't worry, honey. I had people telling me I'd never make it out here in this sea of size-zero-don't-eat-food-just-live-off-of-coffee females. Here I am, though. Huh?! Huh?!"

"Word!" says Paris, snapping her fingers.

"That's right, girlie!" I add.

"Before I forget, I got some juice," interrupts Joanne. "You know that tape of Juliette the singer? The one of her screwing the baseball player?"

"Yeah," we all say.

"My man Lenny, his nephew is her manager. Honey, she put that tape out herself. She squeezed every second of her fifteen minutes from that one hit she had a few years ago, so she thought this would get her name back in the papers. And it worked. People talking more about her now than ever before."

"That's a trip," says Amber. "That child needs to get into our line of work. I saw her on television the other night pretending to be tore up about the tape being out for everybody to see. She was crying and going on. She fooled me. That scheming hussy."

"Lenny told me the baseball player is pissed! He just got married and this is causing drama for him at home. I don't think he suspects she's the one who put the video out there, but if he gets hinked, then he's going to blow her out the water."

"Speaking of blowing," I say. "I heard from somebody who saw the tape she was blowing him real good."

"Oh my God." Amber laughs.

"Nikki!" Joanne laughs. "Take your ass home and suck Mario's dick! You still got your mind on that. Lenny was saying the next big publicity tool is nude pictures and sex tapes being released to the public with cries of 'oh it was stolen.'"

I lie back and listen to them talk. Or at least I try to. Their conversation fades in and out as I drift between being awake and sleep.

✦

"Nikki. Nikki. Honey, you want to stay here for the night? Paris and Joanne are crashing here, you might as well, too."

I open my eyes and see Amber standing over me, shaking me. "No, no, no. I'm going home. Where are my keys?"

"Oh Lord!" Amber laughs. "Don't tell me you forgot I picked you up. And even if you did drive over here, ain't no way I'd let you get behind the wheel. Let me call this girl a cab."

I reach over and throw back the shot of tequila I had in the shot glass on the table.

"Nikki, now you're cut off for real. No more. Do you know how much you've had tonight?"

"Girl, I ain't no damn lightweight. I can handle my shit."

"Oh Lord. Paris, pass me the phone. I'm going to get in the cab with her and at least see her to the front door."

I lean back into the sofa and close my eyes and wait for the cab to come.

14

Rosie

I've wasted a whole day hesitating calling Alejandro. I ain't no wimp so I need to quit acting all nervous and just pick up the phone. That boy has been on my mind too tough. Earlier when I took a nap, I had a dream about him. We were back in Detroit at Odell's wedding. Once Odell and Aaron got married, the minister called me and Alejandro up to the altar to take our vows. The shit seemed so real. I even woke up feeling happy. I know I fucked up messing with Crystal again, but I want to pick up with Alejandro. No more bouncing back and forth between my feelings for Crystal and him. I know he's the one. Too bad I had go through this to find that out.

I'll always have something in my heart for Crystal, no matter how much of a bitch she can be; that won't change. Once you feel that kind of love for somebody, it never completely goes away, even if it's just residue. When I was with Alejandro I always had a lingering question in my head of what if Crystal and I could make it. That shit ain't lingering no more, so I can move on. I've never had to wonder with Alejandro. He's always let me know what his feelings were and where he stood. I need that more than ever in my life right now. I used to pretend that I didn't need anybody 'cause I never felt I could count on anybody—well, other than the peeps I can count on one hand. Hell, if your own mother can pretty much turn her back on you, it only stands to reason that you might not be the most open and trusting person in the world. I trust Alejandro, though. That man is the straight-up deal. The only reason I haven't called him is because I felt so guilty. But I'm ready now to one hundred and ten percent focus on my love for him—for good this time. No more of that back and forth shit. It's kind of late to call. It's eleven-thirty here so it's two-thirty in the morning there. Oh well, I've got to call before I chicken out.

I lean over, turn the light down low, and pick up the phone and dial his number. Damn, why is my heart racing and shit? I feel like a little girl calling a boy for the first time.

"Hello?"

"Hey, babe. How are you doing?"

"Rosie?"

"The one and only."

"Oh. I saw the name Mario Esposito on the ID and had to think for a minute who it was. How's California?"

"It's cool. I like it even more than when I first came out here. Um, I have the photo shoot with *Silk & Velvet* next week. After that I just have to wait and hear something back from them."

"That's nice."

"What's up? You sound kind of funny."

"Really?"

"Yeah."

"No, I'm cool. How did things go with your mother? I saw Chico and his girl at the movies and he said you were going to New York to see her."

"Things are still the same. She couldn't give me any good reason for doing what she did. I told her I'll pray for her but I can't be a part of her life. I'll talk about that some more when I see you in person. I called to talk to you about something else. I miss you, babe. I can't get you out of my head. I think about you nonstop. I know I said I needed some space 'cause I had to sort out some things, and I've done that. I love you and I want us to get back together. Can we start all over, please?"

He doesn't say anything for a few moments and that puts me even more on edge. "Do you really want to get back together because you miss me and love me or am I sloppy seconds 'cause Crystal doesn't want you?" he says finally.

"What?!"

"You heard me, Rosie." His voice sounds controlled. Like he's stopping himself from going off. "Crystal came into the store yesterday to see me. She said ever since you ran into her a few weeks ago you've been harassing her, calling and telling her how much you love her. She said the reason she stopped talking to you the year before last was you tried to make more out of what happened between you and her that night. She also said that's why you broke up with me—you thought you could convince her to be with you and you wouldn't accept the fact she's not interested in women and was just experimenting that night."

That lying bitch! I know on our last conversation we didn't end on the best note, but I still can't believe she'd do some shit like this! Why?! Why would she betray me by going to Alejandro with a bunch of half-truths? Why would she go to him at all?!

"I know Crystal has her own motives for telling me all this. I didn't tell you, but she came by to see me a short time after that night the three of us were together. I'm just going to put it out there: She came out point-blank and said she wanted to sleep with me and asked if I'd be down to do it again without you in the mix. I turned her down because I wasn't about to do something behind your back even though we weren't going together yet. I never mentioned it 'cause I knew you two had been friends for years and I didn't want to cause any conflict. She was very persistent, but I did my part, which was to remain loyal to you. What I want to know is, what about your loyalty to *me*? All I want is a yes or no answer to this question—did your breaking up with me have anything to do with you having feelings for Crystal?"

I can't even talk right now. I see my chance of getting back with Alejandro disappearing before my eyes.

"Rosie? Yes or no?"

"Yes," I reply softly.

There's silence for a minute.

"Rosie, you've always said that you need to be sure the person you're with is down for you. That it's the most important thing to you. You had that in me, but I guess you were so caught up in having somebody be loyal to you, you didn't think about being loyal yourself. For the last two years you've been my life. I never did anything without thinking of you first. I'm sitting up here like a fool planning for our future. My sister and brother have been bugging me for a while to move out there to Hermosa Beach but I haven't done it because you said you weren't interested in moving out there. I live for you, Rosie—or at least I did. But as much as I love you, I need to be with somebody who has the same love and loyalty for me that I have for them. That person obviously isn't you. I hope you find whatever it is you're looking for out there. I wish nothing but the best for you, but I need to get on with my life—without you in it. This is already hard enough so make this your last call to me, okay?"

The line clicks. I hang up the phone. It would've been a lot better if he'd screamed at me and called me all types of bitches and shit. I could've rolled with that better. To hear the hurt in his voice and the resolve that he was through with me is more than I can take. I'll never forgive Crystal for this! That bitch went to him not once but twice! The first time I might be halfway willing to give her just a tiny bit of slack. Her going to him a second time, after we'd been kicking it, is totally unforgivable. And then to lie like she did… I was harassing her?! That bitch was ringing my phone damn near every night wanting me to come over and fuck. She wanted to make sure I couldn't get back with Alejandro and she succeeded. That vindictive *sucia*.

I wanted to try and plead my case to Alejandro and get him to understand. But I could tell from his voice it wouldn't have done any good. He's through with me. It's my own damn fault, too. I had a certain love and left it to run after an uncertain one. How could I be so motherfucking stupid?

I hear a knock on my door. "What?"

"Rosie?" says Mario. "Can I come in for a minute?"

"Yeah, come on in."

"I'm going back out to pick up some burgers from that all-night diner down the street. You want something?"

"No, thanks."

Mario walks in and over to where I'm sitting on the bed. "Hey sis, are you okay? You look like you're about to cry." He sits down next to me and puts an arm around my shoulder.

"Everything's fine. I just completely destroyed my relationship with Alejandro, that's all. Other than that…" I shrug.

"What happened? If I'm not being too nosy."

"I don't feel like getting into the whole thing again. The *Reader's Digest* version is I cheated on Alejandro with Crystal because I still loved her. I broke it off with him to explore things with her. I found out once and for all things would never work with her. Once I came to that realization I called Alejandro to try and patch up things, but it seems Crystal went to him with a bunch of lies. Between that and my own shit he wants nothing more to do with me." I cover my face with my hands. "Mario, man,

I can't believe what I did. Alejandro didn't deserve that. I look back on it and don't know why I did what I did."

Mario puts his hand on my head and places it on his shoulder. I put my arm around his waist.

"Everybody messes up once in a while. Sometimes you have to lose what's important to truly appreciate and value it. I did the same thing when I came out here to go to school. I just assumed Nikki and me couldn't make it in a long-distance relationship and made the decision that we should see other people. There are some beautiful women out here and I dated my share but I didn't meet anybody who I connected with like I did with Nikki. I didn't know what I had until I didn't have it anymore. Luckily, when I went back to Detroit and got her to finally come out here, our connection wasn't broken. We couldn't be happier. There's always a chance Alejandro can come around."

"I won't hold my breath. He sounded so final, man. Like 'keep stepping, bitch, 'cause I'm moving on.'"

"Don't give up hope. You never know what might happen one day."

"What the fuck is going on in here?!"

We look up to find Nikki standing in the doorway.

"Nikki," Mario says.

"Answer my damn question! What the hell are you two doing?!"

"Nikki," I say, "what is your problem?"

"Oh, *I* got the problem? I come home and find my cousin and my man all hugged up and shit on the bed with the lights turned down! I'm surprised y'all motherfuckers don't have Marvin Gaye or Sade pumping on the stereo!"

Mario and I stand up. I walk over to her.

"I don't know what the hell is wrong with you, Nikki, but you need to check yourself." I catch a whiff of alcohol coming off her. "You've obviously had enough to drink to make you lose your goddamn mind. Mario was only comforting me because I called Alejandro and found out he doesn't want anything else to do with me. That's all!"

"Oh, so now you fucked up with Alejandro and you think you can find comfort with my man?! I don't think so! You better flip your mattress and go find some pussy!"

I clench my fists. I've never wanted to lay a hand on my cousin but right now it's taking every last bit of willpower I have to not slap the living shit out of her. Mario walks over to Nikki. He gives her a look that shows he's just as mad as I am. He turns to me. "Like I said, we couldn't be happier." He brushes past her and walks out the door.

"How much have you had to drink tonight, Nikki?"

"None of your business. When you got pissy drunk in New York did I question your ass? No! So don't question me. I'm a grown-ass motherfucking woman!"

"Get your drunk ass out of my room! Right now, before one of us does or says something we can't take back."

"Ain't this some shit? You're kicking me out the room of my fucking apartment. You ain't running thangs up in here. Whatever. I don't want to be in here anyhow."

She turns, wobbles slightly, and leaves the room. I slam the door. I can't believe her! I would never do what she's thinking. Shit, to do anything with Mario would feel like incest. She looked drunk as a damn skunk. Still, for her to say some mess like that is fucked up. Wait till in the morning when her ass sobers up. Girlfriend is going to get an earful from me.

15

Nikki

Oh, God. My head is killing me. I have to strain to open my eyes because they're crusted with sleep matter and mascara. Ugh. I rub my eyes. How did I end up on the couch? I look over at the clock on the wall. Twelve-thirty? I get up and go to the kitchen. I open the cabinets till I find my remedy: two aspirin with milk of magnesia. I get some orange juice from the fridge to wash the chalky taste from my mouth. I walk through the apartment and find I'm the only one here. I take off my clothes and prepare to take a shower. I hope the steam helps me with this hangover.

As soon as I finish my shower and walk out the bathroom I hear the key in the door. I walk down the hall to the living room. Mario and Rosie come in with grocery bags.

"Hey, you two. I didn't even hear you leave."

"You were so out of it, you wouldn't have heard a stampede of elephants leave," Mario retorts.

Rosie rolls her eyes at me and goes to the kitchen. What's up with her?

"I see you guys went to the store. It's a good thing 'cause we're low on food."

"Yeah, we went to the store and on the way back we stopped at a hotel for a quickie," he says, his voice dripping with sarcasm. "Hopefully the ice cream hasn't melted."

"What? What the hell do you mean by that?"

He ignores my question and goes into the kitchen, too. I follow.

"What's wrong with you guys? Are you mad at me or something?"

"Mad at you?" Rosie asks as she stops from putting food in the cabinet. "Why would we be mad at you? Just because you walked up in here last night sloppy drunk and accused Mario and me of getting ready to fuck?! Naw! Why should we be mad about that?"

"Huh? I what?"

"You don't remember?" asks Mario.

"No! Wait…" I search my mind. I do kind of recall walking in and seeing them sitting on Rosie's bed and me cussing at them. Oh shit!

"Mario was consoling me because I called Alejandro and found out things are completely over for us. I was already going through it over that and here your ass come in with some bullshit!"

"And then," adds Mario, "you had the nerve to try to come to bed with some gin and juice. I told you to take that shit out to the living room somewhere."

"I'm so sorry. I apologize. I—"

"What all did you have to drink over Amber's house?" Mario asks.

I do some more mind searching. "I had Hpnotiq and then I made a couple of Incredible Hulks out of that and Hennessy. I had a daiquiri and that's it," I lie. I don't tell him about the tequila shots, the Long Island Iced Teas, and the beers. I'm already in trouble.

"You need to slow your roll on that drinking shit if it's gonna make you act like that," Rosie says. "You come accusing us of something that nobody was even thinking of doing and calling us motherfuckers on top of that."

"I'm sorry—for real. Please forgive me." I look earnestly at them. Even though I'm truly apologetic, I realize this is a good time to let a tear fall. So I do.

Mario walks over to me and looks me square in the face.

"Don't you *ever* accuse me of anything like that again," he says in a measured tone. "Do you understand me?"

I nod.

"You have no idea how much you insulted us last night. It was only because I knew you'd been drinking that I didn't pack my shit and go to a motel for a few days."

I wrap my arms around him and put my head on his shoulder. After a few agonizing seconds, I'm relieved when I feel him return my embrace, albeit reluctantly. I raise my head and kiss his lips. He raises his hand and wipes the tear from my cheek.

"I love you," I say.

"I'm still ticked at you."

"I love you," I repeat.

"I love you, too, Nikki."

I turn to Rosie, who has resumed putting up groceries. I go up to her and hug her from behind.

"Go on, Nikki," she says.

"Do you accept my apology? I'm not letting go till you say yes."

She moves to put a box of cereal on top of the refrigerator. I hold on to her and move with her.

"Girl, if you don't let me go!" I can hear suppressed amusement in her voice.

"Not till you accept my apology."

She moves back to the bags on the counter and I move with her again. She goes to the sink and bends down to put the dish liquid under the sink. I move and bend down with her. I finally hear her laugh.

"Okay! Okay! I forgive you. Damn!"

"Turn around and give me a hug."

She turns around and has a smirk on her face. "Can't stand you." She hugs me back.

I'm still tripping over what I did last night. I guess I'd better take it easy next time I go out drinking. Or else I might do or say something and I won't get out of the doghouse this easily.

Big Time
(I'm on my way,
I'm making it)

16

Everything has been such a whirlwind. Shit is crack-a-lacking big-time. People at *Silk & Velvet* said the issue featuring me on the cover and in the centerfold has been the bestselling one in four years, since pop sensation Brooke Samson shed her bubblegum image by posing for them. After my spread blew up like it did, I got offers for videos and calendars, and to be the spokesmodel for a popular cognac. Nikki turned me on to an agent and an attorney to help choose projects and to negotiate the contracts.

I'm having a blast. I have thrown myself into the L.A. party scene with a vengeance. A lot of this is new to me, like rubbing elbows with all kinds of celebrities, and I'm enjoying every minute of it. Mainly because the more time I spend occupied the less time I have to mope over Alejandro. I wanted Nikki to be my hanging partner but she's all in settled-down mode. Girlfriend was even about to sell her bike till I convinced her to let me use it while I'm here. So my hanging buddy has been transplanted East Coast rapper Mission.

We met when I was picked to be his love interest in one of his videos. We hit it off from jump because we have a lot in common. We both like to party, we like the same types of music—most music anyway. I tried to turn him on to salsa but he wasn't feeling it. Another thing we have in common is we're family. Yeah, he's bi too. His image is so hardcore you'd never guess it. He's tatted up, has the thug MC Kill-A-Nigga swagger and the sneer always on his face. His hardcore persona isn't an act because he'll step to anybody who's disrespecting him or his peeps in a minute. He's not like a lot of punk-ass rappers I've seen out here who start shit, then run for cover behind their bodyguards. Unlike other rappers, he doesn't have a huge entourage following him everywhere. Mission is good people. On a personal level he's cool to chill with, and on a professional one, it's worked in both our favor that the press has tagged us as a couple. I provide him with a lovely woman to squire on the red carpet and he provides me with extra exposure.

I found out a couple of weeks ago one of his lovers is a neo-soul singer named Tre-Smooth. There has been some talk about Tre being gay ever since some grainy sex photos alleging to be of him and a male lover ended up on the Internet. You really can't tell if it's him. I only know for sure 'cause Mission confirmed it to me. Come to find out, a spiteful ex-lover who was bitter over their breakup put the photos online. A pit bull public relations firm went to work on Tre's "romantic lover of women" image. He went from telling interviewers he was too busy to date to squiring starlets and models around town. Any indication of Tre's homosexuality was also shot down by the denial of hundreds of thousands of swooning women who refused to believe the man whose face they emblazoned in their heads while fucking their men could be anything but a one hundred percent pussy-loving man. Lucky for Tre, his ex didn't have any clearer photos stashed away. There was still talk about him of course. I've noticed out here that once a rumor about a celebrity's sexuality, be it true or not, hits the pavement it's hard for them to shake it.

I became suspicious about Mission's preferences one night when we were dining out. A gorgeous man eating alone sat at the table next to us. I couldn't keep my eyes off him—and I noticed Mission couldn't, either. That was my first clue. My second clue, if you want to call it that, was a few nights later when I crashed at his place after a night of drinking and doing E. That was the first time I met Tre. He was in town to collaborate with Mission on some songs. I knew right off that Tre had sugar, honey, *and* molasses in his tank. He comes off all butch when you see him in videos and interviews. But when the cameras are off, a bit of the queen comes on. He's not flaming like my boy Odell, he just lets the mannerisms flow enough to pick up on. I also caught a vibe between him and Mission that made me think their collaborating wasn't just in the studio.

After we sat up for a while listening to music and me taking turns dancing with them in the living room, I went to one of the rooms to crash. That morning I woke up and went looking for Mission. I didn't see him in his room or any of the other guest rooms. I finally found him in the living room. Him and Tre were passed out naked on the floor, lying on pillows and cushions from the couch. Mission was lying on his stomach and I had to cover my mouth to keep from laughing out loud: Dude had a condom hanging out his ass. Now that shit was a trip! If I had to place bets I would have pegged him as a pitcher and not a catcher. I went back to my room to shower.

Later on when we were eating, he asked me if I'd seen anything. I knew exactly what he was talking about without him having to elaborate. I let him know I'd seen him and Tre together and that it was cool—I wasn't going to flap my gums or anything. What happens in Vegas stays in Vegas. He already knew what I was about and even though I don't hide it, I let him know I wasn't going to open the closet door on him. He trusts that my word is bond.

He also let me know he's attracted to me. I'm feeling him on a physical level, too. I told him about Alejandro and how I'm not interested in getting serious 'cause my heart is elsewhere—but that doesn't mean we can't get down. I said I didn't want to rush it just 'cause we both put it out there. Let shit happen naturally. As much as we get high together, I'm sure we'll fall into bed eventually. He is sexy. He's not extra fine or nothing but he's got a certain raw sexuality to him that makes him hot. He's dark reddish-brown-skinned, bald, about 5'11" and because he hits the gym every day, he's in great shape—big muscles rippling everywhere. I pick up my cell phone when it rings. Aw, dude must've heard me thinking about him.

"What's up, dawg?" I say.

"Shit. What's going on wit' you, Ma?"

"I was just sitting up here thinking about your ass."

"Oh for real." He laughs. "You thinking about finally lettin' me tap that?"

"As a matter a fact I was. You're finally returning my call, huh? I left about two messages for you."

"Yo, sorry 'bout that. I had two muthafuckin' interviews this morning that my sorry-ass manager didn't tell me about until the last minute. So I was runnin' around like crazy and shit. Never hire fam to handle yo' b'ness. Then on top of that, I found out I got these niggas is beefin' wit' me."

"Who?"

"Niggas from the PD-Click. I'm on the radio givin' a interview with Tammy Turner and she come wit' all this shit these mofos done said about me. Talkin' 'bout I jacked they beats and style. I ain't jacked shit from 'em. But you know, they on the come-up and whenever niggas is tryin' to make a name for theyselves in this game or get some extra shine, the way they do it is by lookin' at who's hot and startin' beef and shit. They last joint went triple wood and since they next piece just dropped, they tryin' to stir up some attention. What better way to do that than hit up the nigga whose shit is playin' everywhere?"

"If that new song they premiered on *106 & Park* is any indication, they need all the extra publicity they can get. That shit was straight garbage."

"I'm sayin'. I ain't sweatin' it, though. Them bitches ain't even in my league. Everybody see what they doin'. You gotta always watch yo' back, it's a lot of jealousy in this mix."

"I hear you. What you got going on tomorrow night, papi?"

"Damn, I love it when you call me that. What you wanna do? It's all about you, Ma. How come you don't wanna hang tonight?"

"I got dinner plans with my cousin. But tomorrow let's just hit the strip, you know—club hop. And we'll take it from there. Is Tre still in town?"

"Yeah, why? I thought it was just gonna be me and you, girl."

"I like Tre. I wouldn't mind hanging with him."

"I hope you don't like him like that, 'cause that's a lost cause right there. I loves me some pussy but that nigga don't go for any at all."

"I didn't say like him as in I want to fuck him. I just strictly like him."

"All right then. I'll call him and see if he can roll wit' us."

"You sound so cute when you're jealous—thinking I wanted to screw him."

"Shut up, girl." He lightly chuckles. "When me and you gonna do that for real? I been a good boy for a minute now. Nah mean?"

"What did I tell you? Just let things happen. If we end up doing our thing tomorrow night, then so be it. But let's not force it, okay?"

"All right. I feel you. How 'bout I swoop you up 'bout nine o'clock?"

"I'll be ready, papi."

"See? Mm-hmm. All right, girl, I'll hit you up later."

"Bye." I hang up the phone smiling. I'm only talking shit 'cause I like the anticipation of what's about to drop. I know something will end up happening tomorrow tonight. And I can't wait.

"Hey, girl," Nikki says, peeking her head in my room.

"Come on in."

"Who were you in here gabbing with?"

"I just made plans with my boy Mission for tomorrow."

"You two have been hanging tight. You getting serious about him?"

"Honey, you know who got my heart. Mission and me just cool like that."

"Mm-hmm. Tell me anything. We'll be ready to go in about half an hour."

"I'll be ready, too. I just got to put on my outfit."

"All right." She begins closing the door.

"By the way, you've got to check out my website. The guy who designed it did a fierce job."

"Yeah, I'll go online tonight after we get back and give it a look-see. I don't know if I told you but Mami and Papi are in Italy now. Ain't that something?"

"It sure is considering Tío Miguel doesn't like to go anywhere but down the street."

"I think he's used to doing a little traveling now. Each time they go somewhere, he complains less about packing and taking planes."

"That's good. I'm glad he's getting with the program. I know you were worried about them."

"That's one less thing to stress about. All right, I'm going to finish getting ready."

"You know it. Wait! Don't forget my taped interview airs on KTLA in the morning. I'll be at a meet and greet when it comes on. You remember what time?"

"Yes, girl. I remember." She closes the door.

Jealousy

17

Nikki

D amn, I hate feeling this way. As much as I try not to, though, I can't help it. This is really fucked up! I love my cousin to death and I'd do anything for her. All I want is for her to be happy and for good things to happen for her. I know it's selfish but I'm having a hard time dealing with good things happening for her on my turf. In the six months since her cover shot hit the stands, she's surpassed me as far as becoming known in the industry. Six months! She comes out here showing her titties and bush and she's already had a billboard advertising her *Silk & Velvet* cover on Sunset Boulevard, she's doing television interviews and has a website. I don't even have my own fucking website yet.

What really annoyed the hell out of me was when she got offered a part in an Antonio Muras movie. Everybody and their mother want to get a part in this movie. She didn't take it because she felt uncomfortable trying her hand at acting. But it was the thought that they would even offer the part to someone who never spent so much as an hour in acting class that got to me. One of the things I hate about this business is a lot of times style wins out over substance. Almost anyone with any notoriety, be it a former lover of a famous figure, a so-called reality TV personality, or someone like Rosie who is only known out here for her face and body, can get a gig that actors such as myself have to pretty much beg and plead for. I'm the one who had to fight my parents left and right about choosing to act. I'm the one who sat in class after class drawing from deep within to bring out the essence of characters. I've studied my craft for years. I'm the one who had to be hit with rejection after fucking rejection, scared to death I wasn't going to get anywhere out here.

Scared that my parents were right and that I should've went to college and got a so-called real job. And I'm still trying to make it.

Right now I know I'm not exactly doing Shakespeare, but I put my heart into every episode. As much as I love working on *Tapestry*, I want to make my way into film, too. Not only in front of the camera but behind it. I know every actor says they want to direct but that's what I'd love to end up doing eventually. I also want to write and produce. Back in high school Mario and I said we would collaborate on a screenplay one day and I still want that to happen. I worked hard to get to where I am right now and know I have to work even more to get to that higher ground.

I could deal with working against the competition—other real actors. But I hate having to fight through all this other bullshit like having to contend with my non-acting cousin for roles. Did I mention the fact that I couldn't even get a reading for the movie Rosie was offered a part in? Yeah. Ain't that some shit?

I know it's not her fault. Like I said, I just find it hard to deal with her having such quick success in my arena. I truly, to the core, abhor feeling this way. The feeling of jealousy is a horrible one. Particularly when it's directed at someone you love dearly.

"Baby, what are you thinking about with your face all scrunched up?" asks Mario.

I was so caught up in being an envious bitch I didn't even hear him come in.

"Nothing. I just have a lot to do over the next few days. We're running late. I was rushing Rosie and I've got to take a quick shower."

"I'll take one with you."

"We don't have time to be messing around."

"I know." He takes my hand and pulls me off the bed and toward him. He wraps his arm around me. "I want to tell you something now that it's official."

"What's that, babe?"

"I gave my notice to *Urban Report* today. I accepted an editor position with *Community* magazine. It's a lot more political than what *Urban Report* is turning into. You remember Mike Pierson, right?"

"Yes."

"He knew I was putting out my feelers and he put in a good word for me. As soon as I got a firm offer I typed up my letter of resignation and took it to the big office."

"That's great, baby. I'm glad you found something else. I know you haven't been happy where you are. I've never read *Community* magazine. You think you'll like working there?"

"Definitely. I had only read a couple of issues but I went and got a bunch of back issues and they are just what I'm looking for, Nikki. They seem pretty confident in taking me on as an editor. Now that I've cleared up this gray area as far as my job situation, we can start looking for a house."

"Good! 'Cause I'm really sick of this apartment. I want more space. We'll start checking the Sunday paper in the morning and I'll get us a real estate agent on Monday." I kiss him briefly on the lips. "You've made my day."

"Is Rosie still going with us?"

"Yes. Now that I think about it, I should've asked her if she wanted Mission to join us."

Mario rolls his eyes.

"Come on, babe. He seems like a good guy."

"He may be a good guy but trouble seems to follow cats like that."

"As much as you like hip-hop I didn't think you'd be prejudiced against a hip-hop artist. So is it they're okay to listen to but not to be friends with?"

"Please. I'm not prejudiced against hip-hop artists. My book is about how police make unfair assumptions that *all* people in the game are violent thugs who need to be followed and have dossiers. But I also know there's a dangerous element about certain people—like Mission. They attract a violent vibe. You know somebody shot up his car when he was in Atlanta last year. And he's known to be affiliated with gangs out here." He touches me on the nose playfully. "Besides, Mission isn't a hip-hop artist, he's a rapper—there's a difference."

"Oh here we go." I let out a laugh. "I'm not about to get into that debate with you again."

"Better not, 'cause you'd lose."

"Whatever."

18

Nikki

Whard Mario, Rosie, and I enter Koi, I inform the waiter of our reservations and that we want to sit on the back patio. As we're escorted through the restaurant Rosie tugs on my sleeve.

"Oh my goodness, Nikki. This joint is love-ly!"

"I know. It's one of my favorite spots."

We pick a table with booth seating and settle in.

"Rosie, I'm glad you finally got to come here with me. You're hardly ever home and we don't get to spend nearly enough time together."

"Is that a statement or a condemnation?"

"Whatever it is, heifer, you could spend more time at home. If I can find the time to chill at the crib, then so can you."

She leans over and looks at Mario.

"Are you hearing this? Is it just me or does she sound like a nagging wife?"

Mario puts his hands up as if to say he was keeping out of it. I lightly pinch Rosie's arm.

"Ow."

"Quit making fun of me then."

Suddenly her face lights up. "Oh my fucking goodness! Is that who I think it is?!"

I look over in the direction she is and spot international film star Jon Waver. He's in his forties but has still managed to maintain his boyish good looks. With him is his younger girlfriend, actress Kelly Lowan.

Rosie says, "I just saw on *Access Hollywood* that they were dating."

"*Mija*, that's P.R."

"P.R.? Public relations?"

"No. Publicity relationship."

"For real?"

"Whenever you have a showbiz couple pop out of nowhere and start proclaiming their undying love to anyone who'll listen, I guarantee you one or both of them have an album or movie that's about to drop or lagging careers that need a shot in the arm. Matter of fact, I'm surprised they're not over at the Ivy. That's where half the town's paparazzi hang out. It would've been a perfect photo op."

"Girl, I'm here thinking they're really in love."

"Please," I tsk. "This is the role of that chick's life. You can't believe anything coming out of the machine that is Hollywood."

"Baby," Mario says, "you're sounding kind of cynical. Are you getting disillusioned with acting?"

"No, of course not. I'm not disillusioned with acting. Just the acting *business.*"

I'm not naïve or anything. Before I moved out here I knew how things worked from reading and listening to the stories from actors on the play circuit who'd had a taste of Hollywood. Another point of contention for me about this business is the smoke-and-mirrors aspect. I hired one of the top P.R. firms in the city and was pleased with them until they suggested an orchestrated romance with a high-profile NFL player. He'd just hired the firm to repair his scandal-laden image. He had run-ins with the law due to drugs, solicitation, and roughing up a groupie after a one-night stand. He had already lost some endorsements—if he wanted to be considered for others he needed an image overhaul. Since I have a pretty clean reputation, the meeting of the minds thought it would be a great idea if we hooked up. I would be the woman whose love changed him into a better man.

When it was presented to me I looked at everyone in the room like they were out of their ever-loving minds. I then proceeded to remind them that I was madly in love and living with Mario. They said that was no problem. I would just show up to various events holding hands with Mr. Quarterback and I could keep my relationship with Mario— just on the down low. Because the football player was so famous he didn't want someone who would outshine him, so I was perfect. Plus, it would take me up a notch or two on the publicity ladder. Many in the business had arrangements like this. I not so politely informed them that I wasn't about to be one of those people. I found another P.R. company after that.

"Here comes Benjamin and Amber," Mario says.

They walk over to the table hand in hand.

"Hey, people," Amber greets us as they slide into the booth.

"What's up, everybody?" Benjamin gives Mario dap. "Rosie, on our way here we saw you on another billboard. You've really blown up. You came out of nowhere and now I see your face all over."

"Thanks."

"Where's Paris?" I ask. I'm so not in the mood to hear about how Rosie has blown up so quickly.

"She's on her way to Vancouver, girl," Amber replies. "Jabari called and asked her to fly out to visit him on the set."

"I ain't mad at her," I say.

"Me, neither," says Amber.

"Add me to the 'I ain't mad at her club,'" replies Rosie. "Jabari Thompson is scrumptious."

"Oh man," Mario grumbles. "I don't know why you women go so gaga over that fake Billy Dee, Jr."

"I know that's right," agrees Benjamin. "He ain't all that."

I tilt my head up and sniff the air. "I don't know, girls. I smell a certain scent in the air. I can't quite tell what it is, though. Oh, I know. It's called Eau de Hateration."

Rosie and Amber giggle.

"I think you're right," says Amber.

Benjamin shakes his head. "Ain't nobody jealous of that dude."

The waiter brings us our water.

Amber leans into Benjamin and strokes his cheek. "He's got nothing on my sweetie pie." He plants a kiss on her forehead.

Mario looks at me with a raised eyebrow. "Well?"

"Well what?"

"Aren't you going to say he has nothing over me?"

I grin and give him a wink. "I know. I'm just teasing. He doesn't have a damn thing over you, baby."

"All right then."

"You see how our women are, Mario?" says Benjamin.

"How's that, bruh?"

"When we have our tongues hanging out over some hottie they expect us to let them know we find them just as sexy."

"Exactly."

"They don't realize we want the same thing sometimes."

I raise my hand. "Guilty as charged."

Amber nudges Benjamin. "Speaking of tongues hanging out, tell Rosie about your brothers."

"Oh yeah. They are dying to meet you. We're having a get-together at the house next week and hopefully you can make it."

"Sounds good to me. I'd love to come."

"Even though I've been doing television work for years and have been in a few movies, that hasn't impressed them nearly as much as me knowing Rosie Moreno."

"I heard you're going to be on the cover of *Maxim*," says Amber.

"Yes, I am. I'm so excited about that. My agent has been kicking ass for me. She's got so many things lined up…"

This is where I tune out the conversation. I take in the beautiful feng shui-inspired decor of the restaurant as I do every single time I come here. I listen to the light jazz playing. I think about how I'm going to order my usual—tuna tartare with avocado on crispy wontons and a bottle of Kamoizumi Madoka sake. And I loathe myself for feeling the way I do right now about one of the people I love most in the whole world.

Erotic City

19

Mission and I are driving down Wilshire Boulevard in his customized Escalade. Music from his upcoming CD is blasting away on the stereo system.

"All right, miss," he says as he passes me the blunt. "I got good news and I got bad news."

"What's up?" I take a hit, holding the smoke in my lungs as long as I can.

"Tre had to fly back to New York as a last-minute replacement for a benefit concert, so he ain't gon' be hanging with us. The good news is I got somebody even better to fill his spot."

"And who might that be?" I pass the blunt back to him.

"Keilana."

"Keilana? Who's that?"

"Present company excluded, Keilana is one of the most beautifulest women I ever laid eyes on."

"Most beautifulest, huh? Tell me more, Keith Murray."

"I met her on my last tour. She was in the front row and she caught my eye big-time. I pulled her up on stage and after the show I had her brought back to the dressing room. She told me she lived in Honolulu but visits her sister that lives here a lot. After we got all the small talk out the way, we headed back to my place and fucked like jackrabbits. That girl is real special. Whenever I decide to settle my ass down, she might be the one I do it wit'."

"Hmm. I'm not going to be a third wheel, am I?"

"Aw, hell naw. She love you." He looks over at me and grins.

"Oh, really?"

"Yep. She gots a huge crush on you. Ol' girl said she got yo' poster and everythang."

"Hold up! Keilana. I thought that name sounded familiar. Didn't you have me sign a copy of my *Silk & Velvet* issue for a Keilana?"

"Yeah, that's her. She bugged the shit outta me till I had you sign it. Then I had to overnight it to her."

"All right. That's cool. And she's a fan? A beautiful fan at that. Interesting."

Mission pulls into the driveway of a condominium. My buzz must be kicking in 'cause I didn't even notice we'd turned into a residential neighborhood. He throws the truck in park.

"You down to finally 'let things happen,' as you say?"

"If I didn't know better, I'd think you were trying to 'let things happen' with you, me, and Keilana."

"You done that before, right?"

"A few times. It's been a couple of years since I last did it, though."

"I think it's about time you had a refresher course." He leans over and plants his full, soft lips on mine. An electric shock shoots straight to my pussy. Mmm, he's one of the good kissers. He moves his hand to my right tit and moves his thumb in a circular motion across my nipple. I'm wearing a thin silk top and no bra so that shit feels damn good. He moves his mouth from mine. "By the way, I gotta surprise for you later, Ma."

"And what's that?"

"Wouldn't be a surprise if I told you, would it? I'm going to get Keilana. I'll be back in a minute." He takes another quick toke of the blunt and hands it back to me before exiting the truck.

I haven't had anything other than my finger and handy toothbrush since I left Detroit. I've gone months without getting me some. I'm more than down for some action.

A few minutes later, Mission and Keilana are walking toward the truck. From the streetlight I can't really make out her face, but I can tell she's about my height—5'7"—slender, and has waist-length hair. Mission lets her in on his side. The inside light comes on and as she slides in, I can see Mission didn't exaggerate one bit. This woman is beautiful. She has gorgeous tawny, sun-kissed skin; large doelike eyes; a cute little nose; and kissable, bow-shaped lips. Her shiny hair is light brown with dark blonde highlights; the soft curls frame her face. She's wearing skintight jeans and a black leather bustier. Her breasts are full and spilling over the top of her garment. They look real, too. Good, 'cause I hate fake titties. From the sexy smile she's giving me she's just as ready for some action as I am.

"Keilana, this is Rosie of course. Rosie, this is Keilana."

"Very nice to meet you." I reach back to shake her hand.

"I'm so pleased to meet you also," she says seductively. She takes my hand. Her voice is soft, with a husky Demi Moore quality to it.

We continue holding each other's hand and eye contact. The sexual electricity bouncing between us is sizzling. I can't wait to get with this girl. We don't move until we hear the sound of Mission closing the door. I slowly move my hand from hers. Her fingertips lightly caress my palm as I do. When Mission gets back in the driver's seat, he smiles at me and winks. I wink back.

"Keilana, would you like to sit up front?" I ask.

"No, thank you. I'm fine."

You sure in the shit are. "I don't want you to feel alone." I get out and get in the backseat with her. If I could I would sit right up on her, but the seats in the second row are separated.

"Oh, so you gon' leave me up here by myself." Mission laughs. "I see how you are."

"We love you, baby," I coo. "Keilana, I hear you live mostly in Hawaii."

"Yes, I'm thinking of moving to the mainland permanently. I'm still undecided…"

"Girl, I told you, I'd hook you up lovely if you move here. That's my word."

"I know, Mission, and I appreciate that. It'll just be so hard to leave my parents behind. I'm the baby and the only one of the kids on the island. Hey!" She points to the dropped television screens in front of us. "There's the video you two did together."

"Yeah, that's the first time I met this knucklehead." I lightly jab the back of Mission's shoulder.

"Rosie, remember after our love scene, I couldn't get up from the bed right away?"

"That shit was funny. The whole crew was rolling."

"Yo, I be seeing them actors all the time talking 'bout they don't get excited during love scenes. That's some bullshit. I was hard as a rock."

"It depends on who you're having your scene with," I say. "Even though I got hot and bothered with you, it was a totally different story when I did that video with Lil Mane. It was hard as hell to act like I was into him with his smelly, jacked-up-grill ass. He's always rapping about the money he spends on cars and ice when he needs to be dropping some dough at the dentist office and on some soap."

"Ah ha!" Mission laughs loudly. Keilana covers her mouth and giggles. She looks sweet doing that.

"I'm serious. I felt like throwing up. His breath smells like day-old collard greens."

"But I got you wet, though," Mission says, looking over his shoulder grinning.

"You know you did. Now keep your eyes on the road, *hombre.*"

"Where y'all wanna head to?" he asks.

"Since we're on Wilshire, and not too far from La Brea, why don't we go to the Conga Room?" suggests Keilana.

"I'm down with that. Mission?"

"I guess we heading to the Conga Room. I knew she was gon' say that. She love going there. Kei is down wit' that Latin flavor." Mission winks in the rearview mirror.

I look over at Keilana and she looks back at me, flashing an inviting smile. The light from the television screens is illuminating her beautiful face. I lean over and brush her hair away from her cheek. After I move her hair off her shoulder, I softly travel the back of my fingers down her bare arm. I can feel her tremble ever so slightly at my touch. We don't break eye contact for a moment.

"Anybody wanna hit this?" Mission holds up the blunt.

"Yeah, pass it back, *papi.*"

I get it and take a hit. "You want any, Keilana?"

"Can you give me a shotgun?"

I smile at her through the smoky haze. I take a long drag and hold smoke in my mouth. We lean toward each other, bringing our faces close. She parts her lips and I place mine against them. I slowly exhale the smoke into her mouth. Reluctantly, I move my mouth from hers. She holds it in for a few seconds before she breaks into a coughing fit. I rub her back.

"Are you okay?"

"Mm-hmm." She clears her throat. "I'm ready for another one."

I take another hit and put my mouth against hers. Damn, her lips are soft. She breaks into another coughing fit.

"Kei," says Mission. "You know you can't hang with the chronic. Wait till we get to the place. You can order some of those Congaritas you love so much."

"I'm glad you picked The Conga Room, Keilana." I hand the blunt back to Mission. "I've been in town for a while and still haven't gone there. Nikki said she loved it when she went."

"Nikki?" asks Keilana.

"Oh, sorry. That's my cousin."

"That's right! Nikki Moreno. That little bit of grass has gotten to me already."

No one says anything for a minute. Then Mission laughs. "Baby. Did you just say 'grass'?"

I can't help but burst out laughing, too. I was thinking the same thing but I wasn't going to say anything. Keilana even has to chuckle herself.

"Leave me alone, Mission." She giggles.

"That shit remind me of *The Brady Bunch*. 'Greg, your father and I found some grass under your pillow.'"

The way Mission affects his voice to sound like a white female, à la Carol Brady, makes me laugh even more. I'm high as hell now. Every little thing is probably going to have me break into the giggles. I lay back in the seat. A minute later I feel Keilana's hand in my lap. She takes my hand in hers. I smile back at her. Knowing what's inevitably going to happen tonight, I can't help but get a flashback to my last little threesome. This one is going to be different. Even though I care about Mission as a friend, I don't have any strong emotional attachment to him and definitely not one with Keilana. Therefore, if anybody starts tripping the morning after, it ain't gonna faze me. My eyes glide over Keilana's delectable breasts that are almost coming out of her top. Yeah, I'm down for this.

⁂

"Aw snap!" shouts Mission over the music. "My nigga Cochise is here. I'll be right back."

Mission gets up from the table and walks a few feet over to a tall, good-looking dude with cornrows wearing jeans, a throwback jersey, and ice for days. I recall Mission talking about him. He's a hot up-and-coming music producer, married to a beautiful soap actress; they have three kids together. He's also one of Mission's lovers. He told me about the time they got down in the studio one night. Mission and Cochise had to pay a nice sum of money to buy the silence of one of the engineers who came back unexpectedly to retrieve his phone. Dude walked in on them going at it on the floor.

I turn my attention to the beautiful lady next to me. Keilana is sipping on her third Congarita.

"Keilana, do you want to dance?"

"I was hoping you'd ask." She swigs down the last of her drink and gets up. I take her by the hand and lead her to the dance floor and the music of Tito Puente.

With all the indo and drinks in my system, I'd swear I was floating two inches off the floor. Keilana is salsa dancing wonderfully. The only thing wrong with her dancing is it's not close enough to me. I put my hands on her hips and draw her close to me. She puts her arms up on my shoulders. My nipples harden as I feel her tits against mine. We look into each other's eyes as our hips gyrate in unison. I look down at the swell of her breasts, then back into her eyes. I run my tongue slowly across my top lip. She leans in and kisses me. She gives me the right amount of tongue and lips. As we continue kissing our hands roams over each other's backsides. Then I let one hand settle on her luscious ass and the other in her long, silky hair. My *crica* is so hot right now I wouldn't be surprised if I burned a hole through my panties. I want to fuck this girl and I want to fuck her now. I break our kiss and put my mouth to her ear.

"Let's get out of here."

I don't even wait for a response. I grab her hand and we walk back to the table. I notice all the eyes on us but really don't give a shit. When we get to the table, Mission is sitting there looking at us, grinning from ear to ear. Obviously he was enjoying watching us on the dance floor.

"We're ready to break, dawg," I announce.

He laughs. "Y'all fixin' to get this party started? Let's be out this bitch then."

⚜

I'm lying in bed naked waiting on Mission and Keilana to get out of the bathroom. Don't tell me they're in there getting busy without me. Just as I start to get out of bed and see what's up, Mission comes out of the bathroom, closing the door behind him.

"What are you two doing?"

He climbs into bed next to me. "Remember when I told you earlier I had a surprise for you?"

"Mm-hmm."

"Me and Kei was gettin' it ready for you." His eyes glide appreciatively up and down my body. "I've been with a couple of females who posed in *King* and other magazines, but they didn't look nearly as good in person. But you—shit, your body is just as hot live and in color." He licks his lips and reaches out to stroke my legs, stomach, and breasts.

"Let's not forget about Keilana."

"Oh yeah. Now close your eyes."

I do as he says and close my eyes.

"Kei, come wit' it, baby!"

I hear the bathroom door open.

"All right, Rosie. Open your eyes."

When I do I close them again and open them back up. I want to make sure I'm seeing right. Keilana is standing naked at the foot of the bed. She's standing there with a six-inch semi-erect dick. I look to see if it's some kind of strap-on, but it's not. It's all hers. I think this calls for a "what the fuck?" Okay, is she some pre-op transsexual?

"Come here, baby," Mission says to her.

She climbs into bed and lies on top of him and they kiss. Mission then rolls her over to the middle of the bed. I scoot over to make room.

"You see, Rosie," Mission says as he strokes Keilana's dick, "she got the best of both worlds. Open your legs, baby."

Keilana does and now I'm really tripping 'cause when she opens her legs I see a pussy underneath where the dick is. Dayum! A hermaphrodite?! I know I've had too much liquor and weed now. But I don't think I'm hallucinating or anything. My membranes need a minute to soak this up. I've fucked chicks with a strap-on dick and chicks with strap-on dicks have fucked me but this is bugging me out. Though I'm intrigued because, like Mission said, it's the best of both worlds, this is still kind of freaking me out. And it takes a lot to freak my freaky ass out.

Keilana turns to me and strokes my titties. "You're not put off by my extra equipment, are you?"

"No, not at all," I lie.

"Good, because I've been aching to make love to you ever since I first saw you in that magazine."

Dig, this is what I'm going to do. I'm going to let her do her thing on me— with her mouth and hands, though. I'm going to touch every part of her except down there. Maybe later after all this has had a chance to settle in my head, I'll start exploring her down south. Until then I think I'll keep this from waist up.

"Suck my *tetas*," I softly command her.

She drops her head immediately and eagerly sucks them. Most women's breasts are sensitive, but mine are crazy sensitive. The way baby girl is doing it I think I'll come from that alone. Her hard dick—see, that don't even sound right in my head—anyway, her hard dick is rubbing against my leg. Mission is grabbing on her ass—rubbing it down. Mmm. Damn, this girl is working it. I go for her tits and lightly pinch her nipples. I can tell she likes that 'cause she's rubbing up against me even harder. I can't take this anymore. I push her on her back and straddle her chest. I take the index Tíafinger of my left hand and twirl it on one of my nipples wet from Keilana's mouth. With my other hand I spread apart my pussy lips.

"This is what you've been aching to get your mouth on, right?"

She looks at my pussy and licks her lips. "Yes," she says, breathing heavily.

I position myself over her face. Before I can even put it on her face she lifts up her head and attacks my clit with her tongue. Aw shit! This girl knows what she's doing! "*Mama me la chocha!*" I scream.

I grab onto the headboard and grind down on her face. Keilana reaches her arms up and strokes my tits. I take one hand off the headboard and caress her hands. I put one of her hands to my mouth and kiss it. I then take her middle finger, put it in my mouth, and suck on it. She alternates between fiercely tonguing and sucking my clit. I swear in no more than two minutes I'm screaming my head off as I have one of the most intense orgasms I've ever had. I've come quick before but that was a record. When my clit gets too sensitive for her tongue to continue licking it, I slowly get up off of Keilana. My body is literally shaking and my legs feel weak. I flop on my back. Keilana tenderly plants kisses on my neck and breasts. I run my fingers through her hair.

"I know y'all ain't gon' forget about me," says Mission.

I open my eyes. Honestly, I was so wrapped up in what Keilana was doing to me, I did kind of forget about Mission for a minute.

"Never, sweetie pie," Keilana says as she turns her attention to him.

Somewhere along the way Mission has stripped off his pants and is completely naked. I saw him nude before that night we hung out with Tre, but I only saw his backside. I didn't see the incredible package before me now. This dude is hung like he has a third leg. I mean seriously, he can use that *bicho* for a kickstand. He gets on Keilana and they rub against each other. I turn on my side, prop up on my elbow, and just peep the show. Mission moves down to the edge of the bed and settles on the floor in the doggy-style position.

"Where is it?" Keilana asks Mission.

"Right behind you on the dresser."

She gets a condom off the dresser and puts it on. Next to it is a bottle of lube. She squirts some in her hand, then on her dick. She puts the bottle back on the dresser and kneels behind Mission. She looks at me, like she's about to fuck me. I can tell from the look on Mission's face she's begun to enter him. His face is a mixture of pleasure and pain. Soon she starts fucking the hell out of Mission. It's a trip to watch her go from being the sweet yet passionate woman with me and then take on a more masculine persona as she fucks Mission. Her eyes never leave mine. I decide to really give her something to look at. I prop up a leg and lazily play with my still-wet pussy. I pump my hips like she is fucking me.

"Yeah, hard like that!" shouts Mission. "Hell yeah!"

Her movements in Mission grow more frenzied and he's loving every minute of it. Soon Mission lets out a loud groan and shoots a load onto the bed. If Keilana came I can't tell. After giving Mission a few extra pumps, she kisses him on the back of his neck and gets up and goes to the bathroom. Mission is lying on the bed like he's been through the wringer. I get up and go pull his arm.

"Come on."

"Come on where?" he asks in an exhausted tone.

"You got that big-ass shower. Let's all take a shower together."

"I can't move."

"Get your ass up."

He finally does and we head for the bathroom and Keilana. I feel him on being tired. Keilana has worn both of us out. I can't wait to take my shower so I can go to La-La Land.

Confession

20

Rosie

That was in 'In Da Club' by 50 Cent. This is Loco Lou and the Morning Crew. And as promised, in the studio we have an incredibly sexy young woman. *Silk & Velvet*'s Rosie Moreno!"

Lou and Tango hoot and holler. Liza grins and claps. I'm pretty sure she's going to come at me with something. She's known for asking the tough questions. No problem, baby.

"Thanks a lot, guys. Thanks for having me."

"Oh, I'd love to have you, sweetheart," pipes Tango.

"Play your cards right and who knows?"

More hoots and hollers.

"Rosie, your poster is the hottest thing out there," says Lou. "I heard the stores can barely keep them in stock."

"In *Entertainment Weekly*," adds Liza, "they said this is one of the most popular posters since Farrah Fawcett's came out back in the seventies."

"Wow. To have my poster put in the same league as hers is an honor."

"Our partner in crime, Flip, is at home sick and I'm sure he's even more sick knowing he's missing out on meeting you. We love you but that boy *adores* you."

"That's sweet. I would like to have met him, too. He was deejaying a party my cousin took me to a few weeks back. But we didn't get a chance to talk."

"Now, speaking of your cousin. Fineness must just run in your family or something because she's gorgeous, too. For those of you who don't know, Rosie's cousin is actress Nikki Moreno from the sitcom *Tapestry.*"

"Oh yeah!" exclaims Tango. "I never even watched *Tapestry* until she came on there."

"That's one of my favorite shows," adds Liza.

"Thanks. I'll relay your compliments 'cause I think she's doing an interview her-self right now. I wanna send a shout-out to my dawg now that you brought her up. What's up, Nikki? Love you, girl. You, too, Mario. That's her man, by the way."

"No, don't tell me that," says Tango.

"Aww," says Liza. "Are you two really close?"

"Like sisters. We grew up together. We were born in New York—four months apart. Our family moved to Detroit when we were seven and that's where we stayed until Nikki came out here a couple of years ago to launch her acting career. I came out late last year to do some test shots and been here ever since."

"Let me ask you this, Rosie," says Liza.

Uh-oh, here it comes. I've been listening to this show enough to know when Liza says that, she's going to ask a doozy of a question.

"Is there any competition between you two? Do you have problems with jealousy?"

"Oh no, nothing like that. I can honestly say we don't compete with each other and are not jealous of one another. What happens for one of us happens for both of us, you know? We got each other's back and we don't trip like that."

"Okay, that's good. Nikki is African-American and Puerto Rican and you're all Puerto Rican, right?"

"Yep, that's right. Well, my maternal *abuelita*—grandmother—was mixed with a little Chilean."

"Call me crazy," says Lou, "but I didn't think there were any Puerto Ricans in Detroit."

I laugh. "It was about one and a half—me and Nikki. There is a large Hispanic community in the southwest portion of Detroit, mainly those of Mexican heritage. There's been an influx of more Hispanics over the last few years, though."

"Rosie," says Liza. "I read that you were a—um, a dancer back in Detroit."

"Yes. It's okay, girl. You can say it—I was an exotic dancer. Ain't no shame in my game. I did that until I came out here for *Silk & Velvet*. I danced for about three or four years—off and on."

"See that's cool right there," Lou interjects. "Most people come in here trying to front but you seem like a pretty lay-it-on-the-table person."

"I try to be. There's really nothing to front about because it's not too big a leap from dancing to posing for magazines like *Silk & Velvet*. If anything, I'm probably wearing more clothes in my pictures than I did on the stage."

"Well, since you're being all upfront..." Tango chuckles. "What's the dealy with you and Mission?"

"That's my boy. Pure and simple."

"Come on now, Rosie." Liza wags a finger at me. "I thought you were being straight up. What's really going on? You two are photographed everywhere together."

"There's no romance going on if that's what y'all think. We like each other and enjoy each other's company. We have a relationship but we're not in a relationship, put it like that."

"All right, we have to take a minute to pay some bills and we'll be right back with Rosie Moreno. Your time is half past the hour of nine. This is Loco Lou and the Morning Crew!"

<hr />

"We're back about to find out more interesting info on the lovely Rosie Moreno," says Lou.

"Rosie, let me ask you something else," Liza says.

Okay, her first "let me ask you something" question wasn't as bad as I thought so...

"This is going to be a touchy question, I'm going to let you know that right now. I know—even though you're new to the business—I'm sure you realize there are a lot of rumors and innuendo that surround people who are in the public eye."

"Right, right."

"The rumor I've been hearing about you lately is one that plagues many celebrities, and that is that you're gay. How do you address those rumors?"

Bam. She got me. Here goes.

"Um." I brush my hair off my shoulders to my back and take a breath. "No, I'm not a lesbian per se. However, I am bisexual."

I almost want to break out laughing. All three of them have shocked looks on their faces and their jaws are dropped. All we need is the sound of crickets in the background.

"Okay!" says Lou. He grins as he gets his composure. "I didn't see that coming."

"Damn, now I'm really in love." Tango chuckles and puts a hand over his heart. "Daddy ain't got no problems with that. Bring a friend, bring a friend."

"I'm really taken aback," says Liza. "I had to ask the question but I fully expected a denial. It's a question I've asked other guests and it's always denied even when we know it's true. One person even assaulted one of our former deejays. I have to applaud your honesty."

"I don't think I should get props for telling the truth about who I am. It is what it is."

"Is this the first time you've admitted to being bisexual?"

"This is the first time someone's asked me in an interview. I don't look at it as admitting something. That implies I'm guilty of something wrong. Like, 'Do you admit to smoking crack?' or something."

"That's true. Do you have any concerns about how this may affect your career?"

"If it affects it negatively then so be it. I don't go hitting people over the head with who I am but I'm not going to hide it, either. I know too many people who do that. I did it at first when I started to come to terms with my sexuality. Then I just said 'f' it. Life is enough of a battle, you shouldn't come out the gate with a mask on."

"You've got that right," agrees Liza. "Boy, the phones were going crazy before and now it's even more so. We'll take a few calls in a moment."

"I don't want to sound dense," says Lou. "But you have relationships with both men and women."

"Well, duh." Liza softly chuckles. "That's usually what bisexual means."

"Not just usually." I chuckle. "All day long."

"So, which sex do you feel more comfortable being in a relationship with—men or women?"

"Doesn't matter. I've been in love with a man and with a woman. I'm drawn to both. Bisexual, remember, Lou?"

"Yeah, yeah, but I know people who call themselves bisexual and will have sex with both men and women, but when it comes to settling into a relationship, they prefer one sex over the other."

"Yes." I nod as I think of a certain sneaky bitch. "That's correct. And there are those who will have sex with both but don't consider themselves bisexual. Some have sex with men and women but feel more comfortable emotionally with one over the other. Personally, I could easily end up settling down with a man as well as a woman. It's whoever captures my heart."

"Rosie, if you don't mind, we're going to take a couple of calls."

"Sure, Lou."

"Our first call is from Janelle from Fresno. Janelle, go ahead with your comment or question."

"I just wanna say to Rosie, do you boo. My auntie is gay and even though some people be trippin', I don't care 'cause what she do in her bedroom is her business. I got mad respect for you saying the truth about yourself, not all like these other celebrities who be all fake and lying about what they are."

"We thank you for the call, Janelle, but we got to move on to the next caller 'cause the phones are going nuts."

"I want to say thanks to Janelle for her support," I say quickly.

"Our next caller is Esther from San Bernardino. Go ahead with your comment or question."

"Unlike you all and the previous caller, I'm not going to praise this young lady for her sinful ways. I love your show and all but I don't think it's right for you to promote this kind of lifestyle for our young people."

"Excuse me," interrupts Liza. "Ma'am, we're not promoting this lifestyle, as you call it. This is a young woman who has every right to live her life the way she wants without being judged for it."

"And on Judgment Day are you going to stand by her side and say to God that she's lived her life according to His word? Are you willing to lay down your soul for hers?"

"Ma'am, you have every right to believe what you believe, but you don't have the right to judge someone. Only God has that right. He'll be doing the judging, not you or me or any other human being. Thanks for the call. Rosie, I'm sure this woman's point of view isn't any different from what you've heard before, right?"

"No, Liza, it isn't. I've heard this kind of 'you're going to burn in hell' stuff from people before. No disrespect to this lady, but I was half-expecting her to start quoting the passage from Leviticus. It's nothing new. You can't live for other people. Everyone's entitled to his or her opinion. I'm not going to change this woman's mind and she's not going to change mine."

"Our next caller is LaTisha from Compton. LaTisha, go ahead with your comment or question for Rosie Moreno."

"Hi, everybody. I just wanna say I don't really care if you like men, women, or goats. That's your b'ness. My problem is this: I seen you in Mission's video and Lil

Mane's. And I'm sorry, but I get sick of you Latino girls up in our Black men's videos. You turn on BET and it's like, all you see is Spanish girls."

"Exactly what do you have against Latinas such as myself? You and I pretty much in the same boat. We both face prejudice and preconceived notions about us. Are you saying Blacks and Hispanics—who share the same bloodline by the way—should segregate? And I should only appear in videos by Latino artists—like Fat Joe? And then Fat Joe shouldn't put Black women in his videos?"

"No, I don't mean that. I'm saying it's like you know, y'all taking over and stuff. I think it's because the Black men just want girls that are light-skinned and got long hair in the videos and that's not right."

"That's not right if that's the *only* reason they want us in the videos. If that's the case, your issue should be with the Black brothers that do that—not with us. I've been in these videos that had beautiful Black women right next to me. I don't see why we all can't do our thing and not have this divisiveness between us."

"I'm with you on that," chimes Liza. "Thanks for the call, LaTisha. Rosie, do you come across this kind of resentment from Black women a lot?"

"I have. After we moved to Detroit, my cousin and I stood out because of our heritage. We learned to fight at an early age 'cause girls always wanted to scrap with us. It didn't help that we knew we were cute." I chuckle. "But we always got comments like 'y'all think you cute 'cause you got long hair and you're light-skinned.' But we just felt we were cute period, not because of our hair or complexion. And we didn't think we were better than anybody else. It really saddens me that we have this beef that goes on between Latinas and Black women instead of us uplifting one another. It's just stupid."

"We still have division amongst ourselves," says Liza. "So you can imagine what happens when you put another group in the mix. Our next caller is Walt calling from Riverside. Go ahead, Walt."

"I have one question for Rosie. Will you marry me?"

All of us start laughing.

"Get in line, buddy," jokes Lou.

"I'm sayin'. Rosie, you are fly as hell. I don't care if you into females, too, as long as I got a shot. Me and all my boys got your poster and I know this gon' sound corny but I look at it every night before I go to bed."

"Aw, that is so sweet. Thank you, honey."

"Now Walt isn't your real name, is it?" asks Tango. "'Cause it's one thing to be sprung off this young lady, it's a whole 'nother thing to be talking about you be looking at her poster every night before you go to bed at night."

"Oh, leave the boy alone," says Lou. "I ain't mad at him. We have to take another commercial break. Rosie, if you don't mind, we'd like for you to stick around a little while longer and answer some questions from our listeners."

"Sure, I'd love to."

"We'll be right back. Stay tuned as we continue our interesting conversation with Rosie Moreno."

21

Rosie

Maybe I'm a bit touched in the head, but I honestly didn't expect the firestorm that followed my radio appearance. The phone has been ringing nonstop. At first my publicist and agent weren't too thrilled with me announcing my sexuality. Though some have denounced me and my "lifestyle," there has been an overwhelming amount of support for me. Mainstream media like *Entertainment Tonight*, *Extra* and *People Weekly* as well as gay media such as *Out*, *Curve* and *The Advocate* have flooded my publicist with requests for interviews.

It's been a minute since someone on the Hollywood scene has announced they were anything but heterosexual so I guess that's why this is such news. Damn, who's calling now? Oh, it's Mission. I see he's calling from his home number and that means he's back from the concert in London.

"What's up, *papi?*"

"Don't *papi* me, you muthafuckin' bitch!"

"What the hell is wrong with you?!"

"You fucked me! You fucked me, Rosie!"

"Will you tell me what's wrong and what you're talking about?"

Shit, he's really hyped. He's breathing all hard.

"When you were having your little coming-out party on Loco Lou's show, did you stop and think you was gon' be draggin' me into it? Niggas is hipped to my shit now they know 'bout you!"

"What does my speaking on myself have to do with you? Are you worried about guilt by association? Mission, a lot of straight men get involved with bisexual women. Nobody has to know—"

"They do know! Everybody reads that trick Judy's gossip column trying to figure out her blind items. She had one on us and I know it's referring to when me, you, and Keilana was kicking at the Conga Room that night. Lemme read this shit to you. *This new-on-the-scene mamacita has a beauty as soft as silk and smooth as velvet. Her sizzling looks have made her the star of the wet dreams of men coast to coast. But our spies spotted the lovely lass gyrating the night away with another sexy lady at an L.A. hot spot. Said hottie's musical male companion and alleged boyfriend made it his mission to watch the sexual salsa from the sidelines. We guess he doesn't mind a bit since reliable sources say he engages in same-sex sambas himself.*

"Some people had already figured this shit out but now yo' ass decided to air yo' business, niggas is talkin' 'bout it big-time. My peoples told me this is all over the muthafuckin' Net. I had to have my message board taken down 'cause peeps was all over it callin' me a fag. Reporters done started callin' asking me about it. It's all gravy for you but it ain't for me. You know how it is in the rap game. Plus my new CD is about to hit and instead of talking 'bout my music, all these niggas gon' want to talk about is this shit. This is gonna ruin me."

"Mission—"

"Muthafuckas that was keepin' they mouth shut is flapping they gums now you started the ball to rollin'. Even mofos that get down like I do is talkin' mess. And you gon' pay, too. You didn't think about me so I fo' damn sho ain't gon' think about you. I got a homey that offered to take care of you and your big-ass mouth. I might just give him the word to handle that."

The line goes dead.

What the hell?! Mission is supposed to be my boy and now he's calling me up threatening me? It never occurred to me Mission would suffer any fallout over my confession. Lord knows that was never my intention. If people have connected the dots of that blind item then I may have hurt his career. A lot of rap fans as well as other rappers don't take MCs they believe to be gay seriously. It's unfortunate, but that's how that rolls. Man! What have I done?

Any Time,
Any Place

22

Nikki

Just as I enter my bedroom the phone rings. Balls! This phone has been going crazy the last few days. I'm about to turn it off in a minute. It's Mario.

"Hello?"

"Hey, baby. What are you doing?"

"I just got out of the shower and now I'm waiting for my baby to get home."

"I'm leaving the gym right now. I'm going to clear out my office. Or should I say my cubicle. Since I got to come right by the apartment I thought I'd swoop you up and you can ride with me."

"Yeah, I'll put on some clothes right now. I'll be ready in about two minutes."

"Okay. When I get there, I'll call and let the phone ring once and you come on down."

"All right. But ring my cell phone in case Rosie's on the house phone."

"See you in a few, babe."

"Bye."

It's a little thing, but some of the most special time Mario and I spend together is just driving around, even if it's just a quick errand. I reach for my drink on the nightstand and gulp it down. Then start getting ready. Right after I put on a sweat suit I hear a tapping at my door.

"Nikki? Can I come in?"

"Yeah, come on in, girlie."

As soon as I see her face I can tell something is wrong. "What's the matter, Rosie?"

She shakes her head and sits down on my bed. *"Mija.* You're not going to believe this. I just talked to Mission, right? He threatened my life."

"Are you serious?! Why?!"

"You know that gossip columnist Judy? She put out a blind item that I guess everyone knows is—"

"I know, too." I pick up the paper from the bed. "I was getting caught up in reading my rags and I saw it right before I took my shower. I was about to ask you about it but you were on the phone. Even if I didn't know you or Mission personally, I would've figured this one out."

"Mission is freaking out because on top of this, me stating my sexuality publicly has really outted him. I didn't mean to do that at all. But at the same time, even if I knew about this blind item, I can't say I would've lied about who I am when Liza asked. I found out the hard way lying always catches up to you. Anyway, from what Mission said, this is the talk of the Internet. More gasoline keeps getting poured on the fire 'cause if I understood right, a couple of guys Mission messed with have decided to start talking. He feels this is going to ruin his career."

"How did he threaten you?"

"He said a friend of his has offered to take care of me. Mission said he might take him up on the offer."

I sit down on the bed next to her and put my arm around her. "I don't think Mission will let anybody do anything to you. When I've seen you two together, I can tell he's very protective of you. He's very angry right now and I think it's safe to assume your friendship is over. However, letting physical harm come to you, I seriously doubt it."

"I hope you're right."

"It'll be all right. There are other rappers who've been the subject of gay rumors, but besides their egos, it doesn't really hurt them as long as they keep bringing the hits." I kiss her on the side of her forehead, then reach down and get my gym shoes that are lying at the foot of the bed.

"Where are you going?"

"Mario is picking me up to go clean out his things from the office."

"You might want to pop a mint or a piece of gum in your mouth so you don't knock him out with your gin breath."

"My bad." I get up and get a piece of gum from the tray on the dresser and pop it in my mouth. Just then my cell phone rings. I lean over to look at the incoming call. "That's Mario letting me know he's downstairs. We shouldn't be gone long. Why are you looking at me like that?"

"No reason."

"I'll see you later."

"All right."

Rosie is still looking at me like she wants to say something. A little inkling stirs in me as to what it is. I quickly make my way out the bedroom before she decides to change her mind about speaking on it.

23

Nikki

"Baby, I'm blown away that I have my own office at my new job. Not a desk, not a cubicle, but an office. I can't wait for you to see it. I'll probably take you by there sometime this week."

"We're not going tonight? I thought we would get your stuff from *Urban Report* and take it to your new job."

"No, sweetheart. That's almost an hour away from where we have to go. Besides, I'm beat. I killed it at the gym tonight."

"Yeah." I rub his arm. "You're getting even more buff. I think I'm going to have to start coming to the gym with you—keep an eye out."

"I'm about to change gyms. But then again, once we find a place I'll probably set up some equipment in one of the rooms for our own private gym."

"Why do you want to change gyms?"

"I'm not a homophobe or anything, Nikki, you know that. But that place is turning into a big gay pick-up joint. If dudes ain't trying to holla at you, they've got their eyes glued to you. They've driven all the fine women who used to work out there away."

"Good, I'm glad they did. Look out, Mario!"

Some idiot pulls out from a side street in front of us. Mario swerves over into the next lane.

"Stupid bastard! I thought people drove crazy in Detroit, they're worse out here. You okay, babe?"

"Yeah, it just startled me."

"It's a good thing no one was near us in this lane or we would've been screwed."

"Really."

"Speaking of screwing." He looks at me and gives me a devilish smile. "I miss us being able to get busy anyplace in the apartment. Now we're stuck making love in the bedroom with the door closed."

"Rosie isn't there all the time."

"True, but we never know when she's coming home. It's not an extreme big deal—she's a good roomie."

"She is. I'm glad you wanted me to ride with you but I'd gotten all showered and was ready for you to come home. I was craving you."

"Craving me? I like the sound of that. If I came straight home, what would you have done?"

"First round I would've sucked you dry."

"If you sucked me dry, would there even be a second round?"

"Of course. You know I can get those juices flowing again."

"Oh, I know all right." He takes my hand and puts it on his already hardened dick. He presses his hand on top of mine and moves against it. "You see what you do to me, Nikki?"

"Watch what else I can do to you." I unzip his pants and wriggle his dick free through the opening in his boxers. I take off my seat belt, lean over, and take him in my mouth.

"Girl! What are you doing? What if someone sees you?"

I take my mouth off him and look up. "So what if they do. You scared? Are you a guhly mahn?" I ask, giving my best Arnold Schwarzenegger imitation.

"Shoot, never. Go ahead then. You so bad."

I start sucking him again. After a moment, though, I stop and remove the gum from my mouth.

"Woman, I know you weren't doing me with gum in your mouth." He chuckles. "You could mess around and chew the wrong thing."

"Oh, hush. I'm a pro at this."

"Damn, baby. I know with Bush in office times are hard, but you ain't got to conserve gum. You can get it for twenty-five cents a pack."

"Will you shut up?" I laugh. I put the gum in the ashtray.

I get back to business, gradually increasing my suction and tongue-flicking action. I'm rewarded with him whispering my name and squirming in his seat. Then the car comes to a sudden stop.

"Oh shit! Girl, you almost made me run a red light."

I take my mouth off him again. "I guess I'd better stop before we have an accident."

"Yeah, 'cause I was getting into that too much."

I lift my head and see an elderly White woman in the next car over looking dead at me. She says something to the man driving and he leans forward and looks at me, too. I quickly move back into my seat and look straight ahead, anxiously waiting for the light to hurry up and turn green. Mercifully, it finally does and Mario hits the gas. I look at Mario, he looks back at me, and we both crack up with laughter.

❦

We arrive at the offices of *Urban Report* and Mario swipes his security card so we can enter the building. At the front desk is a heavy-set, Black security guard who's surrounded by monitors.

"What's up, Hank?" Mario greets him with a handshake.

"Nothing much, man. How's it going?" He's talking to Mario but he's looking at me.

"I'm just coming to pick up my stuff."

"I'm sorry you're leaving, but you're moving on to bigger and better, dawg."

"Thanks, man. Hey, I don't think you've met my girlfriend before. This is Nikki; Nikki, this is Hank."

"Nice to meet you, Hank," I say.

"Same here, same here." He grins from ear to ear. "My wife is a big fan of you and your show."

"Why, thank you. Tell her I said hello and thank you for watching."

"I sure will. Would you mind signing an autograph for her?"

"I'd be happy to."

"Let me find something." He looks around his desk and opens a couple of drawers.

I glance at Mario and he's gleaming proudly at me.

"Here's something. It's a blank postcard. This will do." He hands it to me along with a pen.

"What's your wife's name?" I ask.

"Verda. V-e-r-d-a."

I write a quick note thanking her for being a fan and hand the postcard back to him.

"Thanks a lot. She's going to be happily surprised."

"No problem."

"Okay, Hank. We're going to head on up. I'll drop off my security card on the way out."

"That's fine. I'll see y'all later."

I wave good-bye. We walk to the elevators and Mario pushes the button for the fourth floor. Mario puts his arm around my waist and kisses my cheek. I turn and kiss him full on the mouth.

"You've already been caught once tonight."

"What do you mean?"

"You saw all the monitors. They have one on this elevator. You trying to give Hank a show?"

"Oh."

"Oh, is right." He gives me a quick peck on the lips.

⁂

"I guess that's everything," says Mario as he looks around his desk.

We've filled up the two boxes we got from the storage closet.

"I'm glad to be leaving, yet I'm bummed at the same time. This was my first steady writing job. It means a lot to me not only because of that, but because it marked the beginning of us getting back together."

"I know, babe." I rub his back.

"Only one thing can make me feel better right now." He looks at me and wiggles his eyebrows up and down.

I playfully slap him on the shoulder. "Aw, you're not bummed nowhere. Talking about only one thing can make you feel better."

"Hey, you're the one who got my engine revving."

"Well, let's go home so I can finish the job."

"No."

"No?"

"Since you're being all adventurous—let's take it up a notch. You heard of the mile-high club, right?"

"Yeah."

"From what I hear there's a club for people who screw in business offices, too. Wanna apply for a membership?"

"Mario, I heard people in the conference room."

"And?" He takes my hand and leads me around the corner and down the hall. We pass the conference room where the meeting is being held. Mario pulls me into an empty office right next door and closes the door behind us. He turns on the light and walks over to the desk to push the armless chair in front of it into the corner.

"Hit the light, sweetheart," he says in a hushed tone.

"Did you lock the door?"

"There is no lock."

"Uh-oh. All righty." I flick off the light switch and feel my way in the darkness over to where he is. The sound of someone talking about circulation numbers is coming through the walls. I walk into Mario. "I'm sorry," I whisper.

"That's okay. You nervous?" he whispers back.

"Yes, but excited, too. Isn't there another office we can go into—one where there aren't people in the next room?"

"Yeah, but that wouldn't be as exciting. Think about it; while they're right next door having some boring late-night sales meeting, we're in here fucking each other's brains out."

Hearing him say that makes me even more horny. "I gotcha."

He takes me in his arms and we begin kissing passionately—wildly sucking and nibbling each other's tongues and lips. Mario moves backward, pulling me with him. He sits in the chair. I straddle him and unzip my sweat-suit jacket, exposing my bare breasts.

"Are you Miss Cleo?" Mario asks. "You knew not to put on a bra."

"No, if I were Miss Cleo, I wouldn't have put on any panties, either."

Mario puts his mouth on my breasts, licking and nibbling the nipples. Before I realize it, a moan leaves my mouth. "Oops. That slipped out."

"Nikki, you have my permission to *not* make any noise." He lightly chuckles. "Get up a minute, baby."

When I do, I hear him slowly unzip his pants and slide them down. I follow his lead and pull down my sweatpants and panties. I realize that in the position we're about to do it in I have to pull them off all the way. If someone walks in on us, I'll be caught literally ass-out. I slip off my gym shoes and get bottom naked. I straddle Mario again. I find his mouth and resume kissing him. I grind my hot, eager pussy on his equally eager hard dick. Knowing what we're doing and where we're doing it gives me an incredible rush.

I lift my hips up, reach down and put Mario's dick right at my vagina. I bear down until he's completely inside me. The initial thrust feels so good I can't help but let out a sigh. I put my arms around his shoulders and he puts his around my waist. We hold onto each other tightly. Other than the traveling voices from next door, the room is filled with nothing but the sounds of our heavy breathing and stifled moans, and the wetness of our lovemaking. Mario licks my neck and that really begins to push me over the edge. I feel my body get closer and closer to orgasm. I move my head down till Mario and I are face-to-face. Our lips touch but we don't kiss.

"You have no idea how good your dick is feeling to me right now. Tell me how much you love fucking me. Tell me."

"You know I love fucking you, baby. Shit, you know I do."

"You're crazy about this pussy, aren't you? Huh?"

"You-know-I-am," he pants. "It's—ohh, it's the best pussy I've ever had."

A short time later I explode. I clench my teeth—trying with all my might not to cry out. I embrace Mario even tighter. He grabs my ass and a few moments later his body stiffens. I hear him strain to not make any noise. A few moments later we collapse against each other. Mario strokes my backside lovingly. I plant kisses on his forehead.

"I'm sure I have a copy in my office," says a male voice in the hallway.

Mario and I straighten up.

"Please don't mean this office," I say softly.

The footsteps walk past. We both sigh in relief. We then hear the door close in the conference room again.

"That was too close," I say as I get off of Mario and feel for my clothes.

"Yeah, but it was worth almost getting caught for."

"Most definitely."

"Hey."

"What?"

"I love you."

"I love you, too. Now show me where the bathroom is." I giggle.

Crossroads

24

Rosie

"Mario, we need to talk."

He glances up from his laptop. "What's up, Rosie?"

"We both can't keep going on like this. Pretending not to see what's happening here."

He raises an eyebrow. "Rosie, I'm a writer, not a mind reader. What are you talking about?"

"Can you shut off your computer? I need your undivided attention."

"All right. Let me save this."

Once he's done I walk over and take his hand. "Come sit on the couch."

After we're seated, I continue holding his hand as I gather my thoughts before I speak. "We need to confront Nikki about her drinking. It's gotten out of hand. Every day she has something to drink. She just bought that fifth of gin three days ago. Do you know it's almost gone already? In three days, Mario. Neither you nor I drink that shit so she's killed almost the whole bottle all by herself."

Mario stares down at the coffee table. By the look on his face I can tell he knows exactly what I'm saying and that I'm voicing things he's noticed and is concerned about.

"Man, back home she used to only drink on weekends, and not even every weekend at that. I would say one or two weekends a month, if that. Now it's escalated to every day. I think we dropped the ball that night she came in acting all crazy and shit. That was absolutely not the Nikki I know. We should've gotten on her harder but we let her off the hook way too easy. By neither of us saying anything we're enabling her. Do you feel what I'm saying?"

He nods slowly. "It's funny how things from your past end up replaying themselves in your future. I don't know if you even knew about this, but my mother is a recovering alcoholic."

"No, I didn't know that!" I'm shocked like a mutha. "You and Chico never told me that. I do recall a couple of times when she came outside acting off the chain. She was stumbling and talking crazy. I never thought she had a problem, though. We saw that all the time at family picnics and parties where somebody had one too many. I figured that's all it was to it."

Mario closes his eyes but a tear still manages to fall down his cheek. I wasn't prepared for this. I hate seeing men cry—it tears me up even more than seeing a woman cry. I let go of his hand and rub his shoulders.

"For the most part, we did a good job of keeping Mom's drinking problem behind closed doors. I guess Chico, our father, and me, by silent agreement, turned a blind eye to her drinking. The times where she was passed out drunk became known as 'Mom's sick.' As crazy as it sounds it was normal to come home from school and find her passed out on the couch or floor. Chico and I couldn't lift her so we just made ourselves something to eat, did our homework, and watched television. We waited until Dad came home and carried her to the bedroom.

"Then one day Nana came over. She was screaming at Dad saying he was standing by and letting Mom kill herself. A short time after that Mom went away for a while. Dad said she had gone to the hospital to get better. She ended up having to go to the 'hospital' a few times. But she's been in steady recovery from the time I was ten."

He lets out a long breath. "You're so right. We're enabling Nikki by not saying anything. I always thought if I were ever in this situation with my woman, I wouldn't be like my father; I wouldn't stand for it. Yet here I am doing what Nana said Dad was doing—I'm helping Nikki slowly kill herself by letting this go on."

"I feel bad because I've been traipsing around town and shit, all wrapped up in doing this and that. I've been seeing things in my peripheral vision but not looking square at it," I say. "I'm done with that. I got snapped to reality with a call I got today. Since then I've been doing some hard thinking about what's happening with my cousin. Our being silent collaborators ends tonight, okay?"

"Okay. What call did you get?"

"They were really calling for Nikki and then we started talking…"

25

Nikki

"Hi, Sa—Mr. Caldwell," I greet our maintenance man. He's a chubby, middle-aged White man with a long gray beard and mustache. He looks just like he could be Santa Claus. Mario and I call him Santa behind closed doors and I almost slipped and called him that to his face. We call him Santa not only because of his looks but also because he's as slow as Christmas when it comes to repairs. If you have a leaky faucet, you'd better set up the drip in a spare bedroom because it's going to be a guest for a while. Something simple like that can take him a few trips. Oh, he'll get it fixed and fixed good but it'll take him a bit to get there. His slowness isn't putting his job in jeopardy because he's married to the daughter of the gazillion-and-one-year-old owners of the building. He's a sweet old man, though. Right now it looks like he's doing something to the door of the building.

"How are you, Miss Esposito?" He tips his dingy baseball cap to me. Right when I moved in, I let him know Mario and I weren't married but he insists on calling me by Mario's last name. I gave up correcting him after the first twenty times. I think he's one of the old-fashioned types who don't want to deal with the unmarried state of two of his favorite tenants.

"I'm doing good. Just tired. What are you working on?"

"This darn door needs some new screws, bolts, and stuff."

Uh-oh. "Will the door be able to lock?"

"That's what I'm working on. We had to disable the electricity to it in the meantime. It'll be all right, this is a good neighborhood."

Please. Anything can happen in L.A., no matter how good the neighborhood.

Which is why I'm hoping Mario and I can outbid another couple for the house we want in Studio City. It has security patrolling the area 24/7.

"Okay, take care. Tell Mrs. Caldwell I said thanks for the squash casserole. It was delicious."

"Will do. Have a good evening."

"Thanks, you, too."

As soon as I open the door to our apartment, Mario, sitting stony-faced on the couch, meets me. I put my purse and grocery bags on the chair closest to the door.

"What's up, Mario? Is anything wrong?" I close the door and lock it.

"Nikki, babe. Come sit down." Mario pats the empty space next to him. I walk over and sit down.

"You are scaring me. What's going on?"

"Rosie!" Mario calls out.

Rosie comes out of the kitchen and sits down next to me. She's looking equally as serious.

"Will somebody tell me what's going on?"

"We need to talk to you, cuz."

"About?"

"About you."

"Me? What about me?"

"It's your drinking, Nikki. It's getting way out of hand," Rosie says.

"Yeah, babe. You're heading for a serious drinking problem and you need to put a stop to it. We're both worried so we decided to finally confront you about it."

I know my face is red 'cause I'm getting heated. "Confront me? What the hell is this? Some kind of intervention?"

"Yes, it is. Rosie and I have been talking all afternoon about this and we want you to go get some help. You could probably do it on your own, but we think you should get some professional support."

I fly up off the couch and step over Rosie. She grabs my arm and I jerk it away.

"Let me go, goddamn it! You two have your motherfucking nerve putting your little heads together, having a powwow about my so-called drinking problem! Fuck both of you! Rosie, you got a boatload of gall trying to step to me all the nights you stumbled your ass up in here high as a kite. And I know you've been doing a lot more than drinking and smoking herb. I ain't stupid!"

I look at Mario. "She put you up to this shit, didn't she? 'Cause I know you didn't come up with this on your own. She planted this in your head."

Rosie stands up. "Wait one damn minute! You're making it seem like I'm conspiring against you or something! Girl, you straight trippin'!"

"Nikki, she only pointed out what I'd already noticed but didn't want to see," says Mario.

"I'm not the only one, either! Amber called here this morning looking for you. We got to talking and she said she was concerned about how much drinking you've been doing. Both her and Paris are worried. She wanted me to talk to you. So what, you think I put it in her head, too?"

Tears are threatening, stinging my eyes, but I'll be damned if I let these two traitors see them. Amber and Paris? I thought those were my girls and they're gossiping about me, too. Can't trust no fucking body.

"Listen up, you two. Yeah, I drink. But so do you. Mario, when you want to have some Henn, do I look at you like you have a problem? No! Rosie. We've already tapped on the shit you do. Still, I don't come at you ready to throw you in rehab. I don't believe this! You both act like I've passed out drunk on Sunset Boulevard or something. I'm thinking I'm coming home to—instead I get hit with this!"

"Babe, you drink every day now," says Mario.

"I've had a lot of shit on my mind. Sometimes I need a little something to relax, so maybe I'm drinking a little more than usual. It's not a big deal."

"A little something? A little more than usual?" Rosie asks. She leaves the room and goes to the kitchen. She comes back holding the fifth of gin I bought recently. She stands in front of me holding it up like some smoking gun.

"A little something, cuz? You just bought this three days ago and it's got about four drops left. This is hard liquor, *mija*. This ain't no light beer." She puts the bottle on the table. "And let me tell you something. You are jeopardizing everything you place a bit of value on." She points to Mario. "This man would give his right arm and left nut for you. You're out here making it in Hollywood like you've always wanted and now you're about to throw it away. I'm not saying you're an alcoholic. Yet. But you're on the train to, baby. We're just trying to derail you before you reach that destination. I'm hoping you can stop now but if you keep on like this it's gonna be harder."

"What the fuck are you talking about? Train? Derail? Ain't nobody trying to hear your little stupid transportation analogies, Rosie."

"You'd better hear something! You know exactly what I'm talking about. You were concerned about your parents but they're cool now. Your career is going like you want it and you're happy with Mario, so what possible reason could there be for you to have to do the drinking you're doing? Hell, if anyone has justification to drink it's me. You know all I've been through."

That's it. The button has really been pushed.

"Oh here we go! You don't have to tell me about all you've been through! I've been well aware of that shit for over twenty years! Do you think I could ever forget? Our whole family has revolved around Rosie and what Rosie's been through. We revolved around the fact that Rosie was molested; that Rosie's mother all but abandoned her. Don't you think maybe I needed something to revolve around me once in a while?! Maybe I needed some extra attention now and then? But no! Everything was always about making Rosie feel loved. There were times when I felt like a bothersome stepchild. But you know I fell right in line—focused on making sure Rosie was all right. Fuck how I was feeling. Even your boy Mario said we sit up and co-sign on any and everything you do whether we think it's wrong or not. All we seem to do is look out for Rosie. Nod our heads at everything Rosie does, even if it's something we don't even agree with because it's all about making Rosie feel loved and secure. I'm sure if Alejandro were here he'd attest to that, too. He gave you all his love and devotion but you see where it got him. I'm sick of me and everyone else kowtowing to you and your needs!"

"Cry me a fucking river," she says. "And I know my name. I don't need to hear it fifty times in a row." Her tone is nonchalant but I can tell by her eyes that I've hurt her. That's just too bad. Now we're even.

Mario comes and stands in front of me. "Your drinking is getting out of hand, Nikki. I see it. Rosie sees it. And your friends have begun to see it. Somewhere deep inside, you see it but are too stubborn to admit it. There's a place located little over an hour from here. My co-worker Luke went there to detox. You can go there and clear your system and your head. I've already called and they can take you tomorrow. It's a very good place."

"Oh really? It's a good place, huh? Well, take my bitch-ass cousin and drop her off. She needs that place more than I do. She's the one who's been coming up in here drugged up, not me." I turn toward the door and grab my purse out of the chair.

"Nikki, you walk out that door and we're over."

I stop in my tracks.

"I mean it. You know the situation with my mother. I'm not going through that again. I love you with everything in me, but if you're not going to get help, then I'm not going to stick around and watch you destroy yourself. I'll call Nancy and have her withdraw our bid on the house and I'll move out. I'm not bluffing, either."

I turn to him. "Do you, babe. You're not bluffing and I'm not caring. Um, wherever you go, make sure you have an extra room for my dear cousin. I don't want to lay eyes on either of you!" I unlock the door and leave out. To where, I have no idea.

26

Rosie

Mario and I keep staring at the door, like we're expecting Nikki to walk right back through the door. Somebody could've thrown an anvil at my chest and it wouldn't hurt as bad as this. So this is how she's felt about me all these years? That I was some interloper who got in the way of her getting all the love and attention she needed from her parents? My Tío and Tía went out of their way to make me feel a part of their household, but I didn't think they did it to the exclusion of Nikki. I guess she saw things differently. Perception is a mother. She's acting like it was all about me, yet I thought it was always me and her, Los Morenos, against the world. How wrong was I? And on top of all that she calls me a bitch. We've called each other that before in a playful manner, but there was nothing playful about the way she called me that tonight. The Nikki standing here a few minutes ago wasn't the Nikki I know. I feel like I've lost not only my cousin but my best friend. I reach out, touch Mario's arm.

"You okay, man?"

"No, I'm not."

I tug his arm so he can turn around to face me. I hope he isn't crying 'cause I'm right on the edge of losing it myself. His eyes aren't filled with tears, but pain.

"There are so many things I wanted to say to her, Rosie. I was having a hard time 'cause…"

"No need to explain."

"Maybe we went into the rehab stuff too soon. We shouldn't have gone in for the kill like that. You can't just start talking rehab to somebody right off the bat. I don't know."

I wrap my arms around him and hold him. As hurt and angry as I am with my cousin, I pray she'll be okay.

27

Nikki

I press the doorbell a couple more times. I know it's one-thirty in the morning but this is important. Finally the door opens and Amber stands there tying her robe together, her hair disheveled.

"Nikki, girl. What are you doing here this time of night steady ringing my bell like a Jehovah's Witness?"

"So you and Paris think I have a drinking problem?"

She looks at me for a moment. "Get in here out of the rain." She grabs my hand and pulls me into the house. "Honey, you are soaking wet. Why in the world are you out here in this monsoon?"

I hang my trench on the coat stand and go plop down on the couch.

"Let me get you a towel for your hair."

She comes back a minute later with a big, plush lavender towel. Just as she comes over to me, Benjamin appears at the top of the stairs.

"Baby? What's going on? Nikki, you all right?"

"Hi, Ben. I'm sorry for coming over so late. I'll be all right in a little bit."

He looks at me, puzzled. I have to suppress a grin and turn my head when I notice the huge erection pressed against his pajama bottoms. Shoot, I feel bad interrupting them.

"Amber, we can talk about this in the morning," I say, standing up.

"No, it looks like we need to talk right now." Amber looks up at Benjamin. "Honey, I'll be back up in a while. I really need to talk to Nikki. Okay?"

"Mm-hmm," he says disappointedly, as he turns back toward the bedroom.

"Your timing sucks. I'm in here getting me some. I was this close," Amber whispers, putting her index finger and thumb together. "Now sit back down."

I do as she says. She takes the towel and starts drying my hair.

"You were only out there a short time. How did your hair get this wet?"

"I was down by the beach a few blocks over and before I could make it to my car I was done. I'm still waiting on an answer to my question."

Amber stops drying my hair and puts the towel across my shoulders. "Yes, I think you have a problem."

"Rosie said you and Paris felt that way. What about Joanne?"

"Child, Joanne is a hard drinker her darned self. She's dancing on the edge, so no, she doesn't think you do. We gonna need to have a talk with her behind in a minute. Listen, I'm not comparing you to my crackhead sister, don't think that at all. But being around her and my boozing uncles I've gotten good at recognizing the symptoms of people heading for addiction. And you ain't that hard to spot."

"Thanks."

"Honey, I don't think you realize how much you drink. I've seen you put men under the table. Your tolerance is so high you can throw back about eight drinks before I notice it even have an effect on you."

"If I have such a problem, how come I can go into work and read my lines perfectly? As well as handle all my responsibilities, like going to meet and greets and premieres, photo shoots…"

"For now. Girl, you do have a problem. No matter how you try to cut it, it comes out the same. All the people who see it are the ones who love you. We're not your enemies. We're not all sitting around plotting to make up shit about you."

"I know."

"How long were you on the beach?"

"Ever since I left home. Six hours ago," I admit.

"So you had a while to think, right?"

"Oh, yeah."

"Even though you're here trying to find a little crumb that proves you don't have an issue with alcohol, you know you do, don't you?"

After a long pause I finally answer. "Yes."

"Hallelujah! Thank you, Jesus!"

She says it so loud, it startles me. She throws her arms around me, giving me a big hug and laying her head on my shoulder.

"Girl, you just don't know! We've overcome the biggest stumbling block right there with you recognizing you have an issue. When I talked to your cousin this morning, I just knew we were going to have to hunker down and wait it out while getting you to admit…Whoo!"

I lean my head into hers. "Amber, my cousin has always looked out for me and I hate myself for some of the things I've said and been feeling. For instance, she was so happy for me when I got hired on the show. When I called people back home to tell them, they already knew—she had beat me to the punch spreading the news. But when she came out here and things started happening for her, I'm ashamed to admit how jealous I was. Smiling to her face, pretending to be happy when I was really pissed because things started happening for her quicker than they did me."

"Really?"

"Yes. This is the first time I've admitted this. I haven't even told Mario. It's just been simmering in me. It's a lot of other things going on in me and maybe I need to purge it through therapy or something. I said some fucked-up stuff to Rosie and Mario tonight. Mario said if I didn't agree to go detox, he was leaving. I told him, 'Peace!'"

She lifts her head to look at me. "Nikki Moreno, you didn't!"

"I did. I hope when I get home they both are still there. You know, I've always paid attention to signs. Today, of all days, is when I get confronted by Mario and Rosie, when something else already had me doing some life assessment."

"What was that?"

"I'll tell you about it later. The thing is, I still hate how I went off on both of them. I was so defensive. Whoever said the truth hurts ain't never lied." I get up from the couch. "I value what I have too much to lose it. I'm sorry I bothered you. I guess I just needed reinforcement. Get that extra piece of the puzzle in place."

"No problem, girl."

I walk over to the coat rack and put on my trench. "I'll let you get back to handling yo' b'ness," I tell her with a grin.

"That's right. Shoot, it's almost that time of the month and you know how you get real horny right before—"

"Amber, you giving me a little bit more info than I need." I lean and kiss her on the cheek.

"You be careful, honey. It's still messy out there."

"I will."

"This was perfect timing."

"What?"

"You taking care of this now. We're on hiatus so you don't have to worry about missing work."

"True. I had planned on going after some movie auditions during this time off, but I guess that'll have to wait for now. I'll give you a call when I get to the—facility."

"Please do, the first chance you get. Take care, girl."

"I will."

28

Nikki

I can't wait to climb into bed. But I've got some unfinished business to take care of. Thankfully, I saw Mario's ride still in his parking spot. As I enter the bedroom, I expect to have to wake Mario up, but the table lamp is on and he's sitting up in bed.

"You've had your cell phone turned off."

"Yeah, I know."

I kick off my shoes and sit on the bed next to him. We sit in silence for a few minutes.

"What time do you want to take me to that place? What's the name of it, by the way?"

"The Helena Baisden Center," he says in a surprised tone. "You're going?"

"Yes, I'm going."

The look on his face is such a mixture of happiness and relief it makes me want to cry.

"I can't believe the shit that came out of my mouth. I guess I felt so on the defensive 'cause I thought you two were turning against me. Most of all it was because you both were telling the truth—the ugly truth. Tonight I took a long look at where I'm headed and I don't like it any more than you and Rosie. I have too many blessings to mess them up."

He leans over and gets something out of the nightstand drawer. He places it on the bed between us. "Is this the main blessing, Nikki?" he asks.

I stare at the home pregnancy kit.

"I looked in the bags to make sure there wasn't anything perishable and saw this." He reaches over and takes my hand. "So we might really need to get a bigger place, huh?"

"Maybe. I don't know yet, obviously. But I'm late and my cycle is usually like clockwork. To tell you how unclear some of my thinking has been, I didn't even realize how late I was until today."

"You've been taking your pill every day?"

"No," I sigh. "I've been real stupid lately. I've been missing days here and there. A lush on the Pill makes for a bad combination. Oh my God! If I am pregnant, what if I've harmed the baby?"

"We just got to hope and pray that the alcohol you've consumed up to now hasn't had any adverse effect." He gives me an assuring kiss on the forehead. "Nikki, I know we're both busy with our careers, but this happened right on time. It's got you to stop and take a good long hard look at yourself. The question is—if you're not pregnant will you still—"

"Yes. I don't want to lose you. And I'm doing this for myself as well. I didn't work as hard as I have to mess everything up. I can do this. I *will* do this. I can't tell you how horrible I feel for what I said earlier."

"You know as hard as I try sometimes, I can't stay mad at you for long."

"Would you have really left me?"

He lets out a breath and runs a hand through his hair. "I was ready to start packing. But when I came across the pregnancy kit, that threw me. I didn't know what I was going to do. All I know is that I love you."

"I love you, too." I lean over to him and we share a lingering kiss.

"When are you taking the test?" he asks, as he pulls away from me.

"I'll do it now and then I'm hitting the sheets. As tired as I am I won't be able to sleep until I find out the results. They say it's best to take the test in the morning, but I can't wait. Besides, technically it is morning."

"Can I ask you something?"

"Yeah, sure."

"Do you feel loved by me? I know I get caught up in my writing for the magazine and researching my book when I have free time. What I mean is, do I show it enough?"

"Mario, yes! Why would you even ask me that?"

He shakes his head. "I don't know. I guess I thought maybe that's why you were drinking because I—never mind."

"Baby, look at me. You have nothing to do with this. It's all me. And I'm going to get myself together. I did a whole lot of thinking tonight an' I know my drinking started getting out of control right before I got *Tapestry*. I was getting so stressed-out because my career was going nowhere. I would drink to calm my nerves, but even after I got on the show I continued drinking. By then it was more out of habit than stress. So this has nothing to do with you, baby. All right?"

"Yeah."

"Where's Rosie?"

"She was pretty hurt by what you said. She wanted to get out and take a breather. She said she might stay the night at one of her friends'."

"Let me call her before I do anything else." I reach for the phone. The call goes straight to voice mail. "Now she has *her* phone off."

"Of all times for you both to have your phones—"

I hold up my index finger to him. "Hey, Rosie, it's me. I just want to tell you how sorry I am but I don't want to do it over the phone. Please call me as soon as you get this message. I really need to talk to you. Please. I love you." I mark the message urgent, click the phone off, and put it back on the base.

⁂

The next morning I sit on the couch mindlessly clipping coupons. I don't even know what I'm clipping; I just need something to keep my hands occupied. That way I don't notice so much how badly they're shaking.

"Nikki," says Mario as he enters the living room buttoning his shirt, "I think we should get ready to go."

"I still haven't heard from Rosie. I don't want to leave until I talk to her."

"Didn't she say something about a photo shoot this morning? She probably went straight there from wherever she stayed last night."

"Oh, damn it. You're right. It was for today. I wish she'd come home last night."

"Baby, I told you I'd bring her up there so you two can talk face-to-face."

I sigh. "I can't stand the way I left things. I really need to tell her how sorry I am about the horrible things I said."

"You will, Nikki. But for now let's go and get you settled in."

"Okay. I know you're already going into work late as it is."

He walks over and takes the pile of coupons out of my lap.

"Depends?" he inquires. He looks at me, grinning. "You got a little bladder problem you're not telling me about?"

"Oh, brother. I didn't even realize I clipped that."

He places the coupons and the scissors on the couch next to me and holds out his hand. I take it and he pulls me up. I pick up my purse from the coffee table as he gathers my two suitcases and we walk out the door.

29

Rosie

"Hello?"

"Rosie?"

"What's up, Mario?"

"Where are you?"

"I'm almost home."

"I'm at work trying to make this deadline. Listen, I dropped Nikki off at the center earlier."

"Are you serious?! Thank God! I got her message this morning but I've been tied up. Where is this place located again? I want to see her."

"We found out when we got there that they don't want her to have outside contact for the first forty-eight hours. I've got to get in touch with Amber and Paris and let them know that, too. We'll drive up there day after tomorrow."

"You don't know how relieved this makes me, man. After the way she was illing I figured we'd have to drag her to rehab. I sure as hell didn't expect her to check in the very next day, especially after how she reacted to your ultimatum."

"Yeah, uh, I'm sorry, Rosie, it looks like we got a little emergency going on here. We'll finish talking when I get home, all right? Just know that everything's working out."

"Thank God. I'll see you later."

This is an answer to my prayer. I don't care what she said to me or how she acted toward me; nothing could ever stop me from wanting her to be okay. Besides, some of what she said to me was on target. I do need to take a look at myself. You can always smell somebody else's shit before your own. I'm going down the same path I'm trying to rescue my cousin from. I've been too wrapped up in partying and all that comes with it. Back in Detroit, I did my share of drinking and weed smoking but it wasn't nearly as often as it is now. Since I've been out here I've been drinking and smoking on the regular. I've even tried E and a few lines of coke. I still can't believe I tried that shit. It's something I said I'd never do.

Things ended fucked up with Mission but I think that was wake-up call number one. I'm a grown woman but I was influenced by the dope shit he did. Mission was cool people but just because somebody is cool don't mean they're supposed to be in your life. As much as I hate to admit this shit, coming off what happened with Crystal and Alejandro, I was—well, vulnerable. That leaves you wide open to doing crazy stuff. Hollywood can be an exciting place to be, but it's also a dangerous one if you're not careful. It's easy to get caught up in some wild shit. This is no place for the vulnerable or the weak. And all that's going on with Nikki, that's like, "All right, bitch, since you didn't hear the first bell here's another. Look in the mirror." I definitely have to make some changes in my life. I already know I'm not the same person.

It's funny, but when I was about to get down with Keilana and Mission, I said I wasn't going to trip if one of them had morning-after regrets. So it took me by surprise when *I* was the one who woke up feeling regretful. Before, I could fully enjoy being sexually adventurous and not feel strange or anything—despite what happened to me as a kid. Trust me, it's something I had to work on. But even though I enjoyed my encounter with Keilana and Mission, it left me feeling empty. Later that night when Mission tried to get things going again, I pretended to be knocked out and listened to him and Keilana have sex. Imagine that. I don't want to sound like one of those romance novels Nikki reads, but I think it's because love wasn't a factor. Now that I've known what it is to make love and not just fuck, fucking comes up short. I need more because I've had more.

I don't regret any of my sexual adventures. Hey, it's something I can look back on and say, "Damn, you was a wild bitch." It's not like I'm hanging up the freak drawers. Oh hell no. I'm just going to be a freak for that one special person, whoever he or she may be. Funny how I used to run from love and pretend I didn't need it, but now I'm at that point in my life where I can't lie to myself anymore. I want to love and be loved. Maybe I can be lucky enough to find what I felt for Alejandro and Crystal with someone else. I can hope.

I don't think I've ever been so happy to see this apartment. Now, that was a rough photo shoot! If only people knew the hell we go through to get the right shot. Plus, my mind was still on last night so it was hard to keep my focus. And the photographer expects you to hold these impossible poses for the longest time till your damn muscles practically lock up. That bathtub is calling me for a long-ass soak. I almost stop at the kitchen to get a drink until I realize Mario and me tossed out all the alcohol last night. Besides, I don't need anything to drink. Didn't I just say I was going to make changes in my life?

Once I get to my room, I take off my shirt and toss it on the bed. I lean over to turn on the table lamp, but I stop midway when the hairs on the back of my neck stand on end. Something isn't right. I feel like I'm not alone. As if to confirm it, a scent hits my nostrils, like faded cologne and perspiration. Just then the door slams behind me, and the overhead light switch is flipped on. I whip around and come face-to-face with someone I never wanted to see ever again.

"What the hell are you doing here?!" I try to sound forceful when really I'm close to fainting.

"I'm here for you, Mamita Rosita."

My blood turns to ice hearing Renaldo call me that. As a child, I knew that meant I was about to get a whipping or at the very least a slap across the face. For him to come all this way and break into this apartment, I know he's got far worse in mind. But what—and why? Even though I would've passed Lupe on the street because she looks so different, I would know this bastard instantly. I wouldn't need photos to refresh my memory of his face. His and Tony's have been branded in my mind forever. Other than a few wrinkles, he still looks the same. The ugly scar that runs from his left ear across his cheek to his mouth, and those mean, black eyes. I can tell his oily hair is dyed jet-black—it should have more than a few gray hairs by now. I look around the room for something, anything.

"I've put away anything that you could use." He taps his head. "Old Renaldo is a smart one."

"How did you get in here?"

He walks a few steps to stand in front of me. "Luck is on my side. The front door was open. And as for getting into the apartment, well...you know I used to work a second job as a locksmith. Remember? Yes, I worked two jobs to help take care of your mother, brother, and you—the little whore. If your next question is how did I know how to find you, I had my girlfriend get Nikki's address off the Internet. I read an interview where you said you were staying with her. With a computer and a credit card you can find anyone."

"Look, you'd better get out of here right now 'cause Nikki and her boyfriend will be here any minute."

He hauls off and slaps me so hard that I fall back on the bed. "Stop lying, you damn *puta!* I saw Nikki and a man pack a car with luggage like they're going on a trip. They didn't look at all like they were coming right back." He pounces on top of me and holds my arms down.

I try to move but I can't. "Renaldo, please. Mario dropped Nikki off somewhere, but he's coming back. Just leave, okay? Why are you here, anyway?"

"Because you killed my brother, that's why!"

"Killed your brother?! What are you talking about?!"

"I'm surprised you haven't gotten the news. Day before yesterday Tony blew his brains out. I found his body. You and your filthy, stinking lies ruined my brother's life. Because of you, people treated him like dirt. The woman he wanted to spend the rest of his life with left him. When he went to jail a few years ago those animals did unspeakable things to him! They took away his manhood! He was never the same after that. When he got out he turned to drugs and…" He chokes up. "You and your lies! You and your lies! You and your lies! You did that to him!"

He spits in my face. "You might as well have put the bullet in his head yourself. You're the only person I'd wish to see what I did. Think about it, Mamita Rosita! Imagine going to check on Raul and seeing half his head blown away! My little brother couldn't take it anymore. He left a note telling me that he couldn't, but I took it and put out the gun cleaner and rags and made it look like it was an accident. I saved my brother his last piece of dignity! I couldn't have people knowing they broke him."

Pausing, Renaldo stares into my eyes with pure hatred. "It sickened me to see you on television and in magazines. Living the good life out here in Hollywood while my brother's life was a living hell! Look at you! You've always been a nasty little whore and you still are. I've seen you posing, showing your stuff."

He takes a hand off one of mine and roughly grabs on my breasts. I wince in pain.

"You like that, don't you? Hmm? Dirty *cuero*," he whispers as he leans his face into mine. I make a fist with my free hand and hit him in his ear as hard as I can. He yelps, "You bitch!" and slaps me hard. I reach up to block the blows with my hand. He pulls down both my hands under his knees. He slaps my face with both hands till I begin to see stars. Mercifully he stops. "I will avenge my brother's life with yours. You're gonna pay for all your lies. When I found Tony I promised him his body wouldn't be put in the ground unless yours was about to follow. His pain began with you and it's going to end with you."

He reaches into his back pocket and pulls out a scarf. "I'm going to strangle the truth out of you if I have to. Now tell me you lied about my brother molesting you. Tell me!"

As scared as I am I can't find the words to tell him what he wants to hear. I know for my own sake, it would be best to go along with this motherfucker, but I can't. Something tells me that it wouldn't matter anyway. He didn't come all this way to hear me deny Tony ever molested me and turn around and leave. No, he's going to do what he wants to do no matter what I say.

"You're not going to admit it?!"

I slowly shake my head.

"You miserable bitch! I gave you a chance."

He wraps the scarf around my neck and pulls it tight. I try to rock my body to loosen my arms from beneath his knees but he bears down on them even more. With as much strength I can muster, I flail my body wildly and somehow manage to free my hands. He tightens the scarf even more. I reach up to press my thumbs into his eyeballs but he jerks his head to the side. I'm losing oxygen—my head feels like it's going to burst from the pressure. I go for his crotch. Luckily he's wearing linen slacks, so I can get a good grip. I grab his dick and twist it as hard as I can. He lets out a howl and loosens his grip on the scarf. I hit him about the face and chest with my fists. I get one of my legs up between his and get him in the nuts with my knee and push him backward off the bed onto the floor. The problem is he falls right in front of the door.

I rush over to the table lamp and snatch the cord out of the outlet. I smash the lamp over his head and he rolls over on his side. I get to the door and open it. He grabs my leg, causing me to fall into the hallway. I kick with my other foot until he lets go.

I run toward the living room to the front door. He tackles me to the floor once I get to the couch. I scream in pain when I feel his teeth sink into my thigh.

"You're not going anywhere but to hell, you bitch!" he screams.

I grab onto the sofa and try to pull myself up to at least get to the phone. Before I know it he's sitting on my back and has the scarf wrapped around my neck again. He's pulling it even tighter than before. I try to grab at the scarf but I can't even get my fingers under it. I can't breathe. I can't breathe. Oh God, help me! Please! I don't want to go out like this. Not like this…

30

Nikki

I've officially become a Hollywood cliché. I'm sitting here in mother freaking detox. Ain't this a blip? How the hell did I get myself into this? At least it's really nice here. It's almost like a resort. I'd better get my system cleared out quick 'cause I'm making good money on the show but not enough to lay up in here for an extended amount of time drying out. And damn, I can't believe all who's here. There are some no-names but quite a few A- and B-list celebrities. The aging blonde actress who had a meltdown on live television is just down the hall from me. It was no surprise seeing her, or the handsome young actor who is known more for wild partying than his acting. Most of the people here who are famous or somewhat famous have been speculated heavily about suspected drug or alcohol use in the press. And their publicists have "heavily" denied that speculation. But that's what publicists are paid for. What really surprised me is the Black award-winning singer/actress who's here. I would've never suspected she has a substance abuse problem. She always seemed so together. Rosie and me used to play dress-up in Mami's clothes and lip-sync in the mirror to her songs, which Mami had on almost constant rotation.

Shit. I look down at my hands. They're shaking even more. I'll be glad when my system is cleared of all the toxins. I didn't realize what a strong hold liquor had on me until now. My body is definitely going through withdrawal. I can do this. Like Rosie said, I'm strong. I've got to concentrate on all I stand to lose.

I look over at the plate that a staff person brought to my room. Are they kidding? Who do I look like, Lara Flynn Boyle? Maybe she can get full off of this, but I need a bit more than a sliver of salmon, a few string beans, and couple of roasted new potatoes. Is this rehab or a fat farm? I wolf it down in about two minutes and then settle back in the bed. I flip on the television and channel surf. I finally settle on Lifetime Television and *The Golden Girls*. I eventually fall asleep to the voice of Rose telling the girls another one of her St. Olaf stories.

31

Nikki

I awaken to the sound of someone knocking on my door. I look over at the clock. After my eyes adjust, I see that it's seven-fifteen p.m.

"Miss Moreno?"

"One moment, please." I grab my robe and throw it on. I pick up the remote and turn off yet another woman-in-crisis Lifetime movie. Then I open the door and see a staff person, a flame-haired middle-aged woman. Her badge says her name is Elizabeth.

"I'm sorry to have waken you, Miss Moreno. You have a visitor."

"A visitor? Who?" I thought I couldn't have visitors yet. Why does she have such a strained look on her face?

"It's Mr. Esposito. He's waiting in the atrium."

"Okay, I'll be out in a minute. Thanks."

With a nod she turns and walks down the hall.

What the hell is going on? Why is Mario here? He's not supposed to be back for a visit until day after tomorrow. Something's wrong, I feel it. I quickly throw on some slippers and head out for the atrium. Mario is standing looking out the window with his hands in his pockets.

"Mario?"

He turns around and I see it in his eyes. Something is definitely wrong. I stop in my tracks. He begins to walk toward me.

"What? Why are you here?" I ask urgently.

He tries to put his arms around me but I push him away.

"Just tell me why you're here!"

"Shh, babe. It's going to be all right."

"What's going to be all right?! Will you fucking tell me?!"

"I was hoping that I could make it out here before you heard anything on television or the radio. Baby, someone broke into our apartment and attacked Rosie."

"What?! No!" I scream. "Is she okay?! Is she okay?! Answer me!"

"Yes, baby, she's okay. She's banged up pretty bad but she's okay. She's at the hospital right now. They might even release her sometime tomorrow."

I fall into his arms in relief. He leads me over to one of the couches to sit down.

"Who the hell would attack her?"

"Renaldo."

"*Renaldo?* Lupe's ex-husband?!"

"Yeah. Rosie told me he blamed her because his brother committed suicide."

"Tony killed himself?" I know I'm repeating Mario like a fool, but I can't help it.

"Yeah. Renaldo tried to blame his suicide on Rosie."

"How the hell is that Rosie's fault?!"

"From what she said, because people shunned Tony after finding out what he did to her, his life took a downward spiral and Renaldo thought it wouldn't have happened if she hadn't said Tony molested her. I'm sure she'll tell you the rest when she talks to you. I left to come tell you in person and make sure you're all right."

"Oh my God. I can't believe this."

"Me neither."

"Renaldo…"

"I didn't know what the hell happened when I got home and found police cars and television reporters all in front of the building. The police weren't letting anybody inside. I finally found out it was our apartment and Rosie was involved. Then the police told me Rosie had been taken to the hospital. I went there and they let me see her for a few minutes."

"I hope Renaldo rots in jail—the dirty bastard!"

"Rotting in hell is more like it. Nikki, Renaldo's dead. He wasn't just there to rough her up. He was trying to kill her but she managed to turn the tables. Thanks to you."

"*Me?* How?"

"He was strangling her in the living room and she somehow got ahold of those scissors you clip coupons with. She stabbed him in the leg and that made him fall away from her a little and then she turned around and got him again in the neck. That did him in."

I keep shaking my head in disbelief. I pinch the inside of my palm to make sure I'm not having one of my tripped-out dreams. "That bastard came out here to kill Rosie?"

"Yes."

"That makes no fucking sense for him to blame her when—I mean, shit, if anything she should've been hunting him down, him and his no-good brother. How the hell...Are you sure she's all right?"

"She's still shaken up by it all. And like I said she's bruised up, but she'll be fine. For real, okay?"

"Yeah."

"Rosie's not too keen on going back to the apartment and tell you the truth, neither am I. The forensics team is probably still there. We're going to be staying at Amber's. Oh, and on my way here I called everybody I could back in Detroit and your parents in New York, before they heard it on the news. I'm glad I did, too, because on the radio I heard someone say that it was Rosie who was killed. They're so quick to say they were the first with the scoop they don't wait for all the facts. Last thing I wanted was for somebody to get the wrong information."

"That's good. Thanks for doing that."

"Of course, baby."

"Hold me, please." He wraps both his arms around me and rocks me gently. I look at him. "I need to see my cousin."

32

Rosie

I f Odell were here, he'd look at me and say, "Chile, you look a hot steamin' mess!" He wouldn't be lying, either. I don't even recognize myself. I'd swear I was holding this mirror up to somebody else's face. My eyes are blood-red from burst vessels. My face is swollen and bruised. My bottom lip is cut. And shit, don't get started on my neck. It's purple. Gross. Thank God I'm here, though. I may look a sight but I'm still here. I just knew I was about to be taken out of this world.

I'm still dazed by all that happened. One minute I'm getting ready to take a bath and the next I'm fighting for my life with that crazy Renaldo. I'm still trying to understand how in even his twisted mind he thought I was responsible for all that happened to Tony. If Lupe hadn't married Renaldo, my whole childhood—my whole *life*—would've been different.

I always felt if I was in a situation where it was either my life or the other person's that I'd take the motherfucker out and not think twice. Yet, here I was put in that exact situation only hours ago; it came down to my life or Renaldo's. And as despicable a person as he was, and even though he was trying to snuff me out, I can't help but feel fucked up that I killed him. I mean, I actually killed somebody. All I keep seeing is when I plunged the scissors into his neck, that and all the blood. My God. I was close to passing out before my hands came on the scissors; I don't know where it came from but somehow I found the strength to use them.

The phone on the table next to me rings.

"Yes?"

"Rosie?"

"Nikki? Hey, girl."

"Rosie, please tell me you're okay."

"I'm doing good, honey. You see I'm all answering the phone and stuff."

"I—" Her voice trembles. "I don't know what I would have done if something happened to you and I lost you." She cries softly.

"Nikki, come on now. Don't cry, please. I'm okay, seriously. I'm just tired as hell and sore. The police were here asking a million questions and that wore me out even more. The doctor said he might release me tomorrow after they run some more tests. For now I'm just chilling and resting. I'm fine."

"I wanted to come see you but Mario doesn't think I should leave here. It's not like I'm not coming back."

"No, Mario is right. You stay there because everything is fine. I'm just gon' be resting up anyway. It wouldn't do me any good to have you fretting over me when you should be there. Please do that for me, Nikki. Stay there, okay?"

"All right. I'm not supposed to use the phone the first couple of days but this is a special circumstance. I'm going to call you throughout the day."

"Oh, okay. Bug me while I'm trying to rest, why don't you. Naw, you call me as much as you want. I'm going to get some sleep 'cause I didn't get any last night."

"Rosie, I'm so sorry for what I said to you. You know in my heart I didn't mean it. Please say you forgive me. Please."

"Girl, I forgave you two minutes after you said it. I know you've been going through some changes. I'm just happy you're getting better."

"I don't know how I would have lived with myself knowing the last words I said to your face—"

"Nikki, I'm okay. Besides, I got your message on my cell phone so your last words would've been you telling me you loved me. Hell, what are we talking about last words for? I'm here, thank God."

"I'm so happy. Okay, I'll let you get some rest. Come see me as soon as you're able. Even if it's before this stupid forty-eight-hour thing is over."

"I will. I love you, brat."

"I love you, too. Talk to you later."

"Bet." I hang up the phone.

One thing that might have been different if Lupe had never married Renaldo is my relationship with Nikki. Her and her parents would've moved to Detroit without me, and more than likely we would not be as close as we are. We'd probably only see each other every other summer or something and be those cousins who laugh and have a good time when they see each other and promise to keep in touch but don't and not have any contact until months or years later. I can't even imagine not having Nik by my side. And not going through all we've been through together—good and bad. I can't even see it. Hmm, I guess God just showed me one of the reasons why things turned out the way they did in my life.

⁂

I stir awake and my mouth feels like I've been eating sand. I got a good night's sleep, though. I'm about to reach for the water glass on the table when I realize someone is holding my other hand. I open my eyes and look over and see a beautiful pair of familiar eyes filled with concern.

"Alejandro?"

He stands up and bends down to kiss my forehead. "How are you? I hope you feel better than you look," he says, flashing me that smile I've missed so much.

"Actually, I feel like shit and look like shit. How long have you been here?"

"I got in about an hour ago."

"How did you find out?"

"Chico called and told me what happened and gave me Mario's cell number. Chico's coming on a later flight, so I had my neighbor drop me off at Detroit Metro and I took the first plane out. Then when I got here, I realized I didn't even know what hospital you were in. I called Mario from the airport and his phone was off. He told me later he couldn't have it on in the hospital. In the meantime I was going crazy waiting to hear from him. He finally checked his messages and called and told me where you were. He's in the cafeteria right now." He strokes my arm. "I'm so sorry you went through this, *querida.*"

"Thanks for being here, Alejandro. I'm so happy to see you. I'm starting to feel better already."

"I'm trying real hard to keep it together for you, but it's killing me seeing you like this."

"I'm alive, baby. That's what matters. Come, lay by me."

"You sure? The doctor isn't going to kick me out, is he?"

"No, crazy. And don't be a chauvinist. How do you know my doctor isn't female?"

"Because *he* came in to check on you while you were asleep."

"All right, you win that round. Now get in this bed." I scoot over and he lies next to me on his side. He puts a hand on my stomach and I put mine on top of his. I look at his watch.

"I didn't know I was asleep that long. I wonder why Nikki hasn't called again."

"Mario decided to have the front desk hold your calls so you could rest."

"Oh. I needed it." I touch my swollen face. "I spent about an hour comforting Odell, assuring him I was all right. It's a good thing I got my shoot for *Luscious* magazine out of the way because I won't be in front of any cameras for a while."

"You did a layout for *Luscious?*"

"Yep. The swimsuit issue."

"I saw your work in *Silk & Velvet*. You were beautiful."

"My work, huh? I never heard T and A called that before." I nudge him in the side.

"Stop teasing me. You looked so sensual. It was very tasteful."

"I'm glad you liked it."

"I'm sure that rapper dude liked it, too. I read he's your boyfriend."

"That goes to show you can't always believe what you read. He's not my boyfriend. He's not even my friend anymore."

"Why's that?"

"When I came out as bisexual, it started the ball rolling on his sexuality."

"Huh?! I know you're not saying what I think you are."

"I am."

"But…but…" he stammers.

"You're going to make me play on words in a minute."

"But, he doesn't look…I would've never guessed. Wait till I tell my sister Talisa. She's always talking about how fine he is. I don't know why women get so proprietary over celebrities they have a crush on. She was so jealous when she thought you two were dating. Just forgot that you were once my woman."

"Were you jealous?" I can't help asking.

"Of course I was."

I shift a little to a better position and close my eyes.

"Rosie, have you called Crystal to tell her?"

The mere mention of her name makes my body stiffen. "No, Alejandro. And I don't plan on calling her either." After a few minutes of uncomfortable silence I decide to let him know exactly how I feel. "I need to clear up some things with you as far as she's concerned."

"Rosie, you don't have to. Now's not the time to get into all that. I shouldn't have even brought her up. You need to rest."

"No, I won't be able to while this is lingering. I'm not going to pull any punches, some of this might be hard to listen to, but it needs to be said." I reach for the glass again and take a few sips of water. "All of us were pretty tight—me, Nikki, Mario, Rhonda, Chico and Crystal. After Mario left for California it seemed like we kind of splintered off a little. When Nikki and me weren't hanging, she gravitated more toward Chico and Rhonda, while me and Crystal spent a lot of time together. It was during that time I started having feelings for her that were more than friendship."

"You fell in love with her," Alejandro states dryly.

"Uh, yeah. I did. I didn't think there was a bit of chance we'd be anything more than friends. She was a pro when it came to hiding her interest in women. Once she moved to the suburbs we didn't spend as much time together but my feelings remained the same. The night the three of us got together was exciting but confusing, too. I was emotionally and physically attracted to both of you. And I'll admit I had some jealousy when you were going at it. Anyway, after that night, she did me foul and tried to say I took advantage of her because she was high."

"Yeah, right," Alejandro says sarcastically. "From what I remember she was all into both of us."

"Exactly. We got into an argument over that and stopped speaking for a long time. Until I ran into her last year."

"When I asked why you two didn't talk anymore, you said it was because she regretted what happened that night. You never told me you were in love with her."

"I know and I'm sorry. I should've been completely honest with you. After that, I just said screw her. I decided to completely open my heart up to you and I did."

"I guess I was the consolation prize." Hurt tinges his voice.

"Alejandro, I won't lie to you. At the very beginning, although I was digging you a lot, I wanted someone to help me forget her. But I can honestly say, as God is my witness, I fell head over heels in love with you. And damn it if that sounds clichéd, but I did. I loved you and, most importantly, I trusted you. I still do. I know exactly where I stand with you—no games or mindfucking. I admire you, too. Your father brought you, your brother, and your sister over here from Cuba when you were nine years old. When he died right after you graduated high school, you stepped up and took three jobs to take care of all of you. You sent both your brother and sister to college. *You.* You didn't even go but you made sure they did. I've got mad respect for you."

"Rosie, if you love, trust, and respect me so much, why did you leave me to chase after Crystal?"

I swallow the lump in my throat as I look into his anguished eyes. "Stupid. I fucked up. I fucked up majorly. I guess I had these unresolved feelings for Crystal I felt I had to explore. When I look back on what I did, I can't believe how dumb I was."

"I got the feeling Crystal wasn't telling the whole truth about you pursuing her. I don't know if I want the truth, but I guess I should get it. Did you two pick up from where you left off that night? In other words, were you two sleeping together?"

Oh God. I close my eyes. "Yes."

He starts to move his hand from my stomach. I hold on to it. "Please don't." Reluctantly, he puts his hand back.

"I'm sorry. I know I sound redundant as hell, but I'm sorry. I found out once and for all about Crystal. She's shown me what a devious, sneaky person she is. Because of our history, I'll always care about her as a person. However, she's killed any love I had for her, so that's squashed forever."

"You've said you don't fully open your heart to many people. That's something we have in common. With you, though, I let you in and loved you like I've never loved anybody else," Alejandro says quietly. "We could be lying in this bed for the next two weeks while I tell you how what you did killed me. It was bad enough when you hit me with the 'I need some space' speech out of the blue. Then I had to find out you broke it off with me to chase after Crystal. And I'll admit my male ego took a bruising knowing you left me to go after a woman. Your bisexuality has never been an issue with me; in fact, it's intrigued me. But I guess I was really naïve to think that once you made a commitment to me I wouldn't have to worry about another man *or* woman coming between us. Crazy, huh?"

"No, that's not crazy at all. Crystal was just that unanswered question I felt I needed to know the answer to. *That* was crazy. Alejandro, all I know is if you ever gave me another chance, I swear to God I'd never fuck it up again. Do you think that's possible?"

He gently rubs my stomach. "We'll see, okay?"

"Uh-oh," I sigh. "That reminds me when I was a kid and I asked if we could stop at McDonald's on the way home and I'd hear 'we'll see.' That was usually something to get me to shut up, meanwhile we'd pass three or four McDonald's before ending up at home—without so much as a cold French fry."

"As much as I've tried not to, I still love you. You'd know just how much if you could've seen how crazy I was when I got that phone call from Chico. Just the thought of any harm being done to you almost made me go out of my mind. So when I say, 'We'll see,' it only means let's first concentrate on getting you out of this hospital and fully recovered and we'll take it from there." He puts his finger under my chin and tilts it to him. "For the record, there's a very good chance a stop at Mickey D's is in the cards."

I smile, the cut on my lip stinging as I do. I don't care. All I know is I love this man with all my heart.

33

Nikki

I'm so happy to be out of apartment living and back in a house. There's nothing like not having to share a wall with your neighbors. This house is not as spacious as I would have liked, but it's big enough. What sold Mario and me on this place is the beautiful panoramic view and the vast, lush landscape that surrounds the property. I'm in the midst of starting up my own little garden. This is very relaxing. I used to help my maternal grandmother back in Detroit with her garden.

I was talking with our neighbor—an elderly woman named Mrs. Chavez—about picking up gardening after noticing her beautiful vegetable and flower plants. She gladly gave me a wealth of tips and instructions she learned back when she first started gardening in her native Peru. Earlier today she brought me over some of her old tools and a big sun hat. She said we people of color have to be careful of sun damage, too. I've spent most of the morning preparing the soil where I'm going to try my hand at growing tomatoes.

"Yo, Nikki!" Rosie shouts from inside the house.

She and Mario are back from house hunting a place for her.

"I'm out here!"

They both come out to the patio and stop in their tracks. They begin laughing raucously. Rosie bends over, she's laughing so hard.

"What the hell is wrong with y'all?"

"You," Mario replies. "Babe, where you get that hat from?"

"Mario, you know who she looks like? Katharine Hepburn in *On Golden Pond*." She plops down on one of the chaise lounges still laughing.

"She does, doesn't she?" he chortles.

I press my lips together. "Why y'all clowning my hat? Mrs. Chavez gave it to me so I wouldn't get sun damaged."

Mario walks over and holds his hand out to help me to my feet. He pulls me into an embrace, still chuckling.

"How's my baby doing?" He puts his hand on the little swell of my belly. "How are both my babies doing?"

"We're fine," I grin. "I was a bit queasy earlier but it passed."

"You sure you should be out here doing this work?"

"Honey, I'm just preparing the soil, not pulling a plow."

"All right, just don't exert yourself."

"I won't."

He moves to kiss me but is blocked by the rim of my hat. He shakes his head and pulls up the rim and gives me a kiss. "I'm going to hop on the computer to look up some info for the book now that I've gotten some time to start working on it again. You need anything?"

"Some iced tea would be nice."

He turns to Rosie. "You want anything while I'm getting Nikki some tea?"

"I'll have some of that, too. Thanks."

"I'll be right back."

I go over the chaise lounge opposite Rosie and settle in.

"*Mija*, I won't be able to keep a straight face until you take that whoopsy-doopsy hat off."

I crimp my lip, but take off the hat and lay it on the bottom shelf of the little table between our two loungers.

"That's better. I forgot to tell you I talked to Odell and he said he and Aaron are coming in Friday night."

"Good. I look forward to seeing him and finally meeting Aaron."

"Girl, I can't get over what a nice view this is."

"I know, me too. By the way, how's the house hunting coming along for you and Alejandro?"

"His sister Talisa came across a townhouse for sale a few blocks away from her. It was the first place we went to see. It's on Bayview Drive—two blocks from the beach. That joint was really nice."

"Shit, is there anything that isn't nice in Hermosa Beach?"

"That's true. I fell in love with it right away so that'll probably be the one we end up in. It's only about forty minutes away from you, which isn't too bad. That's a lot closer than Detroit."

"Ya know?"

"Alejandro finally found a buyer for the store, so hopefully he'll be wrapping that up soon and get his butt back out here. Whenever he's ready, I'll head back to Detroit and scoop up the rest of my things."

I reach over and take her hand. "I'm so pleased you two are working things out."

Her face lights up. "No more pleased than I am. I know this is a trial run and he's still really hurt over what I did. Not that I blame him. I'm going to have to prove myself to him and show him I'm worthy of his love and trust. You know I'd planned on going back to Detroit eventually, but I know he's wanted to move out here to be closer to his brother and sister for the longest time so I don't mind putting down stakes here. Plus, you're here."

"Oh, why I gotta be an afterthought?" I tease her.

"Don't even. I'm really hoping that Alejandro can get past what I've done and this won't end up being a temporary situation. I'm crossing my fingers."

"I'm not going to lie. It might be a while before he rebuilds his trust in you, but I believe he'll get there eventually. That he's even making an effort to make your relationship work says a lot."

"Here you go, ladies." Mario comes out of the house carrying a tray with a pitcher and two ice-filled glasses. He puts it down on the table between Rosie and me.

"Thank you, sweetie."

"Thanks, Mario."

"No problem. Let me know if you need anything else." He bends down and gives me a kiss before going back inside.

"Nik, Chico sounded so pitiful when I told him my stay out here would be permanent. He was like, 'Dang, all y'all moving out to Cali.' I told him maybe he should move out here with Bisola but he said, 'Naw, man. I'm not moving out there with them rolling blackouts, earthquakes, and shit. Y'all niggas gon' be shaking in the dark.'"

I shake my head. "That boy is crazy. When he gets out here next week he's going to stay a few days. We'll work on him and try to change his mind. You didn't think you'd ever want to live in California and here you are."

"Part of me wanted to run back to Detroit and stay after what went down with Renaldo," Rosie reminds me. "I thought I was going to go crazy with everybody wanting an interview to talk about what happened. I wanted nothing more than to put that shit behind me as quickly as possible and every time I turned around some *pendejo* wanted to ask a thousand and one questions about it. Before I do interviews now I make sure they know what happened is off limits. I'm sure they'll still find a way to work it into the interview."

"Yeah, but the bright side, it brought you some nice press, too. You're like f'ing Xena the Warrior Princess to a lot of women."

"I only did what I had to," she says solemnly. "I'm not comfortable with people trying to make me out to be some hero."

I don't want to see her get back down about Renaldo so I decide to lighten the moment. "Did you ever know that you're my hero?"

She looks around. "Do I hear a Bette Midler song somewhere?"

"Did you ever know that you're my hee-rooo," I sing off-key.

"Ahh! Be quiet, Alfalfa," she says, laughing and covering her ears. "*Mija*, just be happy you're a great actress and don't hold your breath waiting for Jimmy Jam and Terry Lewis to come knocking on your door."

"Shut up, heifer."

"Next week is going to be crazy with everybody coming into town. I wish *Abuelita* was well enough to travel."

"Me, too. I miss her so much. We have to make a way out to see her."

"Wait a minute. Where are you and Mario going for your honeymoon?"

"We were thinking about going to Catalina Island for a few days."

"Why not spend your honeymoon in San Juan instead? That way you can see *Abuelita.*"

I smack my forehead. "Duh! Of course! Why didn't I think of that?"

"'Cause you're nutty, that's why."

I give her the finger. "That's a great idea. San Juan it is! Mario's always wanted to go and check the place I've told him so much about so I'm sure he'll be down."

"My cousin is getting the old ball and chain."

"Yep. If I had to be chained to someone I couldn't pick anyone better."

"And you got a little bambino cooking in the oven. You're killing two birds with one stone. At least now you don't have to put up with your parents bugging you about getting married and having babies. Just me and Raul are getting the drill."

"Don't tell me they've started in on Raul."

"That's what he said."

"Oh, give me a break. They're still griping about me, though."

"You? Why?"

"Mami and Papi just can't be happy that not only am I giving them a grandchild and getting married; they're tripping that we're not having a big ole church wedding. Papi said, 'I pictured walking my daughter down the aisle of a church, not stepping over seashells and getting sand in my shoes.' I told them this is my wedding and I don't want a big to-do. I just want a nice, intimate ceremony off the beach with a small circle of friends and family. I want you and others to walk down the aisle before me but I don't want bridesmaids or groomsmen per se. And I also just want a short exchange of vows. I'm more focused on the marriage, not the wedding. You know what else Papi isn't pleased with?"

"What?"

"That I'm not going to be married by a priest. That TV judge Evelyn Mathers made a guest appearance on our show and we hit it off. I asked her to officiate the ceremony."

"I know Tío Miguel wasn't pleased but he'll get over it. Hell, he's marrying off his daughter and getting a grandkid. It's going to be wonderful, kid. The weather forecast for the rest of the week looks great."

"Our producer Leo graciously offered his Malibu estate for the ceremony and reception. Wait till you see this place—talk about beautiful. Oh! Is everything straight with the caterer?"

"Yes. I told you I'd take care of it and I did. All the food and—uh, drinks are set. Nikki, are you sure you want there to be liquor? It wouldn't be that big a deal if we had a dry reception."

"I'm cool, really. I don't want to deny everyone else from sipping on the sauce because of me. So don't worry. I can handle being around alcohol, okay?"

"Okay. Now this is totally off the subject but I think I'll call Lupe tonight."

"Really? What made you decide that?"

"Alejandro. I hurt that man, yet he decided to work at giving me another chance.

That showed me no matter how bad someone fucks up, if they're truly sorry, you should give them at least another chance. The hurt I did to Alejandro is on a different level than what Lupe did to me; still, I was given a second chance at life and love so I don't feel right not returning that favor to somebody. Raul said Lupe was really worried about me. She said for him to tell me Renaldo got what was coming to him. A part of me was surprised because I thought she would be sad that he was dead. I don't know if Lupe and I will ever be close like a mother and daughter should be, but I think I should open that door and see what happens. Know what I mean?"

"Of course I do. I'm happy to hear you're going to at least try." I take her hand again and kiss it.

"Oh, brother." She grins. "What do I always tell you about that mushy stuff?"

I grin back at her. "Yeah, but I know you don't mean it."

"Did you find out what the producers are going to do?"

"Erica told me the show will more than likely have me doing the 'hide your pregnancy' by carrying bags or standing behind plants. I knew Leo wouldn't have a problem with it; it was the others I was concerned with. They're not too happy with my pregnancy and aren't interested in writing it into the show. That's fine by me, though. Just as long as they're willing to work with me."

"That's cool. I told you it'd work out. Those guys don't want to be looked on as heartless assholes who canned a woman for getting pregnant. Never mind that it's illegal."

"Mm-hmm. I remember how bad it looked when that actress took the producers of *Townsend Hills* to court when they fired her after she got pregnant. She got a nice piece of change, too. Rosie, as much as I want this baby, I'm still hoping I can juggle family life as well as still climb up the ladder in my acting career. I gotta lot of things I want to do— producing, directing—"

"You can and you will. Don't start bugging out about that. It'll be hard at times but you can do it. All right?"

"Yeah. You don't think Mario will flip on me, do you?"

"Flip on you how?"

I peek around and make sure he isn't near the patio door. "You know how some men start off as being supportive of their wife's career but then turn around and want them to stay home full-time. I don't want that to happen."

"Why do you do that?"

"Do what?"

"Worry about shit before it even happens?"

"I'm just expressing a concern, Rosie."

"No, you're being a fucking worrywart as usual. Just enjoy being in the now—if the problem comes up, deal with it then."

"Okay, okay. You're right."

"Now back to me. Stop smirking, heifer. I'm starting a new venture soon."

"What's that?"

"Don't laugh, but after I do the guest performance with the Pussycat Dolls I'm going to meet with these music producers. They approached me about doing a CD."

"A CD? You're going to be a singer?"

"No, I'm going to piss in the wind. Yeah, I'm going to give it a shot."

"You never said anything about wanting to sing before. When did all of this come up?"

"It was back when I was hanging with Mission. I was at the studio with him and I was singing along with the hook of one of the tracks and the cats there told me I had a nice voice. They said they wanted to produce some new talent and since I had the look and all, we could pop it off. I thought they were talking shit until they called me last week."

"I'm so surprised. I never would've thought you wanted to do something like that. I've heard you sing along with the radio and always thought you had a nice voice, too. It's better than mine, that's for sure."

"That ain't saying much."

"Oh, fuck you. Try and pay a compliment…Hell, go for it. I'm rooting for you."

"Thanks. You know, if they'd approached me about this before the thing with Renaldo, I would've said no. Now, I see how short life can be so I'm going for all I can. If it works it works, and if it doesn't it just doesn't. It's not going to hurt to give it a try."

"You've got that right, *mija.*"

"Um, there's something else."

"What?"

"Uh, my agent is in talks with the people over at *Girlfriends* about me doing a couple of episodes. Are you cool with that if it happens?"

"Rosie, we've talked about this in the counseling sessions—"

"I know. I just don't want to make you uncomfortable."

"Don't make me hit you. I'm cool with that. Don't let those jealousy and insecurity issues of mine affect what you want to do, all right? I'm past that, okay?"

"You sure?"

"Yes. I'm positive." A little twinge in me lets me know what I just said isn't completely true but fuck it—I'll deal with it. I'm too happy that my cousin is sitting next to me and is not six feet under.

"Okay. I'm loving trying the new things coming my way but at the same time I don't want to get involved with too much so that it affects things between Alejandro and me. We're at a make it or break it stage in our relationship and I don't want to jeopardize it in any way."

"While he's settling down here and getting his thing going—opening up another store or whatever, just make him a part of what you're doing somehow. For instance, bring him along to the studio or something. That way you can do what you want but still make that time with him. He used to be a concert promoter and he's great in business, so perhaps he can help you in your career in some capacity."

"Yeah, that's a good idea."

We fall into silence.

"You know what I thought of?" Rosie finally asks.

"Hmm?"

"Next week you won't be a Moreno anymore. We'll no longer be the Moreno girls."

"I'll still use it professionally. I was going to hyphenate, but Nikki Moreno-Esposito has too many 'o' sounds to it . I'll just go by Nikki Esposito."

"Really. Here, let's make a toast." She pours tea into the two glasses and hands me one. "Here's to us. We've been through some shit and we made it, baby. And anything else that gets thrown our way, we gonna handle that, too."

"I know that's right."

"Here's to me, you, and the little one. Who are we always and forever?"

"Los Morenos."

"What? I didn't hear you."

"Los Morenos!"

"Damn right."

This Is My Promise To You

The wedding ceremony of
Mario Dimitri Esposito and M. Jisela Nicole Moreno
Malibu, California

34

Mario

"Mario, man, let me do it." Chico takes over from me and begins fixing his tie. "You need to chill, bro. Your hands are shaking like crazy."

"I know you're supposed to be nervous on your wedding day, but this is ridiculous."

"No reason to be that nervous. You're marrying a hell of a woman."

"You don't have to tell me that."

"I can't believe my brother and my sister are finally getting hitched."

"All right, that sounded a little bit backwoods."

Chico chuckles. "You know what I mean. Nikki is like my sister. Who knows, maybe you all will be heading for Detroit for a wedding in the next year or so."

"What? You and Bisola getting married?"

"I haven't asked B yet. But I'm thinking about doing it over the Christmas holidays."

I pat him on the arm. "I'm happy for you, man. I haven't met Bisola yet, but just by talking to her over the phone, she seems like a winner, like she's got her head on right and everything. And seeing the way you light up as you talk about her, I can tell she's the one for you."

"She is, dawg. B wanted to come but she had a bunch of houses to show this weekend. But I'll bring her out when we take our vacations in a few weeks."

"Cool. You know Rosie and Nikki are on a mission to convince you to join all of us out here. I've got to say, I wouldn't mind one bit having my big brother out here with me."

Chico shakes his head. "As much as I miss all y'all, I can't leave the D. My girl is there, and despite the fucked-up economy, Esposito and Son is doing real well. I know Pops is going to retire soon and I'll be running everything. Plus, it would kill him and Mom if neither of their sons were around."

"I hear you."

"But you know I'ma be out here as much as possible when my little niece or nephew get here. How does it feel? You know, impending fatherhood and all?"

"It feels good, a little scary but good. Every time I see Nikki's little stomach poking out and knowing that's a life we made growing in there, I'm amazed. Man, you should see me talking to her belly…"

When I see Chico stare off with a sad look coming over his face, I figure I shouldn't keep going on about the baby. I know he still feels the pain of losing his and Rhonda's baby, Jada. When he told me about it I couldn't help but be shocked. It was already painful dealing with the death of a longtime friend and her child, but then Chico called and told me he was certain the baby was a result of a one-night stand he and Rhonda had had. I was already looking forward to my role as Jada's play uncle and then I found out she really was my flesh and blood. Chico has always connected with kids and I have no doubt he'll make a great father one day.

Right then both of our thoughts are interrupted by a knock at the door. "Come in," I call out.

The door opens and our father peeks his head in. He's got a mischievous glint in his blue eyes. "I heard someone's getting married today."

"Get in here, old man," I reply in jest.

"Old man?" he says as he enters the room. "Don't let this head full of silver hair fool you. I can still take you down."

He proceeds to give me some jabs that I block before grabbing me in a bear hug. He grabs Chico and hugs him as well ."It's not too often the Esposito men are in one room these days. How are my boys doing?"

"Mario is a nervous wreck. Hold out your hand and show Pops how bad you're shaking."

I instead ball up my fist and shake it at him.

"I was the same way when I married your mother. I had two glasses of Southern Comfort to help me calm down. It's not just the bride who gets the jitters. Today I even had to put some *Molinari Sambuca* in my coffee so I can imagine how you feel. But you're not having second thoughts, are you?"

"I know Nikki is the woman I want to spend the rest of my life with. but I have to admit I'm a little worried about our future. Especially since we live in a place where people get divorces like getting a new pair of underwear. Hollywood isn't exactly conducive to marriage. I don't want me and Nikki's relationship to suffer because of our environment."

My father puts his hands on my shoulders and looks me square in the eye.

"Son, whether you're in Hollywood, California, or Haystack, Nebraska, there will be situations that will test your marriage. You and Nikki will have to make your love for each other and your baby your priority. Your mother and I had to fight for our marriage from the start. Let me tell you a story."

"Oh, boy," says Chico, groaning.

I try to suppress a grin. For whatever dilemma my brother and I may face, Pops is sure to have a story for it.

"Watch it, buddy," he says, shaking a finger at Chico. "I promise to keep it brief. My family was very close to our neighbors the Castellanos. From almost the time I was two years old—when Valeria Castellano was born—it became a given that we would unite the two families through marriage one day. I had a crush on Valeria when we were teenagers but my feelings never grew into anything more.

"When I went away to school and met your mother and fell in love with her, that was the end of anything between Valeria and me. My family was heartbroken enough that I came home to announce my engagement to someone else, but when they found out their Sicilian prince, as they called me, was marrying a Black woman…Well, you can imagine. Many were not pleased on your mother's side of the family, either. The only family who came to our wedding from my side was your Nana Sophia and Uncle Vincente and a couple of cousins. Only a handful of people from your mother's side showed up. Over the years most accepted our marriage, but some have not.

"My point is, not having the full support of our families was hard but we didn't let it come between us. We had many other obstacles, but your mother and I put our love first above all else and it's what has gotten us through it all. Plenty of love and *pazienza*. Don't think about what other people are doing, Mario. If everyone around you is getting divorced every day, that has nothing to do with you so don't be concerned about it. *Essiru sempi lu santu fora la chiesa.* Understand?"

"My Sicilian is a bit rusty but basically I should stand outside the choices of others. You're right as always."

He gives me another hug. "You two will make it. If I didn't think you had much of a chance, you know I would tell you. Now that we've got the father and son marriage speech out of the way, all I can say is what an estate! That's what took me a minute to get in here, I was nosing around. I've never been in a home this spectacular."

"It's like something from *Lifestyles of the Rich and Famous,*" adds Chico. "I keep waiting for Robin Leach to walk into the room."

"I know that's right," I agree. I walk to one of the full-length mirrors and check out my attire, make sure everything is in place.

Pops is right. I've got to put my love for Nikki and our child above all else. What I told my father about being concerned that Hollywood would be bad for my marriage wasn't completely true. I couldn't say what my real concern is. Which is wondering if Nikki's drinking is truly behind us. I had a terrible dream the other night. In it I came home from work and Nikki was passed out drunk on the couch and our baby was wandering around the house crying. I literally sat straight up in bed—I could've sworn I still heard the sound of a baby crying for a second. That dream scared the hell out of me and I'm praying it was just my fears put into the form of a dream and not some omen. I don't think I would be as concerned if I hadn't witnessed my mother's problem with alcoholism. Maybe I should take comfort in the fact that even though she had a couple of relapses she's been in recovery for years now.

I'm thankful Nikki's time in detox didn't get to the media because I still haven't told my parents about it. When Chico came out to see Rosie in the hospital, I made him promise not to say anything. Although they went through a similar circumstance, I don't want them to think negatively about Nikki.

Anyway, at this point I don't feel the need to tell my parents since everything's okay. And everything *is* okay. I need to concentrate on that. What separates Nikki's situation from my mother's is we got to her before she fell completely into alcoholism. Today I'm marrying the woman who is the other half of me and who I want to grow old with. Pops always told me and Chico how we would know a woman was meant for us: She's the one we can picture ourselves with in side-by-side rocking chairs in our twilight years. I've dated women I couldn't picture being with two weeks later much less twenty years. I went out with one or two who were great people but they didn't even come close to making me love them the way I love Nikki. Even though she can drive me up the wall sometimes, I can't picture my life without her by my side. Yeah, I'm marrying my baby, and that's all that matters right now.

35

Nikki

I turn my head from one side to the other admiring my hairstyle in the mirror. It's in an upswept style that's held up by a platinum headband laced with violets. Tendrils of curls are falling down each side of my face.

"Odell, you did a spectacular job."

He turns off the curlers and meets my eyes in the mirror. "Chile, why you sound surprised? You know I'm the Oribe of Detroit."

"I know, sweetie. I love it! It's exactly what I wanted." I stand up and give Odell a big hug. "I was scared to ask you to do my hair at first."

"Why's that, Miss Nikki?"

"I thought you might want to come here strictly as a guest and not to work."

"You so silly. If you didn't ask me I woulda been upset. This ain't work. This is helping my sista-friend get ready for her big day."

"Odell, I love you. I've missed seeing you face-to-face. Talking on the phone is cool, but I can't hug you through the phone."

"I know what you mean. I hate that I can't just drop by and see you and Miss Rosie. N'am one of my girls is around."

"I'm glad not only that you're here but I finally got to meet Aaron. I liked him right off the bat. And it's so obvious he's crazy about you."

"Chile, don't I know it. I got him wrapped around my finger. I don't mean that in a bad way or nothin'. I'm crazy about his cute, husky self, too."

"Nikki, come on and get your dress on," Mami says. "Odell, you got my baby's hair so pretty! Rosie, bring the dress over so we can help her."

I slip out of my robe and toss it on a nearby chair. Mami clears her throat and nods over at Odell.

"Oh, Miss Morena, you don't have to worry about me being in here. Nikki ain't got nothin' I want." He looks at me. "No offense."

"None taken."

Rosie brings over my dress from off the bed and she and Mami help me step into it. I'm not wearing a traditional wedding gown much to Mami's chagrin. She found a beautiful white wedding gown in *Elegant Bride* magazine. But I chose a lavender full-length silk dress from Vera Wang. It has flowing chiffon at the bottom and a beaded bodice. Once it's on, Rosie, Mami, and Odell step back and take me in.

"*Mija*, it's so gorgeous."

"Thanks, Rosie."

Mami puts her hand to her mouth. "I'm not going to cry. I'm not going to cry. Sweetheart, you look so…" She fans her face and blinks back tears.

"Miss Nikki, you done picked some kind of dress. I love the way the lavender color plays off the violets in yo' hair, and it looks so good on yo' skin color."

"Thanks, Odell."

"Cuz, I know you're doing everything in your own way, but are we going to do the something borrowed, blue, old, and new thing? I hope not 'cause I forgot to bring something."

"I brought something that's old and can be used for the borrowed part, too." Mami retrieves a small box off a nearby table. "Once you told me the color of your dress, I knew these would be perfect." She opens the box and holds it out for me to see.

I gasp. "Mami, the earrings!"

It's a pair of silver antique droop earrings. They have an amethyst center surrounded by diamonds. These earrings were handed down to Mami from her mother, who wore them on her wedding day. Mami only wears them once a year on her wedding anniversary. Now I have another piece of my late grandmother here. I had my wedding bouquet made from orchids, which was her favorite flower.

"Thank you, Mami." I put the earrings on and give her a hug.

Rosie goes and brings back my shoes. She kneels in front of me and slips them on my feet. I reach down and stroke her hair. She looks up at me.

"Don't start."

"What?"

"You know what." Her bottom lip trembles and she bites down on it and stands up. I grab her and we embrace tightly.

Mami comes and places her arms around our waists. "All right, girls. It's about time."

I let go of Rosie and look at her tear-streaked face and wipe away the tears from my own. "We're going to have to touch up our makeup real quick."

We both go to our makeup cases and repair the damage from crying as best we can.

36

Nikki

T he wedding is set up outside on the immense lawn. Not that we need much
space. Since Mario and I wanted a small wedding, in total there are about
fifty-two guests. Raul and Tía Lupe are absent. Raul took so much time off
to care for his mother that once he got back to Florida, he couldn't take any more
time. And Tía Lupe is still not back in full health and was not up to traveling.

Right now everyone's gathered just inside the door that leads outside. I'm standing
far back, arm in arm with Papi. I glance at him and he's looking at me with such
pride I fear my makeup is in jeopardy again. Everyone is lined up in the order I want
for him or her to exit. The photographer and videographer are snapping away and
taping. Mrs. Esposito turns around and kisses my cheek for the fifth time today.
She's an attractive woman with a tawny complexion, Rubenesque figure, and long
micro-braids that she has up in a bun. I know she likes me a lot and is happy that I'm
going to be her daughter-in-law. However, I think she holds it against me that her
son is still so far away from home. Even though Mario came out here to L.A. long
before me, I think she feels she could convince him to move back to Detroit if my
career wasn't keeping us here as well.

Rosie gives the signal for the deejay to cue up the music. I chose our wedding song
to be "Song for You" by Rodney Franklin. The words speak for me my feelings for
Mario, because not only is he my lover and soon-to-be husband, he's my friend.
Speaking of Mario, he's in the very front and isn't allowed to turn around and see
me. Him not seeing me before the ceremony is probably the only wedding rule I'm
abiding by. He turns his head to the side and then quickly turns it back straight
ahead. I know it's killing him not to be able to turn around.

He walks out the door first to the end of the aisle where he'll wait at the altar. The way I set it up is each couple will walk down the aisle and take a seat in the front row on their appropriate sides. When it's all done, only Mario, Judge Evelyn, and I will be left standing. Next out the door and down the aisle are Rosie and Alejandro, Chico and Paris, Benjamin and Amber, Leon and Joanne, Odell and Mami, and then Mr. and Mrs. Esposito.

Now is when the butterflies in my stomach make their presence known. I look at Papi and he's staring at me again.

"I love you, Zuzu."

At first I'm stunned and wonder if I heard him correctly. But I know I did. It's never bothered me that Papi had such a hard time uttering those three words but right now, actually hearing it, it's the best wedding gift I could receive.

"I love you, too, Papi," I finally respond in a quavering voice. There goes my makeup again.

We proceed out the door and down the aisle. Through my blurred vision, I can see Mario beaming at me. Papi gives me a kiss, leaves me at the altar, and takes a seat next to Mami. Rosie gets up and takes my bouquet. Mario and I face each other and hold hands as Judge Evelyn begins to speak.

"We are gathered here today to celebrate one of life's extraordinary moments, to give recognition to the worth and beauty of love, and to add our best wishes to the words which shall unite Mario Esposito and Nicole Moreno in marriage. Should there be anyone who has cause why this couple should not be united in marriage, they must speak now or forever hold their peace."

Mario and I look out to our guests. I raise my eyebrow and put a little roll in my neck. Light laughter ripples among our friends and family. We then face each other again.

"Who brings this woman to this man?"

Papi stands up. "I do." He gives me a wink and sits back down.

"Mario and Nicole, life is given to each of us as individuals and yet we must learn to live together. Love is given to us by our family and by our friends. We learn to love by being loved. Learning to love and living together is one of the greatest challenges in life and is the shared goal of a married life. Mario, do you take Nicole to be your wife?" asks Judge Evelyn.

"I do," he replies. He gives my hands a squeeze.

"Do you promise to love, honor, cherish and protect her, forsaking all others and holding only unto her?"

"I do."

"Nicole, do you take Mario to be your husband?" she asks me.

"I do."

Mario wipes away the tear rolling down my cheek.

"Do you promise to love, honor, cherish, and protect him, forsaking all others and holding only unto him?"

"I do."

"Wedding rings are an outward and visible sign of an inward spiritual grace and the unbroken circle of love, signifying to all the union of this man and this woman in marriage."

On the altar is a gold, jewel-encrusted box that holds our rings. Judge Evelyn retrieves it and holds it before us. We each take the other's ring.

She nods to Mario.

"I, Mario, take thee, Nicole, to be my wife. To have and to hold, in sickness and in health, for richer and for poorer, and I promise my love to you forevermore."

He places the ring on my shaking hand. I notice his are a bit shaky as well.

"I, Nicole, take thee, Mario, to be my husband. To have and to hold, in sickness and in health, for richer and for poorer, and I promise my love to you forevermore." I place the ring on his finger.

"Mario and Nicole, as the two of you come into this marriage uniting you as husband and wife, and as you this day affirm your faith and love for one another, I would hope that you always remember to cherish each other as special and unique individuals, that you respect the thought, ideas, and suggestions of one another. Be able to forgive, do not hold grudges, and live each day that you may share it together—as from this day forward you shall be each other's home, comfort, and refuge, your marriage strengthened by your love and respect for each other. I now pronounce you husband and wife. Mario, you may kiss—"

Before she even finishes we've embraced each other and are kissing. Everyone begins clapping and whistling.

"Ladies and gentlemen, I proudly present to you—Mr. and Mrs. Mario Esposito!"

The clapping becomes even louder. Mario and I finally break our kiss and hand-in-hand make our way down the aisle. I blow kisses in the direction of Mami, Papi, and Rosie. I place my hand on my belly and feel our baby that's growing inside me. For some reason my mind flashes to when the man I've just married was a little boy torturing me with water pistols and bugs. And now here we are beginning a new phase in our life together as husband and wife and soon-to-be parents. If I can ever be happier than I am right now, I don't think I could withstand the joy.

AUTHOR BIO

Shelley Halima is a novelist/songwriter/screenwriter/poet residing in the Metro Detroit area. She recently completed a screenplay for her first novel, *Azucar Moreno,* and is currently writing her third novel. You may email Shelley at ShelleyHalima@yahoo.com. You may also send mail to her in c/o Santiago Publicity, PO Box 511002, Livonia, MI 48151.

EXCERPT FROM

AZUCAR

Moreno

BY SHELLEY HALIMA

AVAILABLE FROM STREBOR BOOKS

CHAPTER ONE / *Uno*

Saturday, July 14, 2001, 8:30 a.m.

Noooo. Please tell me I'm dreaming about an alarm clock going off and the sound I hear isn't real. No such luck. I reach over and turn it off. I want to hibernate in bed for at least another three hours. But I can't because I have to begin preparing for the baby shower my cousin Rosie and I are throwing for our friend Rhonda. I, by the way, am Mildred Jisela Nicole Moreno. Yes, Mildred. My mother's excuse for bestowing such a name on her child is it was the first name of her former teacher, mentor, and friend who passed away two weeks prior to my birth. She wanted to pay homage to her in some way. That's very touching, but I really wish she'd planted a tree or sent a donation to the lady's favorite charity or something; if she wanted to memorialize her. Out of curiosity I asked Mami what was Mildred's middle name; thinking perhaps I could have gotten off easier. She said it was Eunice. So either way I was screwed. Needless to say, I treat that name like the proverbial pink elephant. Everyone calls me either Nik or Nikki; except for my Papi who calls me Zuzu, which is from *azucar*—Spanish for sugar.

I'm the 26-year-old product of an African-American mother and a Puerto Rican father. Some of my friends tease me and call me "blackerican." It's cool, though, because I truly feel like I've been blessed with two wonderfully rich heritages. I grew up in a world that was a wonderful mixture of soul food and Latino cuisine; Al Green and Hector Lavoe, and celebrating the legacies of Martin Luther King and Pedro Albizu Campos. I'm 5'9", 130 lbs.—that may change after all the eating I'm planning on doing today—and I have dark brown curly hair that falls right below my shoulders. I live on the West Side of Detroit. I was born in New York, but this has been my hometown since my family moved here when I was seven. I work at a private investigation firm as an Administrative Assistant. Basically, that means I change the toner when it's low and keep track of the paper supply. It's merely a day job for me and not my career. But since I've grown attached to having a car to get around, clothes on my back and food in my stomach, I have to keep it.

The true love of my soul is acting. I'm hoping the fates decide to shine my way and one day I'll be able to survive financially from acting alone. Whenever I hear an actor say that when they first stepped on the stage they knew they'd found their calling, I know exactly what they mean. I was in my first play during my first semester of school here. I remember my teacher telling my parents after the recital how I was such a natural and they should consider sending me to a performance arts school where I could get my education, yet hone my gift at the same time. My parents ignored her suggestion.

Although they were proud of my performance, they didn't feel acting was a profession that would get me anywhere so they didn't want to encourage me. They felt, and still feel, that my acting is merely some hobby. I no longer mention any play or local commercial that I've done because, inevitably, their response is, "That's nice, but you need to put your focus on your real job at the firm."

I've never been able to make them understand that my "real job" is only a means of support and there's no way that I can envision giving up acting. People who aren't a part of the artistic world can't understand that corporate life is too confining for someone like me to be happy. I love the testing of boundaries and freeness that I find in acting. My personal hell would be being stuck in a nine-to-five for the rest of my life. I'm an artiste—darn it.

Last year my parents decided to move back to New York so it's been easier to put up with their nagging about my career choice by phone than in person. In addition to bugging me about that, they've still been pressing me for the specifics of why I broke up with my boyfriend. They really liked Jaime, but I don't want to talk about what happened with us with my parents. Jaime and I broke up about three months ago. Okay, two months, three weeks and one day to be precise.

We met in Meijer's of all places. Meijer's is one of those one-stop superstores where you can buy panties, motor oil and chicken all in the same place. I hadn't dated anyone seriously for a while and I was concentrating on my rehearsals for a play. I wasn't looking for love and I sure as hell didn't expect to find it in a store.

I was in the seafood department debating whether or not I wanted to try and cook a live lobster. Actually, it wasn't a question of whether I could cook the lobster but whether I trusted myself with getting the damn thing in the pot without dropping it or losing a finger. I was getting visions of the lobster chasing me around the kitchen, gunning for me with its cinchers. As I was standing at the lobster tank lost in thought, I heard a male voice from behind me.

"I don't know if I'd want to mess with one of those either. I'd probably go to Red Lobster."

I turned around and saw a smiling handsome face. He was about 6 feet tall, with a slim build, caramel-colored skin, a neatly trimmed moustache and a goatee. He had nice large eyes that were rimmed with thick lashes that normally take me two coats of mascara to get and he had a wonderfully engaging smile. His hair was cut close to his head—slightly faded on the sides. I'm a cologne fanatic and he had on one of my favorites—Issey Miyake.

"My indecisiveness is showing that bad, huh?" I said, smiling back at him.

"Yeah, maybe you need me to help you with your shopping because you looked kind of unsure what type of salad dressing to get a few minutes ago."

I turned and raised my hand, pretending to signal someone. "Security, I believe we have a stalker situation here."

"Okay, you got me." He shrugged innocently. "What can I say? A beautiful woman caught my eye and I had to follow her."

"Well, since you put it like that, I'll put off the restraining order for now. I've got a lot on my mind today because I definitely would've noticed a handsome man like you following me."

"My turn to say thank you. So, are you thinking of cooking lobster for a romantic dinner with your man?"

"No, for a romantic dinner with my girlfriend," I said, putting on my most serious face.

His smile slowly faded and he looked at me, as if he was not sure whether or not I was being for real. After a few seconds the quizzical look on his face made me break into a grin.

"I'm teasing you. Payback for following me around the store."

He chuckled. "You had me going for a minute there."

"For the record, I don't have a boyfriend and definitely not a girlfriend."

"That's good on both counts."

"Since you're being so nosy, wanting to know who I'm cooking lobster for, maybe you should at least tell me your name," I said teasingly as I batted my eyes, hoping to God that I didn't have any deposits in the corners of them.

"You're right," he said, extending his hand to shake mine. "I'm Jaime Darrell Dorsey. And you are?"

I shook his hand, then grinned at his playfully formal tone. "I'm Jisela Nicole Moreno. You can call me Nikki."

"Moreno? Is that Mexican?"

I shook my head. "Uh, uh, uh. You'd better be lucky you're fine or else I'd be heading to the checkout lane right about now."

"Aw, man. What I do?"

I chuckled. "For the record, my last name is Latino. Here's a quick cultural lesson. If you meet someone who is or has a name of Hispanic origin, don't automatically put them into a group such as Mexican or Puerto Rican. Just say Hispanic or Latino until you know for sure because there are Colombians, Cubans, Dominicans, Chileans, etc. That's like seeing a Native American and right off the bat calling them Cherokee when they could be Blackfoot or whatever."

"My bad. I hope I didn't offend you."

"No, you didn't. It's a bit irritating usually when people do that, but you didn't irritate me."

"'Cause I'm special?"

"Yeah, because you're special. Of course I don't know yet if it's special as in unique or special as in short yellow bus..."

"That's cold!" He leaned against the counter. "All right, beautiful lady, what's your heritage? I'm curious."

"My mom's Black and my dad's Puerto Rican."

"The mixture sure has given you an exotic beauty. You kind of remind me of that woman Vanity from Prince's old group."

"Yeah, I've gotten that before."

"And thanks for the lesson. I'll be sure to be more careful about lumping folks into a category. You'd think I'd know better as a Black man."

"Um-hmm..." I playfully pursed my lips and cut my eyes. "You're not as bad as some people. I've been asked if I 'speak Puerto Rican.'"

"Now that's bad. Do you live around here?"

"No, I live in Sherwood Forest. And you?"

"Rosedale Park, but I work not too far from here."

"Where?"

"At Office Integrators. I install office equipment, like the cubicles and built-in desks."

"My job isn't too far from here either. I work at Quinn Investigations. We do background checks and investigate insurance fraud and stuff like that." Normally I wouldn't give a guy that I'd just met any personal information, such as where I work or even the vicinity where I live. But I felt so instantly comfortable and at ease with him. No red flags were going up saying, "Possible axe murdering cannibal."

"Uh-oh. I guess you're gonna do a background check on me, huh?"

"Do I have reason to?"

"I guess I might as well fess up about my wife and six kids."

"Oh, man." I pouted. "I knew you were too good to be true."

"You know, I'm just joking with you." He grinned and we held eye contact for a minute. Oh, my stars. I didn't know if it was me or if someone had jacked up the temperature in the store.

"Wait a minute. Office Integrators...is that right off of Lilley and Ford Road?"

"Yeah, it is."

"I thought that sounded familiar. It's next to Vico Engineering, isn't it?"

"Yep, it sure is."

"I used to work at Vico about three years ago."

"For real? I've been working at OI for three and a half years. It's a small world. So there was an overlap of time when we were working right near each other. I never paid much attention over there because I'd only seen guys coming and going. You would've definitely caught my attention—like you did today. Man, that's something. So, what did you do over there?"

"I was the office assistant and the only woman in the office. I liked the guys, but let me tell you, engineers are in a class all their own. They can put the brain power on high and put together the most high-tech designs, but then will turn around and ask you how to use the pencil sharpener. 'You stick the pencil in which way?'"

He nodded. "You're right. My uncle's an engineer and even though he's smart as you know what, sometimes we wonder how he finds his way out of bed without some kind of manual."

We both expressed amusement.

"You certainly aren't doing much shopping," I said. I noticed that he only had about three items in his handheld basket. "Unless you're barely getting started."

"Nah. I was in the area and came in to get a couple of things. I can't get much in the compartment on my bike."

"You ride a motorcycle?"

"Yeah, I have a Yamaha."

"Cool! I ride a Ducati."

His jaw dropped open. "What? Are you serious? You're not playing with me again, are you?"

"No, I'm a hundred percent serious. I wouldn't lie about something that's nearly caused my parents to have simultaneous heart attacks."

"Damn! You ride?!"

"Yes. My cousin Rosie and I learned to ride about five years ago. We got our own bikes a couple of years later. We and our friend Chico go riding together whenever we get the chance."

"Man, you've earned some major points and you were already off the meter."

"Thank ya, thank ya very much."

"I won't take away points for that bad Elvis imitation."

We both chuckled.

"So, who taught you to ride?"

"My cousin's ex-boyfriend."

"You say your parents almost bought the farm together, huh?"

"Yes. My cousin and I've put some grays hairs on their heads over the years, but when they found out that we'd bought bikes, that put them over the top."

"I can imagine. My parents weren't too happy with me getting a bike, so I can see how yours would feel by you being female. They don't understand, ain't nothing like riding."

"I know. The feeling of the wind hitting you... You and I know it's a biker cliche, but feeling like you're one with the road, the freedom."

"Exactly. You might think that this sounds strange, but the only other thing that really does it for me like riding my bike is working with the earth. I love landscaping. When I was coming up, other kids used to try to get out of doing yard work but not me. The house I'm living in now, when I first moved into it, you should've seen it. The inside was nice but the yard had been really neglected. Now it looks completely different on the outside." He looked down and grinned sheepishly. "I didn't mean to go on about that. I want to make a good impression and I'm going on about my lawn."

"That's perfectly fine. I love it when people are passionate about something; no matter what it is. And you're making a very good impression, by the way."

"That's good to know. Back to the bikes. I'd like for you and I to go riding one day soon."

I blushed. "That sounds good."

"There's something about you that looks awfully familiar. It's like I've seen you somewhere. And it wasn't at Vico 'cause, like I said, I would've noticed you there."

"I act and I've done some commercials for Scarelli Leather, Solomon Chevrolet, Timeaco's Unique Boutique, Danner Soul Food, WJZZ radio station..."

"That's where! Oh, all right. So you're an actress, too?"

"Yes. My goal is to do it full time."

"What else have you done?"

"I've done some plays. Like *Soul of a Gypsy*, *Sasha's Song*, and the one I'm really proud of, the local production of *For Colored Girls Who've Considered Suicide When the Rainbow Is Enuf.*"

"I'm very impressed."

"And so you should be," I teased.

"You are hella interesting, Ms. Moreno. I'd like to find out more about you. How about we start by trying to tackle a couple of those together?" He nodded toward the lobster tank.

"When?"

"Tonight."

The way he said that one word and the look in his eyes...I felt a jolt hit me in the chest and travel to the southern regions of my body. We stood looking into each other's eyes for a few moments. I couldn't believe that I was actually considering packing up those lobsters and having him follow me home right then.

A grin spread across his face. "We've been formally introduced for about five minutes. I think that's long enough to make a dinner date, don't you?"

"I tell you what. Let's exchange numbers and talk before we go making dinner plans."

"That's fair."

I reached down in my purse for a pen and piece of scrap paper. I found something and began to write my number down.

"You're not giving me a bogus number, are you?" he asked with a grin that I was already in love with.

"Of course not. You'd better not really be married or anything because I'll know something is up if you try to only give me a cell or pager number."

I tore off my number and gave it to him with the rest of the paper and the pen. After he'd finished, he handed me back the paper and pen.

"There, I put my home phone, cell phone, and pager."

"I guess you can go to the lightning round now."

"Is it okay if I call you tonight?"

"It sure is. I look forward to it."

We finished doing our shopping together and talked a bit more in the parking lot before leaving. He scored points with me by not playing it cool and waiting a few days to call. He called that night, as he said he would, and we ended up talking for three and a half hours. I invited him over a couple of nights later and he brought the lobsters. I cooked them without incident. I didn't lose a finger or anything. From that night on, we spent as much time together as possible.

We were together for close to a year until it all came to an end one night about three months ago. Rosie and I had just gotten back from PR and visiting our *abuela*. After I had unpacked and settled in, I called Jaime before going to bed. We talked for a little bit, and then I told him that I was beat and going to turn in. He said that he was going to do the same. We said, "I love you," and hung up.

He called me back a few minutes later, saying that he'd forgotten to tell me that he'd received some Alexander Zonjic concert tickets from his boss. After a few minutes, we hung up again. I had dozed off into a nice slumber when I heard the phone ring yet again. I rolled over and looked at the caller ID and saw that it was Jaime. I glanced at the clock and saw that it was 12:43 a.m.; over an hour had passed since we'd talked. I picked up the phone and before I could say anything, I heard Jaime's friend Antoine talking to someone. He sounded wasted, as usual.

"Aight," said Antoine. "Don't y'all be drinkin' up my Grey Goose. That shit ain't cheap."

I wondered what Antoine was doing over there when Jaime had told me that he was going right to bed. I could hear Najee playing in the background. Then I heard two female voices, giggling and talking. I sat up in my bed, wide-awake.

"Ain't nobody tryin' to hear that," said Jaime. "You be drinking up everybody else's liquor all the time and then you wanna ration yours. Stingy ass nigga."

"Look, man, get ready to take your piece on upstairs so me and mine can have some privacy."

"Who you calling a 'piece'? I know you not callin' me a piece!" That was one of the female voices.

"Ah, baby. You know I don't mean nothing by that. So chill."

"Better not mean nothing by it."

"Is the store still open, dawg?" asked Jaime.

"Oh shit! Hello? Hello?"

I didn't say anything.

"Ain't nobody on the line, man."

"You just now realizing that? Forget it; we got enough to drink anyway."

"We'll have enough if this lush right here don't..." He hung up.

I couldn't move for a few minutes. My heart felt like it was made of lead and was beating a thousand beats a second. When I finally could will my body to move, I got up and walked across the hall to Rosie's room. I peeped through the partially open door and saw that she didn't have company and that she'd fallen asleep reading a book. I went over to her and woke her up.

"Rosie."

She was startled. "Girl, what's wrong? And there had better be something wrong, too—waking me up out of a good sleep."

"I—I..."

"What, *mi 'ja?*"

"I talked to Jaime about an hour or so ago. I told him that I was tired from the trip and going straight to bed and he said he was doing the same. Well, a few minutes ago a call came from his house. I guess his boy Antoine was trying to make a call. Jaime's got this Fisher Price phone that has a tricky redial button. A lot of times you think you're getting connected with the number that you dialed but you've actually accidentally hit the redial button. Remember when I was over Jaime's and I thought I was calling Odell and, by mistake, I ended up calling you back? Jaime kept saying he was going to get another phone..."

"Hon, you're rambling. What's going on?"

"Sorry." I took a deep breath before going on. "Okay, when Antoine called, there was smooth, cozy ass music playing in the background, I heard female voices, and Antoine told Jaime to take his 'piece' upstairs so he could be alone with his."

We were silent for a few moments. Then I saw that flint in Rosie's eyes. She tossed the book from her lap to the chair opposite the bed.

"All right, Nik. Let's put some clothes on. We're going over there. And unless there's a helluva explanation, we're gonna do some damage in the joint. You best believe that. Who does that nigga think he is?! He think he's gonna step out on you and not have to pay for it?!"

Hearing the harshness in Rosie's voice snapped me out of my stunned state and I felt the anger come over me. We both got dressed and got into Rosie's car with her at the wheel.

"Rosie, we should've brought something with us; in case those chicks wanna try and get down."

"*Mi 'ja*, I always carry at least two bats in the trunk. I'm always prepared in case some shit hits. You know that. I've got something harder than that back home; if the situation calls for it."

After a few moments of silence I hit the dashboard with my fist. "That *hijo de puta!* Damn it, I can't believe that motherfucker! How could he do this shit?"

"He's a man and shit is what they do."

"Rosie, I didn't think he was like a lot of guys out here. I thought he was..."

"You thought he was what? Different?"

"Yeah," I said softly.

"*Mira*, you'll save yourself a lot of heartache once you get past the notion that any of these *cabrons* are any different from the next. You know how many females sing that 'I thought he was different' song?"

"I wish that song wasn't on my lips right now."

"Since he put it there, we're gonna go break that nigga's head and anybody else's who gets in the way."

"As mad as I am, I don't want to hurt anybody, Rosie. Not unless somebody comes at us. I feel like smashing his windows or something."

"We're gonna send him a message, after we see for ourselves what's going on. He can't get away with doing this. All right?"

I nodded my head.

Rosie and I are more like sisters than cousins. We're only four months apart and grew up together. She's my father's niece and when Papi's new job moved us from New York to Detroit, she came with us. She's one of the few people I trust and vice versa. We've always been protective of one another. Whenever something is done to one of us, it's done to both of us. So finding out that my man was messing around on me was just like she was getting cheated on.

My cousin is straight-up gangsta, though you wouldn't know it by looking at her. All modesty aside, I'm very attractive but Rosie's downright beautiful. She looks like a Hispanic version of Cindy Crawford—mole and all. She's about two inches shorter than I am, with an olive complexion, long raven hair and a figure that would make J.Lo hate on her.

Jaime lives about fifteen minutes away but with Rosie at the wheel, we got over there in about half that time. When we arrived, we saw Antoine's beat-up red LeBaron in the driveway and a white Taurus in front of the house.

I figured the Taurus must've belonged to one of those tricks. Rosie parked next door. She popped the trunk. We got out and headed to the back of the car and each picked up an aluminum bat. We walked up to the front porch. The window to the living room was open slightly, but the horizontal blinds were closed. There were moaning sounds coming from the living room. Rosie and I looked at each other.

"Mmmm, 'Toine baby."

"I'm about to come in a minute."

Rosie pursed her lips. "Oh well, sorry, but 'Toine is gonna have to put that nut on layaway." She pushed the doorbell and knocked on the door.

I took a few steps back and looked up at Jaime's room. It was dark, except for some flickering of light. Candles. That motherfucker. I looked back down in time to see one of the horizontal blinds move.

"Oh shit!" Antoine exclaimed.

I walked to the window. "Oh shit is right! Open this goddamn door!" I shouted through the screen.

Rosie rang the doorbell again, turned around and kicked the door a few times with the heel of her shoe.

"Who the hell is that?" the female asked.

"That's Jaime's girl."

"His girl? Y'all said he didn't have a girlfriend. That's why I set him up with Tasha. I didn't come over here to get caught up in some fuckin' drama. I don't need this!"

"Shhh, keep it down, all right?"

"Don't tell me to keep it down!"

That *pendejo* Jaime had been going around telling women that he didn't have a girlfriend—having females fix him up with their friends. At that moment he was probably up in his room screwing this Tasha chick—or at least he was about to.

As Rosie continued knocking and ringing the doorbell, I stepped off the porch and loosened one of the bricks that lined the shrubbery. I stood in front of the window opposite that of the living room—the dining room. Jaime hadn't put a screen in that window yet—it was all glass. I threw the brick through the window. That bitch let out a scream; not the woman—Antoine. A few moments later we heard Jaime's voice. He was standing at the living room window pulling a blind to the side.

"Nik, what the fuck is you doin'?!"

"Open the door, Jaime!"

"You tossing bricks through my shit and you want me to let you in? What the hell's wrong wit' you?"

"I'll tell you what's wrong with me, since yo' ass is playing dumb. I know you gotta woman up in there!"

"What? What are you talking about?"

"You know what she's talking about, bitch! Now open the fuckin' door!" Rosie shouted.

Jaime pulled the blind aside farther. "Rosie. Oh, I shoulda known. You probably put her up to this, with your shit-starting ass. This is between me and Nikki and it ain't got nothing to do with you."

"Naw, nigga. If it's got to do with my cousin, then it most definitely has something to do with me! And you ain't seen no shit get started yet!"

"Look, I ain't gonna open the door so y'all can act a fool up in my house. Y'all got bats, too. Aw, hell naw!"

"So you not gonna let us in? What if we toss the bats?" I asked.

"No, I'm still not and if you don't leave, I'm calling the cops. I can't believe you busted my fuckin' window!"

No, he didn't. No, he did not. I knew that he did not say that he was going to call the *popos* on me. I looked over at Rosie and saw from the expression on her face that I hadn't misunderstood. I took one of my deep breaths.

"The reason you're not opening the door is because you have someone in there, Jaime," I said calmly.

"Nik, it's just Antoine and his girl up in here. You know his momma be trippin' if he has females over, so he brought her over here. I'm not opening the door 'cause you need to calm yo' ass down. You all outta control; throwing bricks through my window!"

"Quit being a little bitch over that fuckin' window! Now let me ask you one more time—do you have a female over visiting you?"

"No!"

"Not even Tasha?"

He didn't say anything. I heard the three of them whispering but couldn't make out what was being said.

"Uh, hello? Why you being quiet all of sudden? I said, not even Tasha?"

"Nik, I told you who's all over here."

"Negro, did I just escape from Northville? You're not even going to try and play it off and ask who Tasha is? You have somebody up in your room because you've got goddamn candles lit! And I've known you long enough to know that the only time you have candles lit is when you're fucking, or about to! Now quit trying to play me for a fool!"

"See, that's what I'm saying. You're acting all crazy. I told you I don't have anybody over and if you don't want to believe that, then that's on you. Now, for real, you and your cousin are gonna have to go. If you don't leave within the next two minutes, I'm calling the cops."

"So it comes down to this?" I felt myself choking up but I'd be damned if I was gonna cry; especially in front of him. "I'm supposed to be your woman, the one who a little over an hour ago you were saying I love you to. And now, not only won't you let me in, but you're threatening to call the cops on me? All right, I see how it is. Come on, Rosie, let's go."

"Go? Girl, we ain't going no goddamn where! Fuck him calling the cops! Shit, I've got some peeps on the force. I ain't worried. Let that muthafucka bring it!"

"Still, he ain't worth it. Come on."

Rosie outspread her arms and looked at me with a "what the fuck?" expression on her face.

"Come on, Rosie," I said firmly. I leaned toward her and whispered, "We'll be back."

As we walked off the porch I looked up at Jaime's room again. I saw the shadow of someone walking near the window. I felt my heart drop. I hate to admit it, but there was a tiny part in me that wanted to believe what Jaime had said—that it was just Antoine and his friend over. Stupid; considering what I'd heard Antoine's friend say and the two female voices I'd heard over the phone.

Rosie turned and looked in my direction. "What are you looking at?"

"Who, actually. I saw someone walk past the window."

"Girl, you sure you want to leave? We can kick down the fucking door if we have to. Or we can bust in the screen at the living room window."

"No, I've got another idea."

Once in the car, Rosie asked, "So what's up, Nik? You want to drive around a little bit and go back and surprise 'em again?"

"Not quite. We're going back home and getting some tools out the garage."

"Damn, *Mami*, what you got up? That sounds like some Mafioso shit."

"*Mira*, as angry as I am at Jaime, I'm not going to hurt him. Physically anyway."

"How then?"

"You know what Jaime loves to do?"

"You mean besides the obvious?"

"Yeah. Jaime is a fanatic about his yard. He prides himself on being this master landscaper—always talking about how he's got the best yard not only on the street, but in the whole neighborhood."

"And?"

"And we're going to fuck it up."

"Fuck up what? His yard?"

"Yes."

Rosie looked at me like I'd suggested we take a vacation in Rwanda or something. "Nikki, what kind of lightweight Teletubby shit is that?! That nigga's cheating on you. He's got some *sucia* up in his piece right now and for revenge you want to pull up his flowers?! Are you fucking kiddin' me?"

"He spends hours on that yard and practically goes ballistic if anyone even steps on the grass. Trust me, as hype as he got over me tossing that brick through his window, he'll be even more so at what we're gonna do. You're right; it is a bit lightweight. But he ain't worth the trouble we'd get into if we go with what we really want to do. At least we'll get back at him in some way, Rosie."

"I wish I knew how you can contain yourself like you do, for real. 'Cause if that was mine up in there with some bitch…" Rosie let out a sigh. "All right, we'll do it your way. So, you want to do some creative landscaping of our own?"

"You got it. Let's head back home and get what we need."

Once we got back to our house, we went to the garage. I groped and found the string and turned on the light. Rosie headed straight for a pair of electric hedge clippers and picked them up.

"Oh yeah! I can do some major damage with these, *mi 'ja!*"

I put my hands on my hips and looked at her.

"What? Why you staring at me like that?"

"Okay, Rosie. It's late and all, but why are you picking up some electric hedge clippers? First of all, we want to make as little noise as possible. And second, what are we gonna do—ring Jaime's bell and say, "Hey, we're back. Can you plug in the extension cord for these clippers so we can fuck up your bushes?'"

"Girl, I ain't even thinking. There must be some *indo* still lingering in my system."

"We're going to knock the dust off these old-fashioned clippers. Grab those two shovels over there. We'll take this rake, too. Oh, and some gloves."

"You sure that's all we'll need?"

"Yep. Let's go."

"Hey, I didn't eat on the plane and I'm starving. How about we stop and get something to eat?"

"That's cool. I haven't eaten either, and I'm going to need some fuel for our little job. Where do you want to go?"

"The only place that I can think of that's open now is White Castle. We can go get some fartburgers. Plus, we can kill a little time. I'm sure those fools have an eye out for us."

"Yeah. Hopefully, Antoine and that girl aren't still in the living room. They might hear us."

"That chick sounded pissed. I heard her say something about wanting to get out of there, so she's probably gone."

"Well, if the pussy is gone, then Antoine is gone, too."

"Antoine is the pussy. Did you hear the scream that little bitch let out when you tossed the brick through the window?"

"Uh-huh," I said with a slight chuckle. "As steamed as I was, that shit almost made me bust out laughing. Anyway, let's be out."

We put the tools in the car and ran into the house to wash our hands. Then we drove to White Castle and ordered some burgers, a sack of fries to share, and a couple of drinks. We sat in the parking lot and ate in silence. I was merely going through the motions of eating; I couldn't even taste the food. All I kept thinking in my head was, don't cry. Don't cry. Don't let the universe or anyone in it see you shed a tear over that *cabron*. Don't do it.

"You okay, girl?" Rosie asked.

"Yeah. About as well as a woman can be after finding out that her man is fucking around on her."

"See, I don't know how you're staying so calm. You should be ready to kick some ass or kill somebody."

"That's what I want to do, but I'm only going to let my anger kick in but so much."

"You certainly have gotten your temper in check over the years. You're a good one."

"No, I'm a hurt one. Part of me wants to pack it up and go home..."

"Oh, hell no! Don't even think about that shit. That mofo is gonna pay, in one way or another."

"I said a part of me wants to do that. But the bigger part wants to get back at him in some way. Oh, I'm not backing out. Believe that."

"All right. Good. Girl, you scared me for a minute." She looked at me for a second. "But just in case that other part starts taking over, let's get on over there so we can get some type of revenge on him; even if we only pull up some damn tulips."

Rosie gathered up our containers from the food, got out the car, and took it all to a nearby garbage bin. She climbed back in and started the car. "You ready, cuz?"

"I'm ready."

We drove back to Jaime's house. By then, Antoine's car, as well as the white Taurus, were gone. Rosie parked about two houses down. We got out with everything and went to work. The street and porch light helped us to see a little. We loosened the bricks surrounding the bushes near the porch and placed them quietly on the porch. I raked all the red-colored chips that surrounded the shrub onto the grass. We hacked away at the shrubbery; then the flowers, pulling out the roots. We dug holes in the lawn with the shovels—hurling some of the dirt and grass onto the porch. Luckily, it had rained earlier, which softened the ground, making that portion of the job much easier. By the time we were done, we were two sweaty pieces of funk. We tiptoed to the sidewalk, maneuvering around the holes. We stared at our work, then looked at each other and grinned.

Rosie leaned over toward me and then sniffed. "Whew! You are ripe."

"You ain't exactly a fresh flower in spring yourself, heifer. Let me do one more thing and we can leave."

I walked around to the side of the house and got the water hose. I brought it around to the front and placed it in one of the holes near the middle of the lawn—or what was left of it. I went back and turned on the water full blast.

"Let's go," I said as I came back to the front.

We gathered the tools, put them in the trunk and left. As soon as we got home we went to our bathrooms and took showers. It was weird but, as I was taking my shower, I felt like I wasn't only cleansing my body of dirt and sweat, but of Jaime as well. I felt a bit numb, with little spurts of hurt peeking through, threatening my tear ducts. It was going to take a minute, but I was determined to get over it. To me, infidelity was the ultimate betrayal and I knew that I'd never feel the same way about Jaime.

Still, I did—do love him. Sooner or later those tears I was holding in were going to come full force. I kind of wished that I'd taken the high road, but fuck that. He deserved what we did that night. Shit, fucking up his pride and joy was nothing compared to what he'd done to me.

That morning, the sound of the phone ringing jolted me out of my sleep. I saw from the caller ID that it was Jaime. My first inclination was to ignore the call, but then I decided I might as well get the shit over with. I reached over and picked up the receiver.

"What?"

"Don't *what* me, goddamnit! What the fuck's wrong wit' you? You and your crazy ass cousin fucked up my shit!"

I had to pull the phone away from my ear because he was screaming so loud.

"Look, you need to relax yourself."

"Relax myself? Relax myself? You know damn motherfuckin' well how much time and money I put into my yard! I ought to file a police report and then sue both you psycho bitches!"

"You better watch it with the bitch shit. 'Cause if anybody is a bitch, it's you. Your bitch ass wouldn't even open the door last night." My voice sounded calm and controlled to my ears, but anger was simmering right beneath the surface.

"What the fuck I'ma open the door for when y'all acting all off the chain—throwing shit through my window and standing on the porch with bats?"

I shook my head. "You're still sticking to your story that you didn't have a woman over, aren't you?"

"It ain't no story. That's merely your jealousy and your cousin messin' wit' your head. I told you that it was only Antoine and his female friend over. Goddamn it, I didn't call you to talk about that bullshit! I'm calling to talk about how you..."

"So, if it was only you, Antoine, and his friend over, who was that walking around in your bedroom?"

"What?"

"You heard me. While you three were downstairs, someone was walking around in your room. I saw their shadow by your window."

"We-wha—, I don't know what you thought you saw..."

"Motherfucker, stop trying to play me for a fool!" My simmering anger rolled into full boil. "You know you had a bitch over there, so quit insulting my fucking intelligence! Be a man and own up to yours!"

There was silence on the phone.

"All I have to say to you, Jaime, is number one—fuck you! Number two— you're a lying, cheating, no-good ass bastard. Number three—messing with your stupid yard was the least I could've done. Because if I had let my emotions take over, I would've burned your ass out of that house! And one last thing—fuck you!" I slammed down the phone.

About a week after that, the masochist in me made me drive by his house one night. Parked in his driveway was the white Taurus. There were no lights on in the house. I knew she was there, in his bed—this faceless Tasha. I wondered if they were sleeping the way we used to, naked and on their sides with him behind her, his arm draped across her waist, his face nuzzling her neck. Was he waking her up in the middle of the night to make love again? I drove around a bit until I had to pull over because of my blurred vision from the tears that I finally couldn't hold in anymore. I must've cried for half an hour straight.

Right now I'm getting through the stages that follow a bad breakup. I've gone through the "I want to filet his dick and saute his balls" anger stage. And the "oh God, why does it hurt so bad, how could he do this to me?" crying stage. It's happening a lot sooner than I thought it would, but I'm moving into the "Jaime died? That's too bad—what's for lunch?" apathy stage.

I guess I'd better roll my ass out of this bed. I'm glad we did the housecleaning and some of the cooking last night, because that's less to do today. By *we* I mean Rosie, our friend Chico and me. We share this home, a brick Colonial that I inherited from my maternal grandparents. They died two years ago in a car accident on their way back home from a weekend spent on Mackinac Island.

I love this house. I always have. However, I hate the means by which it became mine. Rosie and I spent many summer vacations in PR but most holidays and week-ends were spent here after we moved from New York. Coming over here is what helped make the transition of the move go much more smoothly. My grandparents were very lively, affectionate people who loved kids. We had more toys here than at home. They always came up with interesting things for us to do. I don't believe that either Rosie or I ever uttered, "We're bored, there's nothing to do." They'd mastered the art of spoiling us monstrously without turning us into spoiled monsters.

As soon as I make the move to get out of bed and head to the shower, I realize that I'm horny as hell. I've been going crazy lately. I haven't had any *pinga* in over three months now. It's been hard adjusting from getting it on the regular to *nada*.

Time to pull out my old friend from the nightstand. I got this little gadget from a sex toy party that Rosie hosted. I call it Hector. This thing can make a repressed Mormon—that was redundant—explode in less than five minutes. You insert the phallic-shaped part inside of you, and attached to the base is this animal, a beaver—appropriately enough, with its tongue sticking out. That rests on your clit. When you turn it on to vibrate—woo hoo!

My trip to bliss only takes about three minutes. Whoever invented this vibrator needs to win a damn Nobel Peace Prize or something. If I knew their name I'd add them to my Christmas card list. It's the least I could do.